"**Linda Winstead is a bright new talent in Western romance!**" —Raine Cantrell

DESERT ECSTASY

"Why is your heart beating so fast?" Annabelle whispered.

"Jesus, Annie. What are you trying to do to me?"

She crept forward until her face was hovering over his. If she kissed him would he push her away? Would it be as wonderful as the other two kisses they'd shared? A tiny smile crossed her face.

"I never should have thrown your makeup into the pond," Shelley said. "I never should have let you out of that ugly damn black dress. I never should have set you on that roan and ridden away from The Silver Palace." There was a hint of anger in his voice.

Annabelle ignored it. "But you did all those things. You can't take them back."

"The worst part is, I'm about to do something else I know damn well I shouldn't."

"You're going to kiss me, aren't you, Shelley?"

"For starters."

Other *Leisure* and *Love Spell* Books by
Linda Winstead:
CHASE THE LIGHTNING
GUARDIAN ANGEL

WEST WIND

LINDA WINSTEAD

For my parents—
who gave me the gift of the knowledge that
all things are possible.

Book Margins, Inc.

A BMI Edition

Published by special arrangement with Dorchester
Publishing Co., Inc.

Printed in the United States of America.

Digest format printed and distributed exclusively for Book
Margins, Inc., Ivyland, PA.

Chapter One

Brayton, Colorado, 1876

Light spilled on to the boardwalk just ahead, and the sounds of merriment grew closer with each of Shelley's steps. As he moved toward the only bright spot in the dark night, the light and laughter called to him. The Silver Palace, Oscar Beddingfield's fine saloon and gaming house, had always been Brayton's one redeeming feature as it was one of Shelley's favorite places to spend a day or two.

Oscar's prices were fair, and he never watered the tequila. It had only been a few years ago that he had added his "girls," whom he named after colors and dressed accordingly. His girls were clean, young, and pretty, and as far as Shelley knew, he employed only three: Cherry Red, Bonnie Blue, and Summer Green.

Shelley grinned as he entered the circle of light

coming from the saloon that spread over the board-walk, and stopped for a moment to listen to the murmur of voices and the enticing ring of bottles lightly touching empty glasses. He heard Cherry Red laugh, a harsh, forced laugh. She'd be glad to see him, and so would Oscar. Shelley always managed to spend a bundle when he stayed a few days in Brayton. Between the tequila Oscar stocked for him, and Cherry, he always left the Silver Palace a poorer man. But a happier one.

He studied the room over the top of the batwing doors. The bartender was pouring drinks and Oscar was lovingly polishing the long bar. The Silver Palace had come a long way in eleven years from the ramshackle saloon Oscar had founded. There was a gaming room in the back, a small stage in the front room, and several comfortably furnished rooms upstairs which customers paid dearly to visit. Dollar whores were available down the street, but Oscar's girls were special.

The front room was packed, more crowded than Shelley had ever seen it. His grin faded. Crowds made him nervous, just a bit. He was always watching his back, and couldn't relax like he needed to on occasion. Cherry was busy, sitting in a bearded man's lap and whispering into his ear as she swung one leg in a calculated move to keep the customers' attentions on her.

"Shelley!" Cherry Red screamed, and half the room turned to watch as she left the man's lap and ran across the room as Shelley pushed his way through the swinging doors. He caught her when she jumped into his arms, wrapping her legs around his waist and clasping her hands behind his neck.

Shelley held her, his arms around her waist. "Hello,

darlin'," he drawled. "I'd a been here sooner if I'd a known I had a greetin' like this waitin' for me."

Cherry planted an ardent kiss on his lips. "It's been ages since you were here, Shelley. Don't you like me anymore?" She pouted, her full and brightly painted lower lip trembling slightly.

"Of course I like you, darlin'."

Shelley lowered Cherry to her feet and smoothed her red silk dress. The skirt ended just above her knees, and she swung one black-stockinged leg seductively, enticing every man in the room. The fair, blue-eyed blonde was a favorite at the Silver Palace. It was no coincidence that Summer was a redhead and Bonnie had light brown hair. Oscar had seen to that. Variety.

Shelley spun Cherry around and patted her on the bottom, sending her back to the miner she'd deserted. "I'll see you later." He ran a hand over his bearded jaw when she turned back to him, pouting. "After I have a drink, a shave, and a bath."

"I can take care of all that for you, Shelley," she offered, but he turned away from her and sauntered to the bar, grinning at Oscar.

Oscar reached under the bar and placed a bottle of tequila on the polished wooden surface. "What have you been up to, Shelley?" he asked as he poured the pale amber liquid into a heavy shot glass. Though he employed a bartender, who was pouring drinks for an impatient group of miners further down the long bar, Shelley knew that Oscar always insisted on serving Shelley himself.

Shelley leaned into the bar and tossed back the tequila. He closed his eyes and savored the first taste. The first of many. "Same old thing. Just turned in Willie Erskine. Slippery fella. Led me a merry chase through half the Rocky Mountain Range."

"But you caught him, of course," Oscar prodded.

He nodded and poured the next shot himself.

"Is he at the sheriff's office here in Brayton?"

"That's where I left him." Shelley was quickly becoming tired of the subject. Yes, that was where he'd left Willie Erskine. His body, anyway. After all, the poster said dead or alive, and Willie had refused to be taken alive.

Oscar smiled, and Shelley could see the man's mind at work. Willie Erskine had been worth 500 dollars.

"I heard you tell Cherry you wanted a bath and a shave. Barber shop's closed. Why don't you let me have the girls fix you a bath upstairs? If you don't want to wait until morning, Cherry can shave your beard for ya."

Shelley grinned and poured another shot. "I might take you up on that offer of a bath later on, but I'll be damned if any woman is gonna take a razor to my face. I can shave myself, thank you."

He leaned on the bar and took a deep breath. The Silver Palace was one of several saloons that were like home to him. He loved the smell of cigar smoke, cheap perfume, and the oil Oscar used to shine the bar.

"What's new around here? Any luck replacing Iris?"

The question caused Oscar to lose his smile. "Ungrateful girl. I still can't believe she ran off with that sodbuster."

Iris White had been one of Oscar's most popular girls, dark-haired and tall and by far the most beautiful girl who had ever worked for him. She had surprised everyone by eloping with a widowed farmer who had four young children.

Oscar's smile slowly returned. "But you haven't seen my newest attraction."

"A new woman?" Shelley raised his eyebrows.

Oscar shrugged his shoulders. "Not yet. At least, not like you think. I've found me a singer."

He grimaced. He had heard some godawful singers in saloons attempting to provide entertainment other than whiskey, women, and cards. "The last singer you hired brought tears to my eyes, Oscar, and I don't mean that kindly."

Oscar laughed. "Hiring that woman who claimed to be an entertainer from New Orleans was one of my worst mistakes. Her voice grated on one's nerves even as she danced half naked on the stage. But this one's got the voice of an angel." He gestured to the crowded room. "See all these customers? Most of them are here to see her."

He grinned lopsidedly. "Is she pretty?"

"Well . . ." Oscar screwed up his face, thinking hard. "Her face is kinda . . . peculiar."

His smile faded.

"I don't rightly know what kinda figure she's got, because she's always wearing this black dress that would probably fit you, it's so big. It hangs on her, and there's black silk everywhere. I tried to get her to wear one of Iris's old costumes, but she wouldn't have none of it. She's a widow, see, from St. Louis. Still mourning, I reckon." Oscar looked pensive. "Every now and then I look at her close and I think she'd clean up real nice."

"Why don't you threaten to fire her if she don't wear what you tell her to? You're the boss." Shelley looked around the crowded room.

"Tried that. She said she'd go, and I believe her." He

11

shook his head. "Stubborn woman. I can't afford to lose her, and she knows it."

"What's her name?"

Oscar laughed. "Ann Brown, and I swear to God I didn't name this one."

At that moment the woman they'd been speaking of walked into the saloon through a side door and headed for the stage. The room broke into thunderous applause to which she gave a brief nod and an even briefer smile. Alfred, the aged black man who had been playing the piano at the Silver Palace for eight years, was already seated at the piano as Ann Brown climbed the steps to the stage.

Oscar's description had been accurate. Her black dress was volumes too big, and buttoned from just beneath her chin to the floor, where it brushed gently as she walked. He'd used the word *peculiar* to describe her face. Shelley thought it merely tired and colorless, though the dark circles under her eyes were odd. Her sable brown hair was in a tight bun at her nape. Shelley thought, before she opened her mouth, that she'd better be a damn good singer.

With no introduction or word to the audience, she began to sing, and Shelley was entranced. He knew nothing about music—pitch, tone, resonance. He only knew that her voice was perfection. Sweet, strong, and somehow uplifting. She began with "Annie Laurie" and went directly into a rendition of "Lorena." Several patriotic songs followed.

Shelley shifted his attention from her to the room. All eyes were on the stage. Miners, cowhands, even the gamblers had left their cards behind and stood congregated in the doorway to the gaming room. The only faces that were less than friendly were on the three women who found themselves suddenly ignored. Cherry, in particular, seemed put out by all the attention Mrs. Brown was receiving. Her red mouth was set in a pursed frown, and when at one point she leaned over to speak to Summer, she was quickly shushed by a nearby admirer of the singer.

Ann Brown sat on a three-legged stool, her voluminous skirt spread around her, her hands folded primly in her lap. Her dark eyes were fixed on a far distant place above the heads of her audience, as if she were singing to an empty room.

When Mrs. Brown finished the evening's entertainment to shouts and whistles and uproarious applause, she left the stage with little visible awareness of the commotion she had created. She walked with her head down, exiting through the side door. Only after she'd left the room did the gamblers return to their cards, and Oscar's girls were the center of attention once again.

Shelley was about to look away from the door the odd Mrs. Brown had disappeared through when he saw a well-dressed and impeccably groomed man, sitting alone and near the back of the room, rise and follow her.

Shelley leaned over the bar and grabbed Oscar's arm. "Who is that fella?" He nodded to the door as the man passed through it.

Oscar shrugged. "Stranger. Showed up here yesterday. Spent a lot of time with the girls." He smiled.

Shelley sauntered toward the side door that he knew opened into a narrow alleyway. It was none of his business that the man had followed the pale singer . . . except that she didn't look like the kind of woman who could look after herself, if it came to that.

"You're not leaving already, are you?"

Cherry stepped between him and the door. He jumped. He hadn't seen her coming, and that wasn't like him. He prided himself on being observant . . . always aware of what was going on around him. In his business it was crucial.

He gave her a charming smile. "Just going out for a bit of fresh air, darlin'."

She winked at him. "How about I keep you company?"

He looked over her shoulder to the door. "Not this time, Cherry. I'll be back in a few minutes."

He brushed past her, but she stopped him, her fingernails digging into his arm through the thin fabric of his shirt. "If you're following her you're wasting your time."

"I'm not following anybody."

"There's been a fella in here asking about her. I think he's an old friend or something. You don't want to interrupt them, do you?"

"Jesus, Cherry," he snapped. "I just need some damn air." He removed her hand from his arm and stepped into the alley.

To his left was the main street. Straight ahead a mere five feet was the side wall of the general store. To the right, he knew, was a flight of stairs that led to a small room Oscar sometimes rented at an exorbitant rate. It was quiet, hidden from the street, and Shelley knew without a doubt that that was where Mrs. Brown lived, so he turned in that direction.

The man he had seen follow Mrs. Brown was leaning against the handrail at the foot of the stairs, a cigar in one hand, his other hand in his pocket. Shelley studied the man as he approached slowly. He was no miner, no cowhand, didn't dress like a gambler. His clothes were more suited to the East than the West, but he was no greenhorn. The stranger reminded Shelley of the man he had met in Kansas City. They'd been after the same outlaw, and the man had been a detective for Pinkerton's Detective Agency.

Shelley took a deep breath, mussed his dark blond hair, and began a drunken rendition of "Annie Laurie" as he approached the man. He tripped over the first step of the stairway that led to the room where he was certain Mrs. Brown was staying, purposely landing on his face. Then he saw her . . . crouched beneath the steps like a frightened mouse. Their eyes met, just for a second, and he winked at her. She was barely three feet from the man she was hiding from. Had it been daylight she would have had no cover at all.

Shelley pulled himself slowly to his feet, grasping the handrail as if for dear life. "Annie!" he yelled as he faced the door at the top of the stairs. He waited several seconds, ignoring the other man, and then yelled again.

The stranger who waited at the bottom of the stairs turned to him in disgust. "She's not there."

Shelley looked at the man as if surprised. "You sure?" He slurred his words just slightly. "I'm supposed to meet her here . . . I think . . ." He turned and stepped cautiously down the few steps to the ground. "Maybe I was supposed to meet her at my place . . . sometimes I forget details like that." He gave the man a searching look. "She gets mad at me when I forget."

Pulling on his cigar, the man peered at Shelley with sudden interest. "You're well acquainted with Ann Brown?"

"Well acquainted?" He grinned. "I guess you could

15

call it that. I've known Annie for a long time . . . a long time."

The man tossed his cigar to the ground and stomped it out with the toe of his well-polished boot. "How long, exactly?"

Shelley knew then that the man was Pinkerton's, or some other sort of detective or lawman. What could a sweet little thing like Mrs. Brown have done to make this man track her?

"Two years," he slurred.

"You knew her in St. Louis, then? Before her husband died?" the man pressed.

He nodded.

"I need to talk to her. One of the ladies told me she'd been here four weeks. Is that correct?"

He shrugged. "I reckon."

"Did you actually know her husband, the late Mr. Brown?" The detective's tone was increasingly authoritative.

Swaying drunkenly, Shelley placed his arm around the detective's shoulder, leaning heavily against the smaller man. He always liked to know what he was up against. There was a pistol in the detective's shoulder holster, and a derringer in his left boot.

"You want to talk to my Annie?"

"I'd like that, yes."

Shelley turned and led the man toward the street. "I'll take you to my place. She's probably waiting there for me right now." He leaned in, placing his face close to the detective's, giving the man a chance to smell the tequila on his breath. "If you're with me maybe she won't yell at me too much for being late."

He pressed heavily against the man all the way down the alley, until he could see the boardwalk that

16

ended in front of the general store. Suddenly he lurched to the side, bringing the man with him, and before the detective could react Shelley's fist connected with his jaw. It was a well-placed, well-practiced blow, and the little man slumped to the ground.

Shelley took the detective's pistol from its holster, drew the derringer from his well-polished boot, and tossed the weapons further back into the alley. Then he turned and all but ran toward Ann Brown's hiding place.

Shelley bent over and peeked under the stairs where she crouched in a dark heap of heavy silk. There was a lot more fabric there than woman. He offered his hand and she took it, slipping out from her shelter with a wary expression on her face. He held her slender hand for a moment before she pulled it slowly away and held it to her breast.

"Is he gone?"

"Otherwise detained." Shelley shoved his hands in his pockets. "But not for long."

"I've got to get out of here."

She turned and ran up the stairs, fishing a key from a pocket in the folds of her skirt. She stopped with the key in the lock and turned to him hesitantly. "Thank you. I don't know why you . . ."

He shook his head. "Darlin', neither do I."

Ann Brown disappeared into her room, reappearing moments later with a worn leather satchel. She was apparently surprised to see him still standing at the foot of the stairs, blocking her path of escape, and she descended the stairway cautiously.

"Where are you going?"

"West," she said, stopping while still several steps

from the ground and him. "Do you mind?"

He stepped back, and she flew to the bottom of the stairs, brushing past him.

"How?" He followed her, even as she took a wide berth around the man who still lay slumped against the wall of the general store.

"Is he dead?" she asked, her voice small.

Shelley continued to follow. "No, so you'd better hurry. You didn't answer my question."

"I don't know." She started down the boardwalk, stepping quickly, until he grabbed her arm and spun her around.

He'd opened his mouth to chastise her, but closed it quickly when he saw that her eyes were full of un-shed tears. "Just stop and think a minute," he said kindly. "You can't just walk out of town."

"I don't have any choice," she said, her voice still small, but steady. "I appreciate what you've done, but . . ."

"Why don't you hire me to take you where you're going?" he offered. The words were out of his mouth before he had a chance to think. Why had he said that?

Ann Brown took a step back. "I . . . I don't have very much money."

"How much?"

"Thirty-six dollars."

He shrugged. "Thirty dollars is fair salary for a month's work as a cowhand."

"Is that what you are? A cowboy?"

He shook his head. "Nah. They work too hard. But escorting a lady to her destination shouldn't be too much work, even for me."

"For thirty dollars?" she asked suspiciously.

He narrowed his eyes and gave her a crooked grin.

"I'll make you a deal. Thirty dollars and you sing me a song every night."

A slice of moonlight lit the lower half of her face, and a smile transformed it pleasantly. "Then we have an agreement, Mr. . . . "

"Shelley." He offered his hand and they shook on the deal. "Just Shelley. Where are we headed?"

"San Francisco."

He took her arm and led her toward the livery. "San Francisco? Hell, woman, you plan on getting your money's worth, don't you?"

"You can back out any time, Mr. Shelley," she offered, and she was sincere.

"Nah. I've got a brother in San Francisco. Haven't seen him in . . . hell, I think it's been five years. And it's not Mr. Shelley. It's just Shelley."

Far behind them he heard the detective's muttered oath, and Shelley quickened his step. The lady beside him needed no encouragement to follow suit.

"I don't suppose you're gonna tell me why that man's after you?" he asked as they stepped into the shadow of the stables.

"I can't," she whispered.

He tied her bag behind the cantle and lifted her into the saddle. He sat behind her, studying her profile as she looked to the ground and tried not to lean against him.

San Francisco. Goddamn.

Chapter Two

They rode most of the night, stopping only when the sky was gray, promising day break. She hadn't complained, even though she was unaccustomed to riding and had never spent so many hours in the saddle. Her body rigid, she held herself away from her escort, and though completely exhausted, she had not once suggested that they stop.

"We can sleep here for a couple of hours," Shelley said, lifting the saddle from his horse and laying it in the grass. He removed his rifle from its sheath and placed it close at hand. He arranged the bedroll for her before he lowered himself to the ground and rested his head on the saddle, crossing his ankles and making himself comfortable.

She remained standing. "We're going to sleep out here in the open?"

Shelley opened one eye. "Yep. It's not like we have

a lot of choices. And you'd better get used to it, Mrs. Brown. There are precious few decent hotels between here and San Francisco." With that he closed his eyes and quickly went to sleep.

Sitting on the bedroll Shelley had provided for her, she looked to the east. She wasn't sleepy. How could she be? She'd stayed in Brayton too long . . . had gotten much too comfortable. Her room had been clean and private, and Oscar saw to it that she was left alone. Still, she had been found. If not for Shelley . . .

A smile, tentative at best, crossed her face as the sky turned pink. How many nights had she stayed awake until dawn? One of the many reasons she loved her chosen profession was the excuse it offered to stay up all night, if she desired. Even as a child she'd often lain in bed, wide awake, long after everyone else was fast asleep. It was her nature to embrace the night, and to sleep away half the day.

How many nights had she danced and drunk champagne until the sun had risen over Paris? Even when she visited New York, or San Francisco, or New Orleans, there were always parties following the opera.

Her smile faded slowly. Those days were gone. Maybe forever. She was a different person. Now she was Ann Brown, a widow from St. Louis, and if she was lucky she would find another singing job in a saloon. But once . . . once she had been Annabelle St. Clair, world-renowned mezzo-soprano, known for her unforgettable performances of light opera.

Three months. It seemed as if a lifetime had passed in that time. She'd had everything a woman could possibly want, and then had been reduced to nothing better than a common thief.

She told herself again that she'd had no choice. She was easily recognizable, given her celebrity and her picture being plastered all over the newspapers. Panic-stricken, she'd wanted only time . . . time to think, to hide, to disappear. The black dress and stage makeup she'd taken . . . borrowed . . . stolen from that St. Louis theater had taken care of that.

Annabelle plucked at the heavy silk sleeve and pulled a handful of material away from her waist. At one time the dress had almost fit. She'd lost so much weight that there was little resemblance to the woman whose face had graced every newspaper in the country in the past three months. No wonder that man at the Silver Palace had been uncertain about her identity.

She, however, had no doubt about his. He'd been at the Denver railway station with three similarly clothed men who shared his determination to find her. They'd stopped passengers and showed her picture to everyone. Even though the passengers had shaken their heads and moved on, she was afraid to show her face there again.

As the sun came up she studied the man who had saved her. That was certainly what he had done. He was sleeping soundly, hadn't moved a muscle since he'd drifted off. His head rested against the saddle with practiced ease. He had a new beard a shade or two darker than the blond or light brown hair on his head. Shelley, the man with the name of a poet, was tall, probably well over six feet, and though he had disdained her assumption that he was a cowboy it was obvious he was no stranger to physical labor. There was no fat on his lean body, and he had lifted her on and off the saddle as if she weighed nothing at all. His long legs, encased in tan twill pants, were still crossed at the ankles. The man hadn't even removed his boots, or the holster that housed a six-shooter at his right hip.

Realizing she knew nothing about this man chilled her. What if he was one of them . . . and he was taking her in? If that were true, he could have handed her over to the man in Brayton the night before. Still, three months ago she wouldn't have considered riding away in the dead of night with a man she'd just met. A man who was a bit too comfortable with that gun at his hip, and a bit too good with his fists. A man who knew that horrid Cherry Red well enough for her to throw herself into his arms. Annabelle had been watching from the shadows of the side doorway when he'd come in, all swagger and smiles. A charmer. A man to be wary of.

"Mornin' Annie." He watched her through barely opened eyes. "You should've given me a shove when you woke up."

Annabelle smiled slightly. "I haven't been up that long." She couldn't tell him that she hadn't slept at all, that she'd spent most of the morning watching him sleep.

Shelley sat up and stretched his arms over his head. His tawny hair stuck out at angles until he combed the mess with his long fingers. "All I've got for breakfast is some jerky. We'll stock up on supplies in the next town."

She took the jerky he offered her with no comment. She'd been living on so little food that even the dried meat tasted good. She'd decided it was more important to save her money to get to San Francisco than it was to eat. It was no wonder she'd lost so much weight.

Shelley saddled the horse and lifted Annie on it as he had the night before. Even with the volumes of silk in his hands he could tell that she was a tiny wisp of a woman. That wasn't exactly shocking. Her hands were delicate, and her face . . .

Her face was almost sickly looking . . . white, with black circles under her eyes, and shadows on her cheeks. But it was a well-shaped face, with high cheekbones, full lips, and big brown eyes. He tried not to look at her face too closely. He didn't want to be caught staring, but even her lips were colorless, gray and pasty.

As he joined her on the roan's back, he hooked his arm around her waist. "I don't suppose you're ready to tell me why that man was looking for you?"

"I can't."

"And I don't suppose I can take you to Denver and put you on a rail to San Francisco?"

"No."

"And I don't suppose you can tell me why?" His voice remained calm throughout the frustrating conversation.

There was a short pause before his passenger answered. "That man . . . the man at the Silver Palace. I saw him a few weeks ago at the Denver Rail Station."

"Looking for you?"

She nodded. "And he wasn't alone."

Shelley thought about this piece of information as they rode at a leisurely pace. "Just so I'll know what I'm up against . . . how many others were there?"

"Three."

"Three, in addition to the man in Brayton," he said thoughtfully. "Pinkerton's?"

Annie looked at the ground. "I think so."

"What the hell did you do?" There was no real anger in his voice, and more than a little humor.

Her answer held none. "Nothing. I swear, I did nothing." She was so vehement in her denial that he let it drop.

After a short while, Annie squirmed uncomfortably in the saddle. She was still working to hold her body rigid and away from him, trying not to touch him at all.

"You might as well lean against me, Annie," he suggested. "We've got a long day ahead of us, and if you don't relax your back is gonna hurt like hell tonight."

"Are you sure you don't mind?" Her questioning brown eyes were wide as she looked at him and sighed, a controlled sigh that told him her back already ached.

"Sure." He lifted his hat and settled it on her head. "I don't suppose you've got a hat in that bag of yours."

She shook her head. "Sorry. I don't."

"We'll have to get you one, but for now you wear mine." His hat was several sizes too large for her, but it shaded her eyes from the bright sun. Her fair skin was certain to burn quickly.

Annie did lean against his chest, and to his amazement was sound asleep a short time later.

He held her relaxed body firmly, astonished that she trusted him enough to fall asleep in his arms atop the moving horse. When he was certain she slept soundly, he leaned over just enough so that he could see her face beneath his broad-brimmed hat. After studying the sleeping woman for a few minutes he smiled, his grin coming naturally and easily to his lips.

To confirm his suspicion, he ran his thumb lightly across her cheek. She wrinkled her nose but didn't wake, and when he held his thumb in front of his face he saw that it was brushed with something oily, grainy, and white. Makeup. And not the kind Oscar's girls wore to make themselves more attractive. No, this makeup had a more sinister use. To disguise . . . to hide . . . to hide what? He had a strong urge to scrub her face clean right then and there . . . but he didn't want to scare her off. There was a settlement little more than four hours away. He had planned to stop there, buy some supplies, maybe spend the night in the boardinghouse. But this discovery called for a change of plans, and he turned the roan to a north-westerly route.

They would pass west of the settlement and head directly to a glade, shaded and secluded, where a clear, cold pond waited.

He felt her awake, her body tensing as she practically jumped from the saddle. He held her tight, but for just a moment she fought him.

"Hold on there, darlin'." He relaxed his grip when she fell back against his chest. "If you're gonna sleep in the saddle you're gonna have to be careful how you wake up."

"I'm sorry," she mumbled. "It was . . . I had a bad dream."

Her face was pale, her dark eyes wide and frightened. She looked as if she'd had an honest-to-God scare. He could actually feel her trembling, a slight but deep tremor. That must have been some dream.

"It's all right, darlin'." He tried to soothe her. "You

26

sleep all you want. Just think of me as the sleeping car on the Shelley Railway to San Francisco."

Annie smiled. "You're a nice man, Shelley."

He tensed. "No, I'm not, and don't you forget it. This is just a job." A job I'm beginning to wonder how the hell I got stuck with, he thought, grimacing.

"I know," she said seriously. "We never discussed . . . do you want me to pay you half now and the other half when we get to San Francisco?"

"Nah. Hang on to your money. You can pay me once we get there."

He didn't give a damn about her 30 dollars. There was the 500 he'd gotten for Erskine in his saddlebags, plus another 50 in his pocket. From the looks of her, she needed that 30 bucks a lot more than he did. He felt that saving her from that Pinkerton agent had made her, in some way, his responsibility. There was no way he could allow her to set out on her own. She'd never make it.

She was looking straight ahead as he led the roan carefully down the steep hill. Below, the grass was brilliant green, the young trees swayed slightly in the breeze, and the sun reflected off the surface of the pond as if off polished glass, still and sparkling.

"What a beautiful place," Annie whispered, not taking her eyes off the water. "Are we stopping for the day already?" she asked as he lifted her from the roan's back.

"Might as well. We can eat a bit, get to sleep early, and then leave while there's still plenty of cool, dark hours to travel. Besides, I never did get that bath I wanted yesterday."

"I'm sorry. It's all my . . . you mean you intend to bathe here?" She looked distressed.

27

He nodded. "Yep. Wouldn't you like to wash up? I promise you there aren't many places like this between here and San Francisco. We'll have the Rockies, the Great Basin Desert, the Sierras . . . you'll be sorry if you don't enjoy this while we're here."

"But . . . but, I don't . . . I can't . . ."

He laughed. "Are you modest, darlin'?"

Apparently, she couldn't believe that he was laughing at her, as she gave him a daunting look. "Yes. It so happens that I am."

He unsaddled the horse, his movements slow, almost lazy. He didn't even give Annie a sidelong glance as he strung a rope between two saplings and hung his blanket from the rope. He stood on the opposite side of the barrier and raised his hands, his palms upward.

"How's this?"

She stepped past him to the edge of the pond and stooped to trail her fingers through the water. "It does feel heavenly."

"I promise I won't peek unless you ask me to," he teased.

"I guarantee I won't ask you to." Annie shooed him away from the blanket, smiling.

"I just mean if you see a snake or something . . ."

Shelley left her standing there, turning his back on the dark-haired woman. He stretched out in the grass, shading his eyes with his hat, and waited until he heard her step into the pond, the still water splashing at her feet. Her satchel was sitting beside the saddle, and he opened it quietly, feeling a small twinge of guilt which he quickly dismissed.

There wasn't much in the bag. She hadn't been lying when she said she had only 36 dollars. There was a comb and brush, a small mirror, and three containers. He opened the first small one. It contained a sticky-looking black goo. The circles under her eyes and the hollows in her cheeks. The next jar held a thick, greasy white glop. Her pasty complexion. The third and largest one held white powder.

He set the three containers in front of him and thought hard, his fingers forming a tepee under his chin. In the distance he heard the soft splashing as Annie bathed in the cool waters of the pond.

After a few minutes he stood, the offensive containers in his hands. He let the smallest jar fly first. It went clear to the opposite edge of the pond, landing with a loud splash close to the bank.

"What was that?" was her startled question, and he heard her hurrying toward the grassy bank.

"Nothin', darlin'," he answered easily. "I'm just tossing some junk into the water."

"Oh," she sighed with relief. "I thought maybe it was . . . snakes or something."

"Is that an invitation?" he asked as he let the second jar go sailing.

"No. Of course not," she answered haughtily, apparently recalling his earlier words.

He let the last jar fly, and this time the widow no doubt looked overhead to see what he was tossing into the water.

"No!" she shouted, too late as the last of her makeup landed in the middle of the pond with a loud splash. Annie stomped to the blanket that hung between them. Her hands grasped the top, her face just clearing the barrier.

"Why did you do that?" she screamed.

He was speechless. She wasn't just pretty without

her disguise, she was downright gorgeous. Her dark wet hair fell around her shoulders, and her face was like porcelain, with rosy cheeks and a mouth the color of a fresh plum. Her eyes flashed at him, dark with anger.

"Well? Have you been struck dumb?" she shouted when he didn't answer.

"With two of us on one horse it's going to be necessary to travel light if we're going to make any time at all." Amazingly, his voice was calm. "Those jars were heavy and useless."

Annie frowned and bit her lower lip. She was giving his explanation some thought before she answered him. "I wish you'd asked, that's all."

He stared at her fingers grasping the top of the blanket. "Darlin', whoever taught you to put on makeup didn't teach you very well. Makeup is supposed to make you look better." He acted ignorant of her reason for wearing a disguise. "Now, I suggest you get dressed and haul your ass out here before I decide to come back there and see what else you've been hidin'."

She narrowed her dark brown eyes. "You wouldn't dare."

He took a step forward. "Don't dare me, darlin'. Don't ever dare me."

Annabelle started to dress quickly, pulling on her chemise while she yelled over her shoulder. "All right, but you stop calling me darling. My name is Mrs. Brown. Not Annie, not darling. Mrs. Brown."

She struggled with the heavy black dress. There were tiny buttons from the high collar to the hem of the too-long skirt, and she refused to step from behind the makeshift curtain until every one of them had been fastened. She hated the black dress. Hated even more that she had traded a perfectly lovely green silk gown for this monstrosity.

When she stepped from behind the blanket she was dressed, and her hair had been returned to a tight bun at her nape. She gestured with one hand. "It's all yours, Mr. Shelley."

He walked past her as she started up the hill. He was already unbuttoning his shirt, and his eyes never left her face. She'd so looked forward to scrubbing the makeup from her face. It had been foolish of her to imagine that her escort wouldn't notice.

"You won't peek, will you, Mrs. Brown?"

Annabelle refused to look at him. "Of course not."

He continued to watch her from behind the blanket as he finished undressing. The top of the blanket barely hit him at mid-chest, and as she seated herself on the grassy hill, she stared at his naked torso and the light, curly hair there.

"What if I see a snake or something?" he asked, his face all innocence.

"I think you're perfectly capable of handling another reptile," she snapped.

He leaned over the blanket slightly. "What do you mean, 'another' reptile?"

"Another reptile like yourself."

Shelley had no sooner turned around than he shouted, "Snake! Snake!"

She leaned back against the lush grass and closed her eyes.

"Aren't you going to save me, Widow Brown?"

She didn't even open her eyes. "I don't think you need saving, Mr. Shelley."

She waited a few minutes before she opened one eye. Shelley hadn't moved. He watched her with casual arrogance. With a start she raised her head.

"Who told you I was a widow?" she snapped.

"Oscar."

She leaned back and relaxed. "So you were talking about me before we ever met?"

"Yep. Oscar was telling me what a wonderful find you were. I'll bet he's really mad today. If he ever finds out I took you out of town he'll never forgive me. There goes my tequila."

She opened her mouth to deliver a sharp retort, but snapped it shut without uttering a word. That control she was becoming so adept at calmed her.

"I would have left, even without you," she said, her earlier fear gone. "But I wouldn't have gotten this far. I probably wouldn't have gotten any farther than the next saloon."

"About that . . ." Shelley started, then stopped. She lifted her head. "That's not a good idea. Oscar's a . . . well, sort of a good guy. Not all saloon owners are like that. Some might try to . . ." His voice trailed off.

She knew exactly what he meant. She'd worked in more than half a dozen saloons in the past three months. Some places it was impossible for her to stay for more than a few days, even with her baggy dress and her makeup.

"Take your bath, Shelley." She returned to her supine position in the grass. "Saloon work is out . . . now that you've thrown out my makeup, you dolt."

She lay there, her eyes closed, for several minutes before she heard him splashing in the water. She loosened her hair and spread it between her hands, rubbing and exposing all she could to the warming rays of the sun.

There in the secluded glade, surrounded by the saplings and lush grass, the pond and Shelley at the center of it all, she felt, for the first time in months, a moment of complete peace. Her thoughts were clear and her heart, while it still beat soundly, had slowed to a reasonable pace. How many times in the past three months had she expected it to come bursting through her chest?

Shelley would deliver her to San Francisco, and Nicky. Nicky would know what to do.

Chapter Three

They camped for the night by the peaceful pond. Shelley built a fire and made a pot of coffee, as he did every night when he was on the trail, and he produced even more dried meat.

"Sorry," he apologized as he offered it to her, but she smiled as she took it from him.

He'd avoided looking closely at her all afternoon, had been grateful for her pensive silence as she stared out over the pond and ignored him. But he had managed to steal an occasional glance at his companion, the demure Mrs. Brown. When he'd finished his bath and returned to the camp, he'd found the feisty woman who had screamed at him gone, replaced by the quiet woman he had rescued from that detective.

It was clear to him that Annie was no ordinary woman. He might have found her in a saloon, but he'd bet his last dollar she hadn't spent much of her life in such common places. The way she held her head, the way she walked, betrayed a gentle upbringing.

He had stepped quietly from the pond that afternoon in time to see her drying her hair in the sun. Dark and lustrous, it hung to her waist. How did she manage to get it all in that tiny bun? It seemed impossible, but she'd done it again, as soon as he let it be known that he was out of the water. He was not normally a curious man. He lived a solitary life of his own choosing, and had no desire to be caught in the complicated workings of someone else's troubles. But he couldn't help wondering what had brought Annie to the Silver Palace.

"So," he said conversationally, unable to stand the silence any longer. "How did you happen to end up singing for Oscar?"

Annie studied his face for a few moments, openly judging him. She folded her hands in her lap and lifted her chin slightly. "After I saw those men in Denver I headed north. Brayton seemed like a nice little town, and I simply went to Mr. Beddingfield looking for a job." She bit her lower lip nervously. "I'm afraid it's all I know how to do. Singing. When I found myself in . . . in a position where I needed to earn money . . . well . . ."

"How many saloons have you worked?"

Annie counted on her fingers. "Nine," she finally said. "I was at the Silver Palace the longest. Some places I stayed no more than one night. Once I didn't even get paid." She grimaced. "The proprietor seemed so friendly, so harmless when he hired me. After the performance he . . . he made an improper advance." She blushed. "I . . . I pushed him away, and I ran. And I didn't look back."

"What's in San Francisco?" He gave her a crooked grin, even though the thought of some dirty old man accosting her didn't sit well with him. He wanted to change the subject . . . make her look forward instead of back. "A career as a famous singer?"

For a moment, Annie looked as if she were going to laugh and cry at the same time. "Family," she finally answered.

He scratched his beard, feeling even more troubled than before. "Can't they help you out? We could send a telegram—"

"No!" she said sharply. "No telegrams and no more railroads." Her voice softened. "I can't explain. I'm sorry."

There was a new tension in the air. Annie watched him across the fire, a hot tin of coffee cradled in her hands. He stared at her frowning when her attention was diverted, then flashed her his most charming smile when she looked squarely at him.

"Are you feeling better?" she asked in a small voice.

He didn't have any idea what she was talking about, and that must have shown on his face, because she clarified her question.

"Your bath," she said, and then she blushed as if she regretted the entire question.

The fire flickered on her face, and he looked down, breaking their eye contact. He fidgeted, his long fingers drumming the sides of his cup, his feet beating a fast cadence in the dirt. "Listen, I've been thinking . . ."

Annie bowed her head. Surely she knew just as well as he did that this wasn't going to work.

"Maybe it's not a good idea for me to take you all the way to San Francisco," he said quickly.

She gazed into the fire, unable to hide her disappointment. "I said you could back out at any time."

"I'm not deserting you, dammit," he said angrily, even though she'd accused him of nothing. It was her innocent face, those big eyes that looked at him with no hopes or expectations. "We'll take that thirty-six dollars and buy you a horse and some supplies. We're headed north to a pass over the Rockies. Somewhere along the trail I can hook you up with a wagon train or a family traveling to California."

She nodded silently.

He felt a wave of relief. That had been easy. She probably had never really expected that he would take her all the way to California. Still, she looked too damn good as the sky turned black and her face was lit by the dying fire. If he could lure her into a safe conversation, something to take his mind off her. Something . . .

"When did your husband die?"

She looked at him oddly for a moment. "Three months ago."

He nodded. Yes, he would have to remember that she was a recent widow. "How did he die?"

"Pneumonia," she said in an emotionless voice.

"What did he do for a living?"

"Bootmaker."

He tossed what remained of his coffee on the fire. She was proving to be damned difficult, with her one-word answers and blank stares. "Get some sleep. We'll head out long before light. Get in some easy traveling before it gets too hot."

She didn't protest or agree, but he felt her censure just the same. Somehow, she had come to trust him . . . he saw that much in her eyes. And in the very short time since he'd first seen her, and heard her sing, he'd come to feel protective of her. He felt somehow obligated to see her safely to her destination . . . and that just wouldn't do.

Again he laid out the bedroll for her, and settled down with his head against his saddle and his ankles crossed. Suddenly his eyes flew open and he looked at her.

"Part of the deal was you'd sing to me. I'll gladly forgo the thirty dollars, since I won't be taking you all the way, but I think the least you could do . . ."

"What do you want to hear?" She sat cross-legged on top of the bedroll, the firelight flickering on her beautiful face. She was especially enchanting when she smiled, as she did now as she stared at him across the fire.

"Annie Laurie," he requested, and then he closed his eyes.

Her voice was as perfect as he'd remembered, clear and strong and lilting, and she sang while he drifted into a deep and dreamless sleep.

He woke hours later, when the moon was high in the sky. She was still sitting there, cross-legged like an Indian on top of the bedroll, watching him. It was definitely disconcerting.

"Don't you sleep?" he asked as he folded his bedroll.

"Not much," she whispered, as if afraid to disturb the stillness of the night.

They rode away from the pond with the moon lighting their way, and at the top of the hill Shelley turned the roan around to look over the glade. The moon danced on the water, bright against the blackness of the landscape.

"I've never seen another place more perfect, Shel-ey," she whispered.

He didn't answer. Why in hell did she have to say his name like that? A whispered caress, as if they'd been lovers for years. He turned the roan and headed northwest, toward the pass that would take them over the Rocky Mountains. With every step he felt closer to whatever party might be able to take her to California. He could hand over his responsibility to the head of a wagon train and be done with her.

They hadn't gone very far when he felt her relax completely against his chest.

"Jesus, woman," he whispered. He got no response, and expected none, since she was sleeping soundly. "I've never known anyone who would prefer to sleep riding horseback than on a perfectly good bedroll."

Still, he kept the pace steady and held her close so she could sleep. Her cheek rested against his chest, and occasionally his gaze was drawn downward. Her long eyelashes brushed against her cheeks, fluttering occasionally. She looked like a little girl playing dress-up, lost in the folds of her mother's dress, falling asleep utterly exhausted.

When Annabelle did awake, as the sun was rising, it was just as she'd done the day before, with a start that threatened to throw her from the saddle.

"Bad dreams, darlin'? I mean, Mrs. Brown?" he amended.

Annabelle wished she hadn't told him to call her Mrs. Brown. The name sounded unnatural to her ear. "Annie" was much better, even "darlin'," the relaxed way he said it. But it was too late to change that now.

"I have nightmares sometimes," she explained.

"Usually not two nights in a row, though."

She lifted herself up and forward, away from the comfort of his chest, and stayed in that uncomfortable position for hours, Shelley's hat shielding her face from the sun, and the heavy silk growing more and more cumbersome as the temperature rose. Shelley made several attempts at starting a conversation, but she was uncooperative.

They stopped in a small settlement, little more than a general store and a saloon in the middle of nowhere, and Annabelle waited on the boardwalk while Shelley did the shopping. She would have waited there until he finished if a man hadn't come riding down the dusty street leading another horse . . . a horse with a man's body draped across it. As soon as she saw the body she ran into the store.

"Come over here," Shelley called when he saw her. "Do you like dried apples?" His smile disappeared when he looked at her. "What's wrong?"

"There's a man outside . . . with a dead body."

Shelley laid down the supplies and stepped out onto the boardwalk while she stayed in the general store. She walked down the aisles and examined all the goods, wishing Shelley would return. She ended up at the front counter, staring into the face of an elderly man wearing a thick pair of spectacles.

"Afternoon, pretty lady," he said.

She smiled at him, but her gaze strayed to the wall behind his head. Wanted posters, at least a dozen of them, hung there, but she saw only one.

Her own.

The drawing, not a very good one, was her likeness just the same. She'd been heavier then, her hair elaborately styled, and her eyes had had an unnatural, evil slant.

> *Annabelle St. Clair. Wanted for murder and attempted murder. Brown hair, brown eyes. One thousand dollars. Dead or alive.*

"You all right, miss?" the old man asked, squinting through the thick spectacles. "You look a bit peaked."

She turned away from him and walked down the center aisle. There, just as she remembered from her earlier perusal, were several sunbonnets artfully arranged. She grabbed the one with the largest brim and returned to the counter. The springy yellow check bonnet had bright yellow ribbons to tie under her chin.

Before she could put on the bonnet, Shelley walked through the door with the ragged-looking man who had scared her.

"The Widow Brown was right concerned," Shelley teased. "Mrs. Brown, this is John Prather, but I'm sure he'll let you call him Beans, like everybody else does."

She nodded slightly, looking at the floor. "How do you do, Mr. Beans?"

That caused all three men to burst into laughter, and she continued to stare at the floorboards.

"Darlin', Beans is a bounty hunter. The man on that horse out there is . . . was a cold-blooded killer. Beans is takin' the body to the sheriff to collect his reward."

Beans reached behind the counter and snatched a poster from the wall. "Might as well take this down."

He studied the wall intently, scratching first his nose and then his wide rump. "Look at this, Shelley." He pointed right at her own wanted poster. "A woman.

Hell, a thousand dollars. I'd like to run across that one."

The dense Beans looked directly at her. "You're right lucky to have Shelley here escortin' you with unsavory characters like this out there." Beans shook his head as Annabelle thought that he was certainly the most unsavory character she had ever met.

"Let's get out of here," Shelley said casually after glancing at the poster his friend had pointed out. He placed the yellow sunbonnet on her head and tied the ribbons beneath her chin.

"I'll get the money for the sunbonnet out of my bag." She turned away from him, but Shelley stilled her with his hand on her shoulder.

"I'll get it. Small price to pay to get my hat back."

When she looked over her shoulder at him he was smiling, and she breathed a sigh of relief. He hadn't recognized her likeness on the wanted poster.

Shelley secured the supplies on the back of the roan, settled her in her seat, and was just about to mount when he stopped short.

"Damn, I nearly forgot." He stomped back into the store, and returned a moment later clutching a bottle of tequila.

She felt a little safer when Shelley was in place behind her. She tried to look straight ahead as they rode away, but her eyes involuntarily strayed to the horse Beans had led into town, and to the body that was slung over it like a sack of cornmeal. Lifeless. Cold. Dead.

Dead or alive.

Chapter Four

They stopped late in the afternoon while still several hours of daylight remained. The landscape was barren in spots, rocky in others, and ragged wildflowers grew on the edge of a muddy trickle of a stream. It was a stark contrast to the paradise they'd camped in the night before.

Shelley promised to cook her a dinner she'd never forget, and Annabelle sat dumbly on the bedroll he'd laid out for her. It had been stupid of her to relax, even for a day . . . even for a minute. Her brief interlude by the pond had been a folly, for now she felt even worse than before. Men . . . men like Beans had her likeness, and were looking for her. A thousand dollars was a fortune to these men, to most men.

Her eyes followed Shelley as he tended his horse, started a campfire, and began to prepare their meal. All the while he barely gave her a second glance, leav-

43

ing her to her dreadful thoughts. She had never known a man like Shelley. Was there anything he couldn't do? Any situation that would break through his cool charm? He said what was on his mind, as open and honest a man as she had ever known. He was, she admitted, attractive, in a rugged untamed way that alternately frightened and thrilled her . . . to her dismay. Of course, in spite of his teasing, he had no interest in a woman like her. If he knew who she was . . . what she had been accused of . . . he would despise her.

Shelley handed her a full plate of beans, bacon, biscuits, and dried apples, and then gave her a cup of coffee. She couldn't eat much—a bite or two of the beans, a taste of the apples. Her stomach threatened to send up everything if she ate another morsel.

"You don't like my cookin'?" He took the plate from her with a feigned frown on his face.

"I just don't feel very well." She had to force her voice to rise above a whisper. "If you'll excuse me, I'm going to . . ." She stood. "I need a little privacy. I'm going over there." She pointed a shaky finger to a large boulder just east of the campsite. "For a few minutes."

Shelley sat back and watched her walk away, her skirt lifted slightly so it didn't drag in the dirt. Lack of privacy was one of the drawbacks of traveling overland, at least for a lady like her who had no business there in the first place. He started to tell her to holler if she saw snakes or something, but the look on her face changed her mind. Damned if Beans hadn't scared the bejesus out of her.

As she disappeared around the boulder, Shelley reached into the inside pocket of his vest. He unfolded the paper slowly to study the drawing once more.

Annabelle St. Clair. Brown hair, brown eyes. Murder and attempted murder. It didn't look like the Widow Brown, not really. Ann. Annabelle. A singer. An opera singer.

The fine print at the bottom of the page identified the surviving victim as Albert Gibson, and he was the one posting the private bounty. Miss St. Clair was to be delivered, dead or alive, to the police station in San Francisco.

There had been a split second, when he'd first seen the poster, that he'd believed his Widow Brown was the murderer Annabelle St. Clair. Though the thought had been fleeting, now he frowned. He didn't believe in coincidence, but what other explanation could there be? Ann was a common name, and the West was full of women with brown hair and eyes. And certainly Annabelle St. Clair wouldn't be traveling to San Francisco.

He tried to push away an intrusive memory of another innocent girl—his little sister Sarah, dead at fifteen simply because she'd been in the wrong place at the wrong time. The burden of guilt he felt every time he thought of Sarah weighed heavily on his soul. If he'd been there when she'd needed him, she would be alive today. He was certain of that.

A bounty hunter acts on instinct much of the time, he reminded himself, pushing his sister's memory to the back of his mind. Annie was in some sort of trouble, that was clear. But what? A jilted lover? Maybe her husband wasn't really dead. Maybe she was running from the not quite deceased Mr. Brown.

No. The Pinkerton agent who had been waiting for her in the alley behind the Silver Palace had mentioned her late husband. What was she running from?

45

He refolded the wanted poster he had snatched from the wall, returned it to his vest pocket, and promptly put it out of his mind.

He opened the bottle of tequila and took a long swig. He could stand to get really good and drunk tonight. That was exactly what he had intended to do at Oscar's place, but Annie had changed his plans. The desire to lose himself in the bottle always seemed to hit him after he'd had to kill an outlaw. Even after all these years . . .

"Shelley?" She was standing over him. He hadn't heard her approaching, but there she was looking down at him with wide brown eyes. A wayward strand of her dark hair had escaped and fell across her cheek, and she pushed it away distractedly. "Can I have a drink of that?"

He passed the bottle to her, and she sat down facing him. The sun was low, so she took off her new sunbonnet and tossed it on her bedroll. Then she set the almost full bottle beside her and wiped the rim with a corner of her skirt.

He raised his eyebrow but said nothing as she lifted the bottle to her lips. She practically choked on the first swallow. Her eyes watered, and when she finished coughing, she laughed.

"What vile-tasting stuff," she said, handing the bottle back to him. But her cheeks flushed prettily, and her eyes sparkled.

He took a long drink and offered the tequila to her again, expecting her to refuse. She didn't. Passing her black sleeve several times over the rim his lips had touched, she raised the bottle. The second drink didn't affect her as much, but her eyes still watered. Her face was flushed, her lips moist where she had licked away the last drop of tequila, and he saw her relax, her shoulders slumping slightly, her face softening. He wished that she had stayed on her own side of the camp, her face set in that rigid mask she'd worn since he'd met her.

When she took the bottle for the third time, she lightly wiped the rim with her sleeve before she raised it to her lips. "Shelley," she said when she lowered the bottle of golden liquid and returned it to him. Her eyes were fixed on a point far to the east, beyond his shoulder.

"Yes?" He took another long drink and gave the bottle back to her.

She didn't bother cleaning the rim before she took a very small sip and then returned the liquor to him. "It wasn't a question, I was just thinking about your name." She looked squarely at him then, brazenly studying his face. That same stubborn lock of her dark hair had fallen again and brushed against her rosy cheek, but she ignored it. "Is that your first or last name?"

He shrugged, took a long drink, and as he lowered the bottle he met her eyes. "I can't remember."

Annie laughed and reached for the tequila. "Actually, this isn't vile at all." She took another sip. "There's a poet named Shelley, you know."

"Of course I know," he said indignantly. "I'm a poet myself." A nagging voice in the back of his head warned him that he should cap the bottle, return Annie to her bedroll, and get to sleep, even though it was not yet dark. She was looking too damn good.

And she laughed as if his claim were the most amusing tidbit of information she'd ever heard. "No, I mean a real poet. 'Ode to the West Wind.' 'O, wild West

Wind, thou breath of Autumn's being . . .' " Her voice was melodious and soft.

"No, no, no." He shook his head. "I never use words like *thou*, *thee*, or *thine*." He ignored the nagging voice, pushing it out of his mind completely with another long swig of tequila.

"All right," the widow challenged him, her chin high, her eyes dancing in the firelight. "Let's hear some of your poetry."

He sat straight up. They were both cross-legged in the dirt, knee to knee. Then he looked her in the eye and said:

"There once was a lady named Annie
   Who dressed like an old gray-haired granny.
   She had chocolate brown eyes
And milky white thighs
   That led all the way up to her fanny."

Instead of being offended, as he'd expected her to be, Annie burst into laughter. He had delivered the lines with a straight face and a deep voice that would have been more fitting for a literary reading.

"That's not poetry. That's a limerick."

"No, darlin'." He grinned broadly. "That's poetry."

She refused the bottle he offered, lifting her palm and shaking her head slightly. Maybe she was afraid her last vestige of self-control would disappear.

"You didn't just make that up," she accused.

He nodded and turned the bottle up once again. Unlike the lady, he was not afraid of the effects of the tequila. Tonight he would welcome oblivion . . . tomorrow he would pay for it.

"I can write poetry anytime, anywhere . . . in my sleep if I have to."

Annie gave him a daunting look that said she didn't believe him, and always relishing a challenge, he decided to take her on.

"I'll prove it to you." He leaned forward, closer to her face. A face that was more beautiful than he ever would have imagined.

"The lady rode in from St. Louis.
With her sweet sounding voice she did woo us.
    The men all came out,
    Every cad, rake, and lout,
And said, 'Annie dear, please won't you—' "

"Shelley!"

" 'Screw us,' " he finished, in spite of her objection.

"That's disgusting." She tried to keep a straight face, but the corners of her full mouth twitched as if she were suppressing a smile. "The real Shelley—"

"I'm real."

"You know what I mean," she interrupted. "The real Shelley wrote real poetry. 'If I were a dead leaf thou mightest bear; if I were a swift cloud to fly with thee; a wave to pant beneath thy power . . .' "

"Hold it, hold it." He held up both hands in protest. "If you're going to use words like 'pant beneath thy power' . . . I'm going to have to kiss you." He leaned forward, close to her.

"You will not," she said, trying to sound indignant but succeeding only in sounding drunk.

"Give me one good reason why I won't."

Annie also leaned forward then, her face mere inches from his. Her eyes twinkled, her nostrils flared, and he noticed details he had missed before—the lushness of her mouth, the way her hair shone in the firelight. He wondered what she would look like in a pretty dress that fit her properly, and realized that he would probably never know.

"Because I've already had a bit too much to drink, and you're a gentleman," she said as seriously as she could manage. "A gentleman never takes advantage of a lady when she's . . . not herself."

"Nobody's accused me of being a gentleman for a very long time." He drank deeply from the bottle. "But if that's the case, I'll have to get good and drunk myself."

They sat there as the stars came out, Annie spouting bits and pieces of poetry and Shelley answering with limericks of his own. By the time the sky was dark, and there was only the light of the fire and the stars above them, the bottle was empty. Annie laughed at everything he said, whether it was funny or not. He was drunk. Not tipsy, not mellow, but gloriously plastered. The widow had put aside her earlier resolve and taken another small drink or two from the bottle while it was still warm from the touch of his lips.

When he finally laid his head against the saddle he demanded a song. "A damn good one," he ordered gruffly.

Annie smiled wickedly, the fire lighting up one half of her face, golden and devilishly angelic. "I might not be able to write poetry, but I do have a talent."

He didn't move as she began to unbutton the several tiny buttons from the neck down, so that the collar revealed her silky skin and the top of her lacy chemise. Then she did the bottom of the skirt up to her knees, revealing a white petticoat, full and ruffled.

He waited for her. She was going to come to him and . . . she stood and loosened her hair, letting it spill around her shoulders and down her back.

She began with a seductive swaying of her hips as she looked down at him, then she began to hum softly as she danced around him, tossing back her head and baring her white throat. "This is my favorite part," she said huskily. "Carmen. I performed it last year at the Opera Comedie. Some of the critics detested it, calling it unfit for the family theater. Women smoking on stage!" Annie stopped suddenly and looked down at him.

"Can I have a cigar? A cigarette?"

He was too drunk to care where or what she had sung. All he wanted at the moment was to hear her sing for him. He rolled over and grabbed one of his long, thin cigars from his saddlebag near his head. She plucked it from his fingers and began to dance again, lighting the cigar in the campfire.

Giving it all she had, Annabelle danced around the fire and sang to Shelley. She lifted her skirts to her knees and spun around until she was dizzy, and she continued to dance long after she had stopped singing, puffing on the thin cigar and blowing the smoke all around her, so that she danced in an ethereal blue haze. Her breath came hard and fast, and she dropped, exhausted, to her knees at his side.

"Do you still want to kiss me, Shelley?" she offered innocently.

He nodded. "I'm afraid I do, darlin'."

She leaned over and pressed her lips against his. She'd expected a sweet kiss, with puckered lips and a little smack, but Shelley wrapped his arms around her neck and held her there, parting her lips with his tongue. She didn't pull away, but opened her mouth to the new sensation. No one had ever kissed her like that, and it made her feel . . . warm and tingly, like the tequila. It was nice, different, made her feel as if she could lie in his arms forever, their lips locked together, their tongues dancing as surely as she had danced around the fire for him.

She pulled away, breathless, staring into his hazel eyes. She couldn't discern their color with only the light of the fire, but she knew they were hazel . . . had seen those hazel eyes bore into her.

"I don't know why I like you so much, Shelley." She laid her head on his chest. She could hear his heartbeat, a comforting sound. To have another heartbeat so close . . .

His hand rested in her hair, and before the moon was at its zenith, they slept.

Chapter Five

It had been a long time since Shelley had awakened with the sun in his face, and he certainly didn't remember it being so painful. Shafts of light as sharp as shards of glass penetrated his reluctant eyelids, eliciting a low groan and a fruitless attempt to roll onto his stomach to hide his face from the intrusive sunlight.

Fruitless because someone was using his stomach as a pillow.

He cracked one eye open, slowly and narrowly, and all he could see was a mass of dark hair as Annie buried her face against his midsection.

The empty tequila bottle lay on its side close to his right hand, and he realized with slowly unfolding wonder that his left hand was buried in Annie's hair. He didn't know how she had come to be there. The last thing he remembered was sitting across from the

53

Widow Brown and making up tasteless limericks while she laughed and lifted the bottle to her lips.

He brushed her tangled hair away from her face, and she wrinkled her nose as the sun intruded on her sleep.

"No," she whispered. "It's much too early, Pierre."

She turned her face into his belly and snuggled as if he were a feather pillow. She tossed her arms across his body so that her upper arm shielded her face and her fingers brushed the ground. She was lying perpendicular to his outstretched body, and he could feel her hot breath penetrating the thin cotton of his shirt, warming his skin.

He came instantly awake. Pierre? Was that her husband's name? Pierre Brown? It didn't seem likely, but anything was possible.

She purred like a cat, and he lifted her arm so that the sunlight brushed her face. She chastised him, first in English and then in French.

He listened to the nonsense that was coming from her mouth buried against his stomach. She didn't want to be pulled awake, but he refused to drop her arm.

He watched, his head resting with little comfort on the hard saddle, as Annie twisted her head languidly and drew her knees up, finally lifting her head and realizing, slowly at first, and then with a start, where she was.

"Good mornin', darlin'," he drawled, determined not to let her realize that he felt horrible.

She pushed herself away from him and sat at his side, both hands covering her face. He lifted his eyebrows and for a moment forgot his pain at the sight of her slender throat and her creamy white breasts threatening to break free from the restraining chemise. Her skirt was unbuttoned to her knees, and while her petticoat covered her, there were a couple of inches of her finely shaped ankle peeking out enticingly as she sat with her legs to one side. Well-worn emerald green slippers covered her tiny feet.

He suddenly wished that he hadn't gotten quite so drunk, because he couldn't remember how she had gotten into such a disheveled condition. Even her hair, the dark hair she was always so careful to keep restrained, was falling wildly around her shoulders and down her back.

It was with great effort that she stood, slowly and uncertainly, brushing her hair away from her face so that it fell straight down her back.

"Look what you've done to me," she admonished, looking down at him.

He gave her a smile, crooked and more of an effort than he would let on. "Whatever I did, I should do it more often. You look . . . remarkable this morning."

The Widow Brown suddenly realized, with a becoming blush, that her dress was unbuttoned, and she turned away from him to repair her appearance. "You know exactly what you did," she muttered under her breath. "I can't believe you would take advantage of me like that."

He frowned. Had he? He looked down the length of his fully clothed body. She was still fully dressed, if a little untidy. Surely he hadn't . . . and not remembered . . .

With great effort he pulled himself into a seated position. "Perhaps you could refresh my memory."

Annie spun around, an accusing look on her face. Her eyes were still slightly swollen and sleepy-looking, and her cheeks were pink, a combination of her anger and a sleepy warmth. Her accusing expression faded, and she smiled.

"You don't recall what happened at all, do you?"

He shook his head, but ever so slightly. Even that was painful.

It distressed him to see his companion's smile grow even wider. "That's too bad," she said insincerely. "I can see you're heartbroken."

She turned away from him and started gathering her hairpins. They were scattered all around the campsite, and he watched with mounting dismay that he couldn't remember how they had become so widely dispersed. She was securing her hair in place, all her glorious hair in a tight knot at her nape, when he questioned her.

"What was your husband's name, Mrs. Brown?"

She twisted her head to look over her shoulder at him. "Why do you ask?"

He shrugged. "Just curious. Do you want breakfast?" he added, to make his inquiry seem trivial.

"God, no," she groaned. "William. My husband's name was William."

"William Brown," he repeated slowly as he came to his feet and lifted the suddenly incredibly heavy saddle. "William Brown, bootmaker from St. Louis."

"Why the sudden interest in my late husband?" she asked sharply.

He ignored her as he saddled the roan, the simple task a chore in his present state. When it was done, he walked with distinct purpose to stand in front of her, and lifted her black skirt slightly. She slapped his hand away, but he was undaunted and lifted her skirt again to barely expose one slipper-clad foot.

"Just wondering why William Brown, bootmaker, didn't make his wife a decent pair of boots." He scowled. "These won't last through Wyoming Territory."

Annie slapped his hand away. "I had several pairs of fine boots," she said indignantly. "But I was forced to leave St. Louis with nothing more than the clothes on my back, and I didn't happen to be wearing boots at the time."

He stood close to her, and she backed away from him, her face paling a little.

God help him, he was becoming far too attached to the increasingly lovely Widow Brown . . . and her story stunk to high heaven.

He shook his head. "So you fled St. Louis with the clothes on your back, and sang your way to Brayton. I don't suppose you'd like to tell me why those Pinkerton agents are after you?"

He placed his hands around her waist and lifted her onto the roan's back. There was something about that simple act he was beginning to enjoy . . . too much . . . and something warned him that he'd better see her on her way to California with another party . . . soon.

Annie closed her eyes. "I don't remember the saddle being so high off the ground before." She clutched at her stomach.

"Well? Are you going to tell me?"

"I can't talk about anything right now," she said as he joined her, wrapping his arm around her tiny waist. She placed the sunbonnet on her head. "I don't feel very well."

He guided the horse at a leisurely pace, and it became clear that Annie was determined to hold her body stiff and away from his. She was quiet as always, and kept her head turned away from him. The sun-bonnet covered her hair and hid her face, and he felt his earlier frustration melt away.

"Mrs. Brown, I know you're feeling none too frisky this morning, and seeing as how you spent last night and most of this morning using my gut as a pillow, I don't think it would matter too much if you wanted to lean back and relax just a bit."

She hesitated, but not for long, before she settled against his chest. It was a surprisingly comforting feeling, more soothing than he could have imagined.

"Thank you, Shelley."

"You're welcome, Mrs. Brown."

She toyed with the ribbons that trailed from her bonnet for several minutes then spoke. "Shelley?"

"Yes, Mrs. Brown?"

"You don't need to keep calling me Mrs. Brown. I'm sorry that I lost my temper and said that you were my employee, and not to call me Annie. Annie suits me just fine."

He smiled in spite of the bright morning light that was presently threatening to split his head in two. He had been calling her Annie in his mind all along. But she didn't need to know that. "Makes sense, Annie, since I'm sharing with you an intimate experience I've never shared with another woman."

He felt her slight tremor at the words *intimate experience*. "What's that?" she asked.

"Why, this hangover, darlin'. I reckon if we make it through the day and neither of us falls off this horse, we'll have accomplished somethin'."

He pulled his wide-brimmed hat low over his eyes. What he really needed was a dark, cool room with a soft bed where he could sleep for a couple of days. But there would be no dark rooms, no cool beds, and no more tequila until he saw Annie safely on her way to San Francisco and out of his life.

She was not his responsibility, he reminded himself. She certainly wasn't his type, as far as women were concerned. She was timid, refined, and far more suited to a city dude, a bootmaker or such, than to a wandering bounty hunter. Hell, he had seen the way she looked at Beans when she learned what he did, had seen the terror on her face at the sight of the outlaw's body. What would she think if she learned that was his chosen profession as well? Would she look at him with the same loathing and fear he had seen in her eyes when she'd looked at Beans?

Shelley had a sudden vision of Annie dancing and singing and smoking one of his cigars, her hair whipping about her head, her seductive smile for him alone. He shook the vision away. A segment of a drunken dream, perhaps, induced by tequila and remembered hazily. Whatever it was, it was best to put it out of his mind, to put Annie out of his mind completely.

There were plans to be made. She would need her own horse, a decent pair of boots, a pair of britches . . . She wouldn't like that, but she couldn't ride sidesaddle all the way to California. Food, a bedroll . . . he made a mental list of everything she would need before he let her go on her own. Well, not entirely on her own. He'd see to it that she hooked up with a responsible party.

It would cost a hell of a lot more than 36 dollars, but he could certainly afford to stake her. In the end, he was sure the cost would be insignificant compared to what he would pay if he escorted her all the way to

California. A price too high to contemplate.

Yes, he'd see her on her way, and then he'd head back to Kansas. Edmund Vaughan had been known to spend time in the cowtowns, and he was worth 300 dollars. The outlaw ran occasionally with Hardy Blount who had a bounty of 500 dollars on his head. So a trip to Kansas was called for . . . yes, Kansas. There was a pretty little redhead in Abilene. Shelley tried to concentrate on her. Big breasts, thick red hair, and big green eyes . . . pretty as a picture.

And who in the hell was Pierre?

Chapter Six

They traveled for two more days before they came to Coldwater Creek, a narrow, dusty town west of Cheyenne. A silent agreement had been reached between them, and they didn't speak of their evening of tequila and poetry by the fire. Annabelle pushed the memory of their kiss to the back of her mind, assuring herself that it could not have been half as wonderful as she remembered. She had been kissed before, after all, and a kiss from one man was no different than from another man. At least Shelley didn't remember . . . either the kiss or her confession that she liked him.

And she did like him. That was what made it so difficult to lie to him. She'd told the story of her fictitious life in St. Louis so many times it almost seemed real to her. Normally the lies came easily to her lips, but not when Shelley looked straight at her and asked probing questions.

The days grew warmer, and she cursed her heavy dress. She'd never spent much time outdoors, and she was beginning to hate the relentless sun. Even though they began to travel well before light, while the air was cool and the aromatic scent of pine surrounded them, it seemed no time at all before the sun rose and threatened to bake the very skin from her bones.

Coldwater Creek was dominated by a large general store, though there was a livery, a saloon, a hotel, a barber shop—all the trappings of a successful town. It was soon clear that everyone there knew Shelley. People on the boardwalk waved and called out to him, and he flashed a smile at everyone he saw.

Annabelle followed him into the general store. A portly man with graying hair met Shelley near the entrance, and she stood behind her escort while the two men exchanged pleasantries and shook hands heartily.

Shelley turned to her, took her arm, and introduced her to Walter Lawrence, proprietor of the general store.

"We've got to get Annie here outfitted for a trip to California," Shelley said, keeping his hand on her arm, almost unconsciously.

Mr. Lawrence smiled admiringly. "I'm surprised a lovely young lady like yourself isn't taking the rail."

Shelley jumped in before she could answer. "Annie here wants to see the elephant. She's a more adventurous woman than you might think, to look at her."

She would have defended herself—he made it sound as if she were some sort of thrill seeker—but before she could say a word, a young girl burst into the room, tight blonde curls quivering about her face, her blue eyes alight as she ran straight to Shelley.

"Oh, Shelley," she said, slightly breathless. "It's just

been forever since you've visited Coldwater Creek."
She looked at him with adoring blue eyes. "Are you
staying long? There's a dance on Saturday."

"Sorry, darlin'. We won't be here but just a little
while." He gave her a crooked grin and tapped a long,
brown finger under her chin. The tiny lines at the corners of his eyes deepened, crinkling his sun-bronzed
skin with that easy grin.

The pretty girl noticed Annabelle and her smile
faded as she narrowed her eyes in Annabelle's direction. "Who is this, Shelley?"

"This is Mrs. Ann Brown, from St. Louis. Annie, this
lovely young lady is Willa Lawrence. Walter's daughter."

Willa was probably no more than 16, and dressed
in a pink and white gingham that was far more suited
to the June heat than the heavy black silk Annabelle
was forced to wear. The young woman looked as cool
as a spring morning, even as she glared at Annabelle.

"How do you do, Mrs. Brown," she said respectfully,
but Annabelle had the feeling she was being insulted
just the same. "Surely you're not—"

"Mrs. Brown is traveling to San Francisco," Shelley
interrupted. "Maybe you can help us choose a few
things, Willa. Annie here needs a good, sturdy pair of
boots, and some britches—"

"Britches!" Willa's hand went to her throat in what
Annabelle was certain was mock dismay. "I just can't
imagine a proper older lady such as Mrs. Brown wearing britches!"

To Annabelle's mortification, Shelley laughed.
"Hard to picture, I know, but it's practical."

They chose a soft pair of tan pants, and a white cotton shirt that looked so cool Annabelle longed to

change her clothes right there in the store. But when it came time to choose a pair of boots, their troubles began. Her feet were too small for the boots Mr. Lawrence stocked. The only pair he had in her size were short boots made of soft, comfortable red leather, that laced snugly around her ankles.

"I ordered these for a lady here in town, but she up and took off for back East before they came in. I swear, I thought I'd never get rid of these boots. I can give you a real good price. They're so small, they're even too small for Willa's feet, not that I'd allow her to wear a pair of bright red boots like these . . ." He stopped abruptly.

Annabelle looked down at the outlandish red boots on her feet. They certainly would serve her better than the emerald green slippers that were already falling apart. She took a few tentative steps in the tightly laced boots, then turned to Shelley and lifted her hem just a fraction. In a synchronized motion they looked at the crimson boots, then lifted their eyes to one another and burst into uncontrolled laughter. Mr. Lawrence and his petulant daughter stared at them as if they were insane.

After a few moments their laughter finally stopped, and Shelley turned to the storekeeper.

"We'll take them."

That wasn't all they took. In addition to the clothes and the boots, Shelley insisted that she purchase a new hat, something more in keeping with her new look. He selected a tan hat similar to his own, and placed it on her head. He gathered together more food and another bedroll, and they hadn't even looked at horses yet.

As Shelley continued to pile goods on the smiling shopkeeper's counter, she chased after him, trying to get his attention in a subtle way. Finally he stopped, and she plucked at his sleeve.

"Shelley," she whispered hoarsely, not wanting to embarrass herself in front of Mr. Lawrence. "This is bound to cost well over thirty-six dollars, and I still need a horse and a saddle."

Shelley looked down at her. She was standing close, whispering softly, lost in the volumes of her ridiculous mourning dress. Her brown eyes looked huge, opened wide, in a face as delicate as fine porcelain.

"Don't worry about it. I'll lend you the money and you can send it to me when you're able." He said the words with apparent indifference.

"But I don't know where you live . . . I don't even know your full name."

For some reason she was still whispering, and his heart caught in his throat. It was all too much, too fast, and he was feeling much closer to her than he cared to.

He gave her his wickedest grin, and he winked at her lecherously. "Just send it to Oscar's place, care of Cherry. I always end up back there sooner or later, and she'll hold it for me."

It worked. Her eyes hardened and her mouth tightened. "I'll just do that." She no longer whispered.

He watched her stride out of the store, holding her skirt off the floor as she left in a huff. He shook his head. Mention a woman like Cherry to a lady, and the reaction was always the same.

The horse he chose for Annie was a sable brown mare, gentle and healthy-looking, and he saddled the horse for her in front of the general store.

"Do you want to change into your new clothes before we leave town?" he asked, watching her stare at the mare as if it were some sort of monster.

Annie shook her head.

"Well, we won't be going far, but you'll be more comfortable riding astride in the britches."

She blushed.

"Put them on under the dress if you're so damn modest you can't stand the thought of anyone seeing you wearing pants, or hike up your skirts and—"

"I can't ride," she interrupted him with a simple statement that left him speechless.

"I thought I would be able to. I really did. I've been watching you, and I thought when I saw my own horse I'd be able to jump in the saddle and do what you do." She never took her eyes off the mare. "But I can't."

"You could have told me," he said, finally finding his voice.

"I know."

He shook his head, took her hand, and led her to the roan. He was so accustomed to lifting her into the saddle he did it almost automatically now, and he did just that as a sulky Willa watched from the window of her father's general store. He led Annie's mare as they rode out of town, and he grumbled in the woman's ear all the way down the dusty street and away from the quaint little town.

When he finally stopped complaining, Annabelle leaned against his chest and closed her eyes. She could never tell him, but she would miss riding in front of him, resting her cheek against his chest, falling asleep to his heartbeat. It was just another secret to keep to herself. One of many.

"You know that little girl is in love with you, don't you?" she asked after a while.

"What girl?"

Annabelle rolled her eyes. Men were so dense sometimes. "Willa Lawrence. She looked at you all afternoon as if you were some kind of . . . hero. A knight who will someday appear out of nowhere on a white horse and carry her away."

"I seem to have that effect on women. Most of them anyway."

She shook her head. "You dolt. Willa's an impressionable young girl. You really shouldn't lead her on—"

"Look," he said sharply. "Willa is just a kid. I've known her and Walter since she was . . . I don't know . . . seven or eight, I guess. And I certainly never lead her on—"

"I beg your pardon, but you do," she snapped, then lowered her voice. "You call her darlin', and flash her one of those Shelley smiles, and tell her how lovely she is—."

"I've done all those things to you, yet you seem immune to my many charms," he said lightly.

"I am twenty-five years old. A woman, not a romantic little girl with dreams of hearts and flowers. Reality will intrude upon Willa Lawrence soon enough, as it does for all women when they find out what . . ." She stopped her tirade. "Sorry. It's none of my business."

There was a moment of silence before Shelley answered her. "No. You're right. I reckon Willa is growing up mighty fast. I'll be more careful about what I say the next time I pass through Coldwater Creek." He waited, perhaps expecting her to respond, but she answered him with stony silence. "I guess I've always had a soft spot for little girls," he said wistfully.

She answered his confession with a decidedly unfeminine grunt of disbelief. "I'll just bet you have."

They stopped for the night on the bank of a shallow creek, and Annabelle strung a rope between two trees and hung the blanket as Shelley had done that night in the glade. She was proud of herself because she was able to perform the simple act unassisted. It was a small accomplishment, to be sure, but for someone who had never had to do anything for herself, had never been expected to do anything but sing, it was a feat.

While Shelley started a campfire and a pot of coffee, she bathed in the creek, washed her hair, and laundered the black dress. He hadn't said a word to her as she'd disappeared around the barrier that afforded her a modicum of privacy, no taunts about her modesty or offers to rescue her if she saw a snake. She didn't know what to expect from her escort anymore. One minute he was grinning and teasing her, and the next he was scowling like a brown bear.

The sun was low in the sky, and with the removal of her black dress the heat seemed to dissipate. The water that flowed gently was almost icy it was so cold, but it felt refreshing, and after a few minutes she was accustomed to the biting chill.

She was loath to leave the water when her dress was washed. She trailed her hand through the waist-high water, then lowered herself so the water touched her chin. With her hands she splashed all around her, turning in a circle and starting to sing in a low voice. A few months ago she might have chosen an aria she enjoyed, but the song that came to mind as she spun

n the water and lightly slapped the surface was "Buf-
alo Gals."

She was certain Shelley couldn't hear her, her voice
was so soft. He was busy setting up camp, and when
she'd last seen him he'd been in one of his surly
moods. There was no telling what kind of mood she
would find him in when she finally emerged from the
creek. When she came to the part of the song about
dancing by the light of the moon, she remembered
now she had danced around the fire for Shelley that
night she had first tasted tequila. It was all she could
do to keep from laughing. At least he didn't remember.
How mortifying that would be!

She continued to sing softly as she dried herself and
dressed in her new clothes. The tan britches were a
tad snug in the hips but otherwise fit well, and the
cotton shirt was heavenly compared to the inappro-
priate black silk she was accustomed to. She finished
off the odd ensemble with the red boots. They were
the most outlandish footwear she had ever owned.

When she stepped from behind the makeshift curtain, Shelley was watching her. It was as if he'd been
waiting for her to emerge. She held her hands aloft
and turned about slowly.

"What do you think?" She completed the circle and
hung her wet dress over the rope, beside the blanket.
When she finally turned to look at him, there was an
angry expression on his face.

"What's the matter?" She looked down at her new
outfit. Nothing seemed amiss. The blouse was buttoned as far as it would go, and though it left her
throat exposed it was decent. It was true that the
britches were decadent, but they had been his idea,
not hers.

"We don't have all day," he snapped. "You get your first riding lesson before dinner, while there's still some light." When she didn't join him immediately, he growled at her. "If you don't mind."

She followed him to her new mare, an animal almost the color of her hair. Shelley showed her how to mount the mare, standing behind her and eventually placing his hand on her derriere. Boosting her up, he cursed, and although she couldn't see him, she knew he was angry with her, though she couldn't imagine what she'd done.

Shelley taught her as if she were a child, his words clipped, coarse, and simple, but he had her riding around the campsite with relative ease before long. The burning rage inside him grew as he watched her atop the mare. She bit her lip and tossed her hair. Naturally she'd left it down to dry today, instead of gathering it at her nape.

He'd grown angrier and angrier as he'd waited on the other side of the blanket and listened to her sing and splash in the water. Damn it to hell, his common sense told him she'd done nothing wrong, but when he'd rescued a terrified, plain mouse from under the staircase outside the Silver Palace, he hadn't counted on being confronted with Annie as she was now. She should have warned him, he thought irrationally, that she would turn out to be so . . . so . . . so tempting.

He helped her dismount, and she smiled at his scowling face as they returned to the campfire.

"That was fun," she said cheerfully. "I think I'm going to like riding."

"I'm happy for you," he said sarcastically. "You can

put your dress back on now. Save your riding clothes for tomorrow."

"I can't. I washed the dress. It was just filthy, and it's still wet. I hope I haven't ruined it completely." She plopped to the ground by the fire. "Besides, these clothes are much more comfortable. That black gown was like an oven."

He groaned as he knelt by the fire. A small pot of beans was warming over the flame, and he turned his attention to it, cursing under his breath.

"You were the one who insisted I buy these britches," Annie said sweetly. "I know they're not very stylish, but I wouldn't expect that to bother you, of all people."

His head snapped up. "You really don't get it, do you?" He forgot about their supper and crossed the short distance that separated them. "Stand up," he demanded, and she did as he ordered without hesitation.

He placed his hands on her shoulders and ran his palms over her slender arms, the thin cotton barely separating his skin from hers. Then he settled his hands on her waist. She was so tiny his hands nearly spanned her midsection. When his hands began to glide slowly down her hips, she pushed them away.

"What do you think you're doing?" she whispered raspily.

He looked up, drawing his eyes away from her body, and their eyes locked. "Why did you hide this under that atrocious dress?"

"Hide what?"

He narrowed his eyes, and his jaw clenched. She was teasing him, and he didn't like it. Not one bit. She wasn't an innocent virgin. She was a woman, a widowed woman who knew exactly how to seduce him.

He pulled her to him roughly, ignoring her palms pushing against his chest. He lowered his head and kissed her fiercely, dismissing her muffled protests. She pursed her lips, trying to keep them tightly closed, but he parted them with his tongue and clasped her to him.

The change that came over Annabelle was slow and certain, like butter melting in the summer sun. Her protests stopped, and her hands that had been pushing him away now grasped the front of his shirt, then traveled up and around to clasp behind his neck.

Her breathing slowed, her heart raced, as she pressed her chest to his. She parted her lips to accept the darting tongue that made her heart pound and caused a funny feeling in her chest, as if a hundred tiny feathers danced inside her.

When she flicked her tongue over his lower lip and grabbed a handful of hair at his nape, the embrace underwent a change. He was no longer trying to frighten her. His lips were firm and demanding, and his hands were gentle against her back. His anger was melting away as surely as her resistance had.

They dropped to their knees, never loosening their firm embrace, their lips locked. The heat of the fire scorched her cheek as the warmth and the flickering light surrounded them. Shelley lowered her to the ground and rolled her away from the heat of the campfire, never releasing his hold on her. They lay in the grass, side by side. She decided that she could kiss him forever. She'd rather kiss than sing. When he moved his hand to cup her breast, she shivered. She was a little afraid. Shelley was going to make love to her, and that was what she wanted more than anything. But she didn't know what to expect. Not really.

She'd heard whispered words about lovemaking, words that conflicted sometimes. Certainly no one had ever told her that kissing the right man could be so absolutely heavenly.

And then she pulled her lips away from his, ever so slightly, and whispered, her breath against his warm lips. "I love you, Shelley."

He stiffened and released her, rolling away abruptly. "Goddamn it, Annie. You had to go and ruin everything."

He rose to his feet with his back to her, and stalked toward the creek and the hanging blanket that shielded a portion of the bank.

At that moment, she decided the best thing to do was to ignore what had just happened between them. One minute he wanted her, the next he didn't. One minute she was pushing him away, the next . . .

"Why don't you wait until morning?" She didn't relish the idea of being left alone by the campfire after dark. "The water's bound to be freezing by now."

She heard a muffled response from behind the blanket, but she couldn't understand him. "What?"

"I said that's good, dammit!" he shouted, too loudly.

Chapter Seven

Wendell was late. He hated being late almost as much as he hated the failure of a well-laid plan, or, in fact, any occurrence that brought disorder to his life. He scowled as he mounted the Denver hotel's plushly carpeted stairs, the thought of that most recent source of irritation in his life intruding unpleasantly. A bounty hunter! He massaged his jaw and remembered the big man who had knocked him out. Knocked him out! No one had ever dared . . . but that was beside the point. Annabelle St. Clair was in the hands of a bounty hunter who might decide at any moment to dispose of her and collect his reward . . . if he knew who she was . . . if Ann Brown really was Annabelle St. Clair.

The door to the hotel room was thrown open moments after he knocked smartly on the door. Maybe he was wrong. Maybe one of his other colleagues had already found her.

"You're late, Yates," Dawson snapped at him before the door was properly closed.

Wendell had never had much patience with Dawson Walsh or his brother Eugene. They drank too much, and complained too much, and their lives were, in general, much too unprincipled for Wendell's tastes.

A quick glance around the room confirmed that the other three agents had been waiting for some time. Dawson and his little brother Eugene had killed almost half a bottle of bourbon between them, and their coats were thrown in a crumpled heap on the single bed, their hats and vests tossed away unceremoniously and quite sloppily. Wendell removed his hat but held it in his hand. Eugene nodded halfheartedly. Neither of the Walsh brothers liked him much, but he didn't mind. He didn't care for them either.

The third agent sat in a chair by the window where the sunlight shone on the open book in his hands. He might have been alone, for all the attention he paid his fellow agents. Wendell had often wondered how Mordecai Butterfield had come to work for Pinkerton's.

As if sensing that Wendell was thinking of him, Mordecai lowered the Bible that was always in his possession and raised questioning eyes to him.

Wendell dreaded opening his mouth. His jaw still ached, and he would have preferred that the others not know exactly what had transpired. But the three of them were looking at him expectantly, and he knew they'd found nothing.

"I think I've located her," he said with as little movement of his jaw as possible, and therefore as little pain.

"What?" Eugene leaned forward.

"I said, I think I've found her," he said slowly, his mouth almost motionless.

Eugene smiled. "What happened? She punch you in the jaw?"

"No, goddammit." He cut his eyes to Mordecai, and received the scathing glare he had expected.

"Well? Where is she?" Dawson snapped. "I hate this assignment. Even if we find her, we can't shoot her . . . and her a killer. We take her to her uncle and . . ."

"I lost her." Wendell finally gave in and moved the joints that still pained him. "I think she's taken up with a bounty hunter named Shelley." He drew her wanted poster from his vest pocket and crumpled it before he tossed it on the floor. "This is useless. She doesn't look like the sketch on that poster anymore."

He had the full attention of the other three men. "I'd say she's lost twenty, thirty pounds. When I saw her she was dressed like a poverty-stricken widow, and she was singing in a saloon."

After a few stunned moments, Dawson regained his voice. "You lost her?"

He didn't like being admonished by men he considered far inferior to him. Eugene and Dawson were both big men, but they had no class, no finesse.

"I wasn't positive it was her, you moron. Did you get those photographs?" he snapped.

Dawson retrieved a small stack—three photographs and several newspaper clippings—and Wendell rifled through them quickly. His eyes fell on what he was looking for, and he smiled. It hurt, but what the hell.

"This is what she looks like. Look at the face." It was a three-year-old photograph of her torso and face only. She'd been a little plump at the time, but the face . . . "She's disguised herself. Quite well, I might

76

add." His voice held a note of respect. She'd fooled him, after all. "Made her face pale, added shadows to make it look tired and gaunt. She's passing herself off as a widow from St. Louis, and to tell you the truth, I wasn't certain it was her until I saw this photograph."

"What about the bounty hunter? Is she in any danger?" It was Mordecai who finally asked a worthwhile question.

"Can't be sure. He seemed to know her well . . . but he could have been lying about how long he'd known her. Could have been a trick to get her away from me."

Wendell knew the other agents were thinking the same thing he was. If she died . . . if this bounty hunter shot her and turned her in for the private bounty posted by her surviving victim . . . there would be no bonus for them. And the enormous bonus promised to each of them for the successful completion of this job was unheard of.

"And you're positive it was her?" Mordecai asked again, his voice low and emotionless.

He hesitated. "Almost positive."

The Walsh brothers exchanged a disbelieving glance.

"Well, what else have we got to go on?" Wendell raised the volume of his voice. "I still say she's headed for San Francisco. If we split up again—maybe in teams this time—we should be able to intercept them somewhere along the route."

"Are you certain they're traveling together?" Dawson asked.

"No. But if you were a bounty hunter, and you got your hands on a mark worth a thousand dollars, would you let her go?" he asked sensibly. "Maybe he knows what he's got. Maybe not. Either way, she's headed in that direction."

Dawson smiled. "Me and Eugene'll take the railway."

Mordecai rose languidly from his chair to his full height, a simple act which always amazed Wendell, for the thin man stood well over six feet, and his acute thinness, the bony angles of his arms and legs, made him look even taller. " 'All wickedness is but little to the wickedness of a woman.' "

Mordecai had the annoying habit of reciting Bible verses whenever he found it appropriate . . . which was often.

"Mordecai and I will travel overland . . . try to track them north and over the southern portion of Wyoming Territory." Wendell was all business. This was his life, and he was damned if a low-life bounty hunter would get the best of him.

"Why that route?" Eugene asked.

Wendell gave him a chilling grin. "Because it's the route I would take. If we don't run across them in a couple of weeks, we'll take the rail from Placerville and wait for them in Virginia City."

"If that bounty hunter Shelley kills her or turns her in before we find her, we might as well turn in our pistols and take up farming." Eugene grinned at the tall man who was slicking back thin, pale blond hair. "Except for Mordy, here. He could become a preacher."

Pain flashed across Mordecai's face, then disappeared and his visage was emotionless once more.

"Don't worry about them, Mordecai," Wendell assured the tall man who would accompany him on his quest for the man who had humiliated him . . . and for

Annabelle St. Clair, of course. "They ain't gonna find squat on the railroad."

Mordecai stared at Eugene. His glare could be daunting when he wished it to be so. His pale gray eyes could bore into a man's soul. "We will find her. 'The path of the just is as the shining light, that shineth more and more unto the perfect day.' "

Wendell placed his hat back on his head and grabbed the lapels of his well-cut coat. Mordecai could be a bother, but he was a better shot than either of the Walsh brothers, and he kept to himself most of the time. Time was wasting. They had the girl to find, and he had that bounty hunter to pay back. He didn't necessarily want to kill Shelley, but he would if he had to. Sometimes people got in the way and got hurt, but that was a regrettable necessity. Wendell Yates prided himself on being a man who got the job done, no matter what it took.

Chapter Eight

If Annabelle regretted anything she'd done in her life, it was her hasty declaration of love to Shelley. He hadn't spoken three words to her in the days that had passed since then, and always rode just ahead of her, more than likely so he wouldn't have to look at her. They traveled fast, Shelley giving little heed to her comfort.

The sun-filled days were cooler, not because the temperatures had abated but because her new mode of dress was much more reasonable for the summer climate. She was constantly amazed by the land that stretched forever ahead of them, alternately green and rocky, hilly and flat, and as the days went by they seemed to come no closer to the horizon as they plodded silently west.

Shelley fell asleep almost instantly every night after supper, sometimes requesting a song, sometimes not.

He woke her while it was still pitch black, usually not long after she'd managed to fall into a restless sleep. How she missed sleeping in his arms in the early morning hours! It was the only time she'd felt safe in three long months.

She knew, of course, that she didn't really love Shelley. She was grateful to him for everything he had done. Surely he regretted his spur-of-the-moment decision to escort her to San Francisco. Poor Shelley. She'd turned his life upside down, and still he hadn't deserted her. But, no, she didn't love him. He was the antithesis of everything she admired in a man. When she fell in love, if she ever did, it would be with a man who was cultured and refined, a man who appreciated the fine things in life as she did. Great poetry, the opera, Shakespeare. And although she didn't consider great looks important, she was certain the man she fell in love with would be dark and tall, but not as tall as Shelley. He could be too overpowering at times. Blue eyes, she decided as she stared at his back, the rhythmic movement of his roan seemingly causing him none of the discomfort her mare was causing her. The man she fell in love with would have blue eyes. Clear eyes with no hidden fury or unasked questions.

He'd been wise to break away from her when he did, knowing the folly of their brief attraction. She knew that she owed Shelley everything. If the thought that she loved him caused him such distress, then before he found a wagon train for her, she had to see to it that he knew she didn't love him after all.

The settlement, if it could be called that, in which they arrived near the end of another day was little more than a roadway stop, a one-story building where a wizened old man sold necessities, whiskey, and an occasional meal. He lived in a small room at the rear of the store, and apparently disdained the touch of water on his body. He was the most odoriferous man Annabelle had ever encountered.

She was beginning to believe that everyone west of the Mississippi knew Shelley. She finally realized that this was an established route he traveled often, and that was why every face seemed to be familiar to him. The shriveled storekeeper greeted him warmly, and ran to the back of the store to grab a bottle of tequila.

"See? I keep a few bottles back 'cause I know sooner or later you'll pass this way again." He grinned, and Annabelle wished he hadn't. The man was missing several teeth.

Shelley shook his head. "Not this time, Pops. Maybe on the way back. Shouldn't be long. I'm lookin' to hook this young lady up with a party traveling to California. Anybody been through in the past couple of weeks?"

Pops nodded vigorously. "Last week there was a big wagon train moving to Oregon. Smaller group came through here yesterday. Three families, I think they said, traveling to the Great Central Valley. Had a buncha kids."

Shelley smiled. "Yesterday?"

Pops scratched his head, not an attractive gesture. "Yesterday or the day before. I'm not sure, now that I think on it."

Shelley's grin never wavered. "They're haulin' wagons, I suppose?"

Pops nodded. "Yep. Nice folks. Buncha kids." He repeated his earlier observation.

Shelley looked at her, really looked at her for the

first time in days. "We can catch up with them to-morrow."

She tried to be as happy as he seemed to be, but she couldn't quite manage it. She would never trust anyone the way she trusted Shelley. The way her life was going, she might never trust another human being again. But she smiled, unwilling to let him know how much she feared traveling the rest of the way without him to guide her.

Shelley quickly gathered together a few supplies, and left her standing at the counter facing Pops. She looked around the grimy store wondering how anyone could stand to purchase the merchandise that had been lying in the filth that surrounded the old man, when she saw the newspaper, the *San Francisco Chronicle*.

"May I buy that newspaper?"

Pops grinned, to her dismay. "Hell, you can have it. It's two months old. Some fella just left it here when he was done readin' it."

She cradled the paper and withdrew a few coins from the front pocket of her britches. "And a bottle of that tequila Shelley likes so much."

When they headed out, she didn't mind leaving Pops' store behind, as she often did the few reminders of civilization along the trail. With the bottle in her saddlebag and the newspaper under her arm, she waited anxiously for Shelley to stop.

She couldn't wait to read the paper. There was still plenty of light remaining when Shelley finally found a place that suited him, and she sat in the open . . . in fact that was all that surrounded them, miles and miles of flat land, and she unfolded the *Chronicle*. There on the front page was an article about her, along with the same atrocious drawing that had graced her wanted poster. Would anyone recognize her, now? She wasn't the same woman she'd been three months ago, and the changes went deeper than her physical transformation.

As she read on, she became more and more disturbed. The article was completely false, and, even more disconcerting, it was only one of a series about her life and her alleged crimes being written by one Samuel Robertson. According to the libelous Mr. Robertson, she was a man-eating Jezebel, a woman who thought nothing of killing one lover and attempting to kill another. The story only reaffirmed her conviction that no one would ever believe her . . . it was Albert's word against her own, and she had made the unpardonable mistake of running.

She forced herself to read the entire article, though it made her physically ill. Thank heaven Shelley didn't know who she really was. Certainly even he would believe everyone else's version of the story.

She turned the pages, devouring every word until she came to the personals. She almost skipped over them entirely, but a bold word jumped out at her.

BRAT,
Please come home. I can help. Love you.

Icky

She smiled. At least she knew there was one person in the world who would believe her. Nicky would believe her. Believe in her.

She ripped the personal from the paper roughly, tearing all around it but leaving Nicky's ad intact.

Then she tucked it inside her new hat, where it would be safe.

Shelley presented her with a plate of beans, and she grimaced at the all too familiar fare.

"Don't like my cookin' anymore?" he asked as he sat next to her—closer than he had been, lately. Usually he settled himself comfortably on the other side of the fire from where she sat.

"It's not that." She didn't want to hurt his feelings. "I'm just tired of beans, that's all."

She ate them anyway, and he reached across and grabbed the paper she had discarded. "Any interestin' articles in here?" he asked casually.

She shook her head. "Not really." She stared into the fire as he began to read the article about her. Fortunately, he didn't seem very interested in news that was two months old, and he soon tossed the paper aside, never realizing that the notorious Annabelle St. Clair was sitting just a few feet away.

"Did you read the article about the opera singer?" he asked, his tone conversational.

She was certain that if he had looked at her just then he would have seen the truth written on her face. "Yes, I did," she finally said coolly.

"I never did care for opera, myself. Bored the pants off of me the one time my brother dragged me to one." He was simply looking for polite conversation, she surmised. He knew they'd probably catch up with the wagon train the very next day, and he certainly wouldn't stick around after that.

She tilted her head to one side and looked at him curiously. "You've been to the opera?"

"I just said so, didn't I?"

"And you didn't care for it?"

"Said that, too. What? You like it?" He gave her a big grin, and she felt so small for not telling him the truth.

"Sometimes."

"Darlin', you've got a prettier voice than any of them stuffy old opera singers. I thought one of 'em was gonna split my damn eardrums."

She was glad Shelley was talking to her again, but she longed for another subject of conversation. Any other subject.

"I brought you a present." She reached for her saddlebags that lay away from the fire.

Shelley grimaced when she withdrew the bottle and held it in the air. "Annie, no. I still remember how bad I felt the morning after we killed off that last bottle of tequila. And I also remember that I forgot damn near everything else."

"Just a swallow or two." She opened the bottle and took the first swig. "For courage."

He took the bottle she offered and lifted it to his lips. "What do you need courage for?"

She took the tequila from him and drank deeply before she answered. "There's something I need to tell you." She passed the bottle back to him and sat on her knees, facing him.

His face took on a pained expression that made her want to hit him. "Darlin', don't."

"I don't love you, Shelley," she interrupted his protest. "I wanted you to know before . . . before you let me go."

"You make it sound like I'm throwing you to a pack of wolves."

"No. I appreciate everything you've done for me. You saved me . . . brought me this far. That's more than any other man would have done. I guess that's why, for a while, I thought I loved you." She discussed her feelings for him as if he were a disinterested third party. "I mistook gratitude for love. It was easy to do . . . you took care of me when I needed it most, Shelley, but I don't love you. I just wanted you to know."

Shelley took another drink. It was one more than he had intended to take. She was saying exactly what he wanted to hear . . . so why did he feel as if she'd just punched him in the gut?

"That's good, Annie. You'll probably meet some great fella in San Francisco and fall madly in love, and he can put you in a mansion and shower you with jewels and silk dresses—no black, please—and you'll live like a queen. No beans and tequila for Annie. Roast suckling pig and champagne instead. Yep, you'll be some pumpkin. The biggest toad in the puddle."

Annie smiled and took another sip. "Sounds wonderful," she said without enthusiasm. "And what about you? Don't you want anyone to love you?"

He took the bottle from her hand. "Nope. I'd make a lousy husband. I never can seem to stay in one place for very long, and I'm too old to change my ways."

"How old?" she pressed.

"Thirty-three."

Annie laughed.

"It's so easy to entertain you when you have a few drinks of tequila in you, darlin'."

"I'm sorry. Thirty-three. That's not old at all!" She made herself stop laughing, pursing her lips together, but her eyes still twinkled.

He shook his head. "I've been thinking—."

"Was it terribly painful?" She laughed, but he was

not amused. He stood and offered her his hand, then pulled her to her feet when she laid her hand in his.

He released her hand and planted both feet firmly as he faced her. "I want you to hit me."

She didn't move. "You want me to do what?"

"You heard me. I want you to hit me. As hard as you can. In the stomach."

Annie pulled back her clenched hand and tapped him lightly in the midsection. "Like that?"

He shook his head in disgust. "Pretend you're defending yourself."

"From what?"

He scowled at her. "Just do it, woman."

She made a tight fist and punched him in the stomach again, but it was pathetic and he didn't even flinch. He just stood there shaking his head.

"Just what I figured. It's a long way to California, and you're a pretty woman, traveling alone. If anybody bothers you . . ."

"If you were with me, no one would dare to bother me."

"Well, I won't be," he insisted, more harshly than he had intended. "You make a fist like this." He molded her hand with his own. "Don't tuck your thumb inside your fingers like that, you'll break it if you ever hit anybody right."

He ran his fingers along her knuckles. "You hit with these, as hard as you can. If anybody grabs you from behind"—he swung her around and held her fast—"use your elbow and bring the heel of one of those boots down as hard as you can on top of the attacker's foot."

"Do you really think someone will try to attack me?" Annie's voice was small, and he didn't dare admit, even to himself, how right it felt to hold her just as he was now, with her back against his chest and her dark hair under his chin.

"Remember that saloon owner you told me about, and that man in the alley behind Oscar's place?" He reminded her with no kindness in his voice.

Abruptly, he released her and spun her around to face him again. "From the front, take aim and kick the bastard right where it hurts the most with the pointy toe of one of those red boots. That'll stop 'im for sure."

Annie frowned and looked at him expectantly . . . and waited. "Well?" she finally asked. "Where does it hurt the most?"

He dropped his head in his hands. "Don't tell me you really don't know."

She shook her head.

"Right between the legs, darlin'." He saw her blush, even in the waning light. "That'll drop a man in a heartbeat."

She looked at the ground. "Thank you. I hope I never need to fight anyone, but if I do I'll remember all that. Everything."

He frowned. Her words made him feel even guiltier. He picked up the discarded bottle of tequila, saw that they had hardly made a dent, and capped it tightly.

"Might as well turn in early." He lay on one side of the fire while Annie laid out her bedroll on the other. She hefted the saddle to the head of the makeshift bed and laid her head upon it. Then she stretched out, crossing her ankles and closing her eyes.

He knew he had abused her, ignored her, pushed her beyond her limits . . . and still he was going to miss her. Just having her there. As hard as he had tried to convince himself otherwise . . . it was an undeniable truth.

Amazingly, she fell asleep quickly. She'd had a hard day in the saddle, and just enough tequila in her blood to lull her to sleep. As soon as he was certain she was fast asleep, he stepped lightly to where her hat lay beside her saddle. He lifted it slowly from the ground and withdrew the folded piece of newsprint he had seen her tuck away.

He read the personal ad again and again by the light of the fire, and his frown grew deeper with every word. Was she Brat? Most likely. And who was Icky? Yes, he would be well rid of this particular woman, with her wide eyes and innocent blushes. One dead husband, Pierre, and now Icky.

The last thing he needed was a woman like her to complicate his life.

Chapter Nine

Shelley couldn't sleep. That in itself should have told him that he'd grown much too attached to the mysterious Annie Brown. Twice during the night he'd fallen into an uneasy slumber that lasted a short while before he woke with a start. He felt as if he were falling into a chasm, only to be jerked up at the last moment. The third time that happened he heard Annie.

She was talking in her sleep, and he didn't even try to return to his disturbed dream. At first he was amused as he listened to her senseless mumblings. Then something changed. She was frightened, tossing and turning in her sleep as if trying to escape from the same chasm that had threatened to swallow him.

"No," she cried out. "Leave me alone!" These words were as clear as if she'd uttered them wide awake.

He crossed by the campfire that was nothing more than a few burning embers, and looked down at her.

Her face was tortured as she turned it back and forth, trying to escape the nightmare. He was debating whether to wake her when he saw the moonlight reflecting on the tears that had begun to stream down her cheeks. He dropped to his knees beside her.

"Annie," he whispered, but she didn't respond to his voice, so he reached out and wiped her tears away with his fingers. "Wake up, Annie. It's just a bad dream."

She came awake so swiftly, so suddenly, that she startled him as she sat up and threw herself into his arms. "I don't want to die," she whispered hoarsely in his ear, clutching him as if to let go would mean death itself.

"You're not gonna die," he whispered. "It was just a dream."

He allowed her to stay there, her face buried against his shoulder, her fear fading slowly. He rubbed his hand up and down her back, removed the few hairpins from her tangled hair that hadn't already fallen out, and held her head against his shoulder. He remembered briefly that this was the very dilemma he had sought so hard to avoid. He felt her pain, a tightening in his own heart . . . after so many years of avoiding messy entanglements.

When she stopped shaking, he attempted to return her to her crude bed, but she held onto him tightly. "Not yet, please. I'm afraid."

He rocked her gently in his arms. He knew it was a mistake, but he couldn't let her go. "What are you scared of, darlin'?"

"Everything," Annabelle whispered. The dream that had been so vivid was fading, but it reminded her that she wasn't safe, would never be safe. She was afraid of dying and never knowing what it was like to really be loved. Of dying and never having a child. Of living and finding out that everything she'd once believed was important was not. Not at all.

"Why don't you tell me a limerick," she suggested. "Maybe that will make me forget that I'm afraid of everything."

Shelley didn't make a sound for a few minutes, then he made a disgusted noise. "I can't think of one. Not a damn thing."

"I don't believe that." She snuggled against him, working her way more firmly into his embrace. If she had her way she would never leave.

"Neither do I. My mind is a total blank."

"Maybe it's too late for reciting poetry." She tried to comfort him.

"Why don't you recite me some real poetry," he suggested.

She moved her head so her ear was directly over his heart. His hand was in her hair, his fingers brushing against her neck. "I can't think of any. Not a verse. Not a line."

Shelley tried again to return her to her bedroll, but she grabbed his arms. "Let me sleep with my head on your chest."

He shook his head. "Not a good idea, darlin'."

"Please," she pleaded with him. "You can lie down and sleep. I just want to . . ." She was about to embarrass herself again, but she didn't care. "I just want to hear the beating of your heart as I go to sleep."

"Annie . . ."

"All those days I rode on your horse and slept with my head against your chest; it was your heartbeat, slow and strong and steady, that lulled me to sleep. I felt safe then. I want to feel safe now."

Shelley laid his head on her saddle and stretched out, muttering the whole while that this was definitely not a good idea. She settled herself beside him and laid her head on his chest, her ear over his heart. She could feel the warmth of him through the thin fabric of his shirt, and wanted to move it away so she could feel his skin against her cheek.

Her intention had been to fall asleep there, to sleep peacefully with Shelley beside her, but the memory of their kiss invaded, and instead of drifting into that peaceful sleep, she became more and more aware of Shelley. Of his heat, his slowly exhaled breath, the hands he kept purposely away from her. After a few tortured minutes she lifted her head and looked into his eyes.

"Why is your heart beating so fast?" she whispered.

"Jesus, Annie. What are you trying to do to me?"

She felt his hands in her hair, and crept forward until her face was hovering over his. He rested his palm against her cheek as she held her face mere inches from his, wondering what would come next. If she kissed him would he push her away? Would it be as wonderful as the other two kisses they'd shared? One he didn't even remember. A tiny smile crossed her face.

"I never should have thrown your makeup into the pond. I never should have let you out of that ugly damn black dress. I never should have set you on that roan and ridden away from the Silver Palace." There was a hint of anger in his voice.

She ignored it. "But you did all those things. You can't take them back."

"The worst part is, I'm about to do something else I

know damn well I shouldn't."

"You're going to kiss me, aren't you, Shelley?"

"For starters."

He pulled her face to his and kissed her, a sweet, slow meeting of their lips that caused her to melt into his chest. When he parted his lips she went to him hungrily, wanting more, wanting all of him. No matter what happened once she reached San Francisco, she would have this one night with him. She would know what it was like to make love under the stars, to experience passion like she'd never known before.

The shirt that had been a nuisance earlier was becoming an unbearable encumbrance. She pulled her lips away from his. "Can I take off your shirt?"

"Darlin', you can do whatever you want."

He hadn't even finished the sentence when she began unbuttoning his shirt. She untucked the shirttails roughly and laid the shirt open, exposing his chest and the curly hair that lightly covered it. She laid her lips over his heart, then pressed her cheek against it.

He sat up and shrugged out of the shirt, letting it fall to the ground. "My turn, Annie."

He unfastened the buttons of her white cotton shirt and it joined his in the dirt. The lacy, short chemise he pulled gently over her head, and as he tossed it aside, he reached out to her.

He ran his fingers over her throat and down to her breasts. He lowered his head and kissed her nipple, sucking softly as she caught her breath and pressed herself against him.

She was amazed at the sensations he was stirring inside her. Every touch seemed to take her farther, higher than before. When he moved his warm mouth over her breasts, she thought she might die. He lit a

fire in her belly, a hunger that was primal and undeniable.

Shelley abandoned all his reservations and lost
himself in the desire that consumed him. He was falling . . . Annie was the chasm that had threatened his
dreams earlier, but now he was falling languidly, wonderfully, with no thoughts of attempting to escape.

He rolled over, laying Annie on the bedroll and tow-
ering over her. He could see her face better this way,
with her dark hair spread out beneath her and the
moonlight on her face. Her lips were slightly parted,
and he had to kiss them one more time before he finished undressing her.

She wanted him as much as he wanted her, he could
see it in her eyes and feel it in her hungry kiss. That
amazed him, because he couldn't remember ever
wanting anyone as much as he wanted Annie right at
that moment. He wondered, for a fleeting moment, if
she was just a hot-blooded woman. Would any man
satisfy the craving she felt? Or just him? Had she been
this way with her husband? With Pierre? With Icky?

It didn't matter. All that mattered was this moment.
This night. The only night they would ever have. Annie
pressed her body against his. Her skin was as silky
smooth as his was rough. Her skin was as pale in the
moonlight as his was dark.

She whispered his name as he buried his face
against her neck and nibbled on her earlobe. She buried her hands in his hair as he kissed the tender skin
at the side of her neck, moving his lips lower to kiss
the base of her throat, then lower still to take one taut
nipple and then the other in his mouth.

He covered her mouth with his when he entered
her, and discovered too late that his Annie, his Widow

Brown, was a virgin. He stilled her initial cries with a kiss, and started again, slowly and with a gentleness he worked very hard to keep hidden from the outside world.

Annabelle instinctively raised her hips. Shelley was lying between her legs in a way that felt wonderfully natural, buried within her so deep he was a part of her. She had heard that there would be pain the first time, but it was no greater than the pain of not having him inside her.

Her initial pain behind her, a pain not nearly so great as she had been told, she lifted her hips to him again. In that moment, surrounded by darkness in a world that ceased to have meaning, he was all hers. And he had instilled a craving in her that only he could satisfy.

She clutched Shelley. She couldn't catch her breath, didn't know what was driving her to such a fever pitch as she urged him to move faster. When she knew she couldn't take any more, a glorious spasm shook her body, and she heard herself call his name as he drove into her deeper and deeper, until she felt his own release.

They didn't move or speak for several minutes. At first, Annabelle didn't think she could. Every ounce of energy was gone, but she felt wonderful, warm, elated.

When Shelley rolled onto his side to take his weight off her, he kept her in his arms, as though he was reluctant to let her go.

"Shelley," she whispered against his chest, her ear above his heart. Her fears about the future and the past were nothing now, mists blown away by the storm they had created. "I don't love you. I promise." She wouldn't say or do anything to ruin the moment for him, or for herself. "But no one makes me feel as good as you do. No one."

He ran his hands through her hair, gazing at the stars over their bed. "I don't love you too, darlin'."

She smiled and kissed his chest. It was the sweetest thing he could have said.

Chapter Ten

When Shelley opened his eyes, Annie still lay with her head on his chest.

"Jesus, Mary, and Joseph," he muttered. Last night's pleasurable activities had taken on a very different aspect in the harsh light of day. A virgin. A goddamn virgin.

Annie lifted her head slowly and looked into his face, a content smile on her own. Evidently she felt none of his regret as she gazed at him. Those big brown eyes were warm and inviting.

"Good morning, Shelley."

He covered his face with both hands and shook his head. "Get dressed, Annie," he said more brusquely than he had intended.

"What's the matter?"

He lowered his hands from his face and stared at her. Her smile and her look of contentment had faded.

How did she manage to look so innocent? His eyes lit on a tiny pink spot on her chin where his beard had scratched her. Annie said nothing, but watched him expectantly. Her lips were rosy and swollen, her creamy soft skin even more perfect by the light of day. He began to remember everything that had happened between them, what was hidden under the rough blanket that barely covered her.

"Why didn't you tell me you were a goddamn virgin, Annie? And how did that happen, 'Widow Brown'?" He didn't even try to disguise the anger in his voice. "I don't suppose you'd like to explain that to me?"

Annie chewed on her bottom lip, and looked—for a moment—as if there were real remorse in her heart.

"I'm not really a widow," she confessed in a low voice.

"Do tell!" He practically shouted, sitting up and moving away from her. "A goddamn virgin. Dammit!"

Annie frowned as she gathered the blanket around her. "You didn't seem to mind last night," she shot back.

"That was last night, and this is this morning. Last night I was obviously thinking with something other than my brain!" His voice got progressively louder, and he almost forgot—almost—that they were both naked and their clothes were strewn all over the campsite.

He turned away from her and searched for his clothes. Muttering under his breath, he grabbed his discarded clothing and dressed quickly, keeping his back to her.

"If you think this means I won't leave you with that wagon train, you're mistaken," he practically shouted. "A goddamn virgin!"

"Would you stop saying that?" Annie screeched. "I was a virgin, not a *goddamn* virgin. And I never, ever, expected that you might change your plans and go all the way to California with me just because we . . . just because we . . . I'm not stupid. I know what last night was to you. Just another roll in the hay. I know you've got a whore waiting for you in every little town, every little backwoods settlement, and you don't want or need any *goddamn* virgin to slow you down!"

Shelley turned slowly to watch her, his only visible reaction to her outburst a slight raising of his eyebrows in what he hoped was a stoic face.

Annie Brown, or whoever the hell she was, somehow managed to look regal as she stood, wrapped in the brown blanket that covered her from her breasts down to her feet. There was color in her cheeks and a surprising flash in her dark eyes.

"Well, I don't need you, either," she snapped, lifting her chin and her nose in the air. "I can't wait to catch up with those families traveling to the Valley."

"Good."

"Fine."

He handed her her clothes. "Then we're agreed."

"Of course," Annie answered, then she wavered. "On what?"

"That last night was a mistake."

"Of colossal proportions."

He turned his back to her while she dressed. He was furious . . . with Annie, with himself. It was good that she was so certain that last night was a common occurrence for him, that it meant no more to him than an evening in any other woman's bed. "A goddamn . . ." he began, muttering darkly,

"Don't you dare say that again," she said, anger lacing her voice. "If you do I'll . . . I'll . . ."

"You'll do what?" he asked coldly.

"I'll kick you where it hurts the most with the pointy toe of a little red boot." Her voice was as icy and detached as his own.

When she assured him that she was dressed, he turned around and frowned. She had combed her hair, but it hung loose down her back. "Aren't you going to do that thing with your hair? That knot at the back of your neck?"

She put her hands on her hips and scowled at him. "If you'd like to dig around in the dirt and find my hairpins I'd be happy to oblige you."

He scoured the dirt around her bedroll but found only two pins. She shook her head when he offered them to her on his flat palm.

"That's not enough, Shelley."

He tossed them over his shoulder in disgust. They'd surely catch up with the wagon train that day, even if it was late in the afternoon.

He had to get her out of his hair. Out of his life. Taking her all the way to San Francisco was out of the question. After all, what would Icky say when he found out his Brat wasn't a virgin anymore? Icky and Brat. How disgustingly cute. At least her nickname was appropriate.

She was being a brat as they rode away from the camp, sulking and refusing to look directly at him. Sticking out her lower lip in a childish pout. What had she expected? That he would swear his undying love for her? That he wouldn't be able to leave her, now? She didn't know him at all if that was the case.

He stayed well ahead of her on the trail, checking on her occasionally, glancing over his shoulder. If she

was too far back, or on the other side of a bend, he
waited until she was closer. As soon as she caught up
to him, he turned his back on her and resumed his
quick pace.

Now as he stopped to wait for her once again, she
didn't appear. He waited and waited, then decided to
backtrack.

It didn't take long to find her. She was sitting in a
shaded copse, her back to a cottonwood tree. Her
mare was tethered to a low branch, and Annie
munched delicately at a piece of dried apple. She appeared to be lost in her own thoughts, with her knees
drawn up and a small frown on her face.

"Goddamn it," he swore lowly. "I turned around and
you were gone."

"Lucky you." She didn't even look at him.

He slid from the saddle, sighing deeply. "I'm not
trying to be unreasonable, but we can't afford to lolly-
gag . . ."

"I am not lollygagging." Annie didn't move from her
place beneath the cottonwood. "I had no breakfast,
my rear end aches from sitting in that saddle all day
every day, and I . . . need . . . a . . . break." She empha-
sized each word. "If you're so anxious to be rid of me,
why don't you just go on back to the Silver Palace, or
wherever it is you're so determined to get to. I'm certain I can find my way to San Francisco on my own."

He scowled at her—he couldn't help it—while her
expression was cool and haughty. This was a side of
Annie he hadn't seen before. She didn't vent her anger
in the ways other women might. She didn't cry, or
sniffle, or beg him to stay with her. God help him, if
she did that he'd be hard pressed to say no.

"You needn't worry about your money," she said

coolly. "I'll send it to the Silver Palace, to your friend Cherry. As you instructed." She gave him an icy smile.

"Forget about the goddamn money," he growled.

Annie arched a fine eyebrow, and her smile disappeared. "And feel like another one of your whores? I don't think so."

He shook his head and clamped his mouth shut. He hadn't intended to get into another argument with her. But when he'd looked over his shoulder and hadn't seen her there, when he'd stopped to wait for her, his eyes on the path that remained ominously deserted, he'd panicked. And all the while she'd been having herself a leisurely picnic, sitting in the shade and taking tiny bites of dried apple.

He didn't say another word as Annie finished her apples . . . with a casual lethargy he had no doubt was deliberate.

When at last she stood and brushed the grass from her britches, he turned to face her. "Can we get movin' now? I'd like to catch up with those travelers before dark."

"You think you're anxious to be rid of me? I can't wait to meet up with that wagon train," Annie said defiantly. "I certainly never intended to be a burden to you, Shelley."

Annie led her mare to the path, walking slowly and holding the reins in her hands as if she'd been riding all her life.

"I never said you were a burden, Widow Brown," he commented, following her on foot, leading his own mount. His boots kicked up clouds of dust around his feet, and with his free hand he scratched his chin.

She spun around, her eyes narrowed, her fresh anger just beneath the surface. Perhaps he shouldn't have called her Widow Brown. It only reminded both of them that she had lied.

"No. You said much worse." She stood in the middle of the well-worn path, her tight britches and tucked-in shirt outlining her perfect figure, her thick hair falling straight over one shoulder. There was little resemblance to the frightened woman he had rescued. If only he'd known that she would turn out to be so delectable, he would have let the Pinkerton agent have her. Or so he tried to convince himself as she confronted him.

"Seems to me the worst I've accused you of was being a goddamn virgin, and we both know that's true, so . . ." He stopped when she stepped toward him and drew back her foot.

He saw her intent, mingled with a flash of fire in her eyes. She briefly hesitated, giving him just enough time to swing his hand down and grab her ankle as it flew upward, before it found its target.

He didn't release her foot. Annie stood there, precariously balanced on one foot while he held the other. A gentle shove would have landed her backside in the dirt.

"If you intend to kick a man in the balls, darlin', don't hesitate." There was no anger in his voice, but Annie still looked as if she expected some sort of retaliation. "If he knows what you're plannin' to do, he just might kill you." He released her foot and she lowered it to the ground.

"I told you if you ever called me a goddamn virgin again I'd . . . I'd do that," Annie stammered.

Shelley shook his head, and Annie lowered hers. She looked at the dirt at her feet, and her tan hat hid her face from him. He placed his finger under her chin and lifted her face.

"You've got to be ruthless to survive a trek halfway across the country, Annie," he said gently.

"Like you?"

He was certain she had meant that as an insult, but he smiled crookedly. "Exactly. If you intend to attack a man, and I know you won't do that unless you feel you have to, it's got to be quick, and you've got to realize you only get one shot. Be timid . . . let him see what's coming . . . worry that you might actually hurt him . . . and he'll get you first. I guarantee it."

"I'm not very good at this," Annie said softly.

"Not very good at what?"

"Survival of the fittest." Annie actually smiled. A small smile, to be sure, but her anger had faded away.

They were standing close—too close—and Annie looked up at him. "A few months ago, if anyone had told me I'd be crossing the country on horseback, eating beans every night, sleeping on the ground and learning how to defend myself . . . I never would have believed it. In the past three months I've known terror like I never knew existed, and everything I was ever taught has turned out to be worthless.

"But the stars in the sky shine brighter than they ever have before, and I never knew wildflowers were so lovely, or that trees could be so tall and green, and . . ."

Annie faltered, and he knew she was thinking of last night. "And I've always had a terrible temper, though it doesn't flare up often." The tone of her voice had changed, from dreamy to practical. He could almost hear an apology in her words. "We'd better get moving if we expect to catch up with that wagon train before

106

dark," Annie said, turning to mount her mare.

He stopped her. "Hold on a minute." He dug around in his saddlebag and came up with a small pearl-handled pistol which he placed in her hand. "This is an over and under derringer. You get two shots. Just two, so you have to make them count. Don't point it at anyone unless you intend to use it. Get as close as you can, because if you miss . . . well, get close."

"I don't want a gun, Shelley." Annie tried to hand it back to him, but he refused to take it. "I couldn't shoot anyone."

"I hope you never have to, but I'll feel better if you take it with you." He folded her fingers around the small weapon.

Annie lifted her eyebrow. "Easing your conscience a little? Showing off your tender heart?"

He shook his head. "Don't have either one."

"Aren't you afraid I'll use it on you?"

He looked down into her face. She was only half joking.

"Nope." He turned his back on her, to prove the point, and looked over his shoulder just in time to see her step into the stirrup and lift herself into the saddle. She didn't need his help anymore.

He followed her for a while as she traveled the well-worn road. He'd accepted the fact that he'd never know who she really was, but he couldn't help wondering what had happened to her. The West was full of people who were running away from one thing or another. They populated the isolated towns and farms, changed their names, started new lives. Annie could do that. She could forget about San Francisco and Icky. She could live among the wildflowers and tall trees she talked about as if she'd just discovered them. She could disappear, and sleep forever under the stars.

With him? He drove the startling thought from his mind and prodded his horse into a trot, passing Annie without a glance in her direction.

Chapter Eleven

They rounded a bend just before sunset and saw the travelers camped beside the road, their wagons in a disjointed circle, more than one fire blazing as the families prepared their evening meal. Annabelle closed her eyes and took a deep breath. The smells that assaulted her were heavenly. Coffee, some sort of bread, meat stewing . . . no beans. She couldn't detect the smell of beans.

As they approached the covered wagons an older man stepped forward. Shelley brought his roan to a stop and slid from the saddle. The man who greeted Shelley wore no weapon, but another man stood behind him casually, a rifle in his hand.

Shelley introduced himself to the older man, and they walked off talking in low tones. She saw the gray-haired man raise a hand to the man with the rifle, obviously a prearranged signal, and that man smiled and returned to his wagon.

Annabelle remained seated on her mare, feeling as if she'd already been deserted. The camp looked comfortable, with washing hung out to dry and three small children chasing one another in no apparent pattern between the wagons and over the gentle mounds that bordered the camp to one side, away from the road. She saw no other children, and could only surmise that three energetic children seemed like a buncha kids to toothless Pops.

After a few moments she dismounted and walked toward the camp for a closer look.

There were five wagons, and the party seemed to travel with all the comforts of home. She stared longingly at a bathtub that had been set up behind one of the wagons . . . filled with bedding. How long had it been since she'd had a proper bath? Too long for her to remember. In the past three months she'd had to make do with washbasins and an occasional wooden barrel—when she was lucky. Then there was her dip in the pond, and her bath in the cold creek where Shelley had later kissed her . . .

The smiling woman who approached was almost upon her before Annabelle realized she wasn't alone. The woman who introduced herself as Suzanne Castleton was not much older than she, a fair-haired lady with sun-browned skin and tiny lines around her eyes that deepened as she smiled at Annabelle.

"I hope you'll join us for dinner," Suzanne said with a sincere smile.

Annabelle never ceased to be amazed at the people who were so willing to accept strangers with warmth and trust and a kind of love. They stuck together, these pioneers. There were no reservations when it came time to share their food, their water . . . their very lives.

Suzanne was the mother of two of the frolicking children, and she tried to point out which two were hers, a boy and the only girl. The little girl, the youngest, ran with an energy that matched the two boys', her skirts seeming to be no encumbrance as she kept pace with the older children.

Annabelle felt an immediate kinship with Suzanne, even though she'd never known a woman like her. She was vigorous and hardworking, her hands red and chapped, her hips wide and her arms well-muscled. Yet there was a beauty about her . . . a peacefulness, perhaps . . . that made her special.

Of course, all she'd ever known were spoiled performers like herself, and the women like Cherry Red she'd met in the saloons where she'd worked. None of them had possessed one iota of the warmth and contentment Suzanne radiated.

Annabelle was pleased to find that the man Shelley had talked with was Charles Castleton, Suzanne's husband. He was several years older than his wife, and was the appointed leader of the small wagon train. Annabelle learned that she would be traveling with the Castleton family, and in exchange would help Suzanne with the children. Suzanne told her that Penny was five and Charlie had just turned seven.

They sat around the fire and ate the delectable stew Annabelle had smelled earlier, and ate biscuits one of the women had managed to bake, using a heavy umbrella to tent the fire and construct a makeshift oven. She was introduced to the other two families. Tate and Elizabeth Manley were newlyweds, a young couple with matching fair tresses, who sat close together during the meal and smiled shyly at her, taking in her strange apparel. Tate Manley had been the one standing guard of Charles Castleton, holding the rifle, until they were assured Shelley was not an outlaw. Annabelle liked them both.

She wasn't so certain about the third couple, Jim and Judith Butler. They were the parents of the third child, a little boy who looked about the same age as the Castletons' son, though he was introduced offhandedly as Little Jim. Although the Butlers sat side by side, they didn't seem to like one another very well. The smile Jim Butler gave Annabelle was much too familiar, and she avoided his gaze. Judith Butler had a tired look that didn't come from working too hard but from living too hard, and Annabelle had a hunch the woman's husband had a lot to do with that.

It was dark before the meal was finished and the children were bustled off to bed. The other fires had been allowed to die down, and the single blaze Annabelle and the other adults gathered around gave off the only light, harsh and radiating a heat that warmed her face and arms. She kept her eyes on the fire, refusing to look at Shelley as he rose and thanked the ladies for the "fine grub," as he called it, and bid everyone farewell.

Everyone but her.

She jumped up and followed him to his roan. "Aren't you going to say good-bye?" she called to his back when they were far enough away from the camp so no one else could hear.

When Shelley turned to her, his easy smile was gone. Of course he hadn't intended to say a word to her.

"Good-bye, Widow Brown. Have a safe trip."

She felt small, lonely, watching him prepare to leave her. "The Castletons seem very nice."

He nodded.

"I like the children," she said, trying to make her voice bright. "That'll be fun. I've never spent much time with children before."

Shelley visibly relaxed. What had he expected? That she would run after him and beg him to take her?

"I wonder if you'll feel the same way by the time you get to California. They seem like a lively bunch."

She wished there was more light so she could see his face more clearly. She didn't want him to leave. No matter how safe she might feel with the Castletons, she'd never feel as safe as she had with Shelley.

And that wasn't all. She admitted to herself as she watched him prepare to ride out of her life forever that she really did love him. Not like she thought she'd loved Henri, comfortable and safe and . . . pleasant. This love was tearing her apart, ripping her heart from her chest.

But he didn't return her love, and that was what made it so painful. To him she was nothing more than a nuisance, an obligation to be gladly transferred to someone else. How would he remember her . . . if he remembered her at all?

"I didn't mean to make you hate me, Shelley," she said suddenly.

"I don't hate you, darlin'," he said gruffly. "Myself, maybe—"

"Don't," she interrupted, her voice urgent. "Please don't. Not because of me."

A good-bye kiss would have been nice, but she knew Shelley wouldn't move any closer to her, and she was afraid if she made the first move he would reject her.

She didn't want to part that way.

"No regrets," she said softly. "Agreed?"

"No regrets, Annie Brown," he said, but there was a touch of remorse in his voice. Then he turned away and mounted his roan.

Annabelle watched Shelley ride away from her without so much as a backward glance. She watched until the darkness swallowed him whole, and still she stood as though rooted to the spot.

"Is everything all right, Annie?" Suzanne's soft question came from directly behind her, and she was so startled she jumped.

"I'm fine." She turned to her new friend, and Suzanne reached out and wiped a tear from Annabelle's cheek with her callused hand.

"You just need a good night's sleep," Suzanne insisted. "We'll put you in the wagon with the children." She placed a motherly arm around Annabelle's shoulders.

Annabelle wiped her face. When had she started crying? Had Shelley seen her tears? She deeply hoped that he had not. "I have a bedroll," she said. "I can sleep outside."

"Nonsense," Suzanne said with authority. "These two wagons are ours. Charles and I sleep in this one." She gestured with her free hand, keeping the other firmly on Annabelle's shoulder. "And you will sleep with the children in this one."

Annabelle stuck her head through the wide opening in the back. "Lots of room," she conceded.

"Tomorrow morning, when we load up again, there'll barely be room to breathe." Suzanne's voice was light. "We get on the road early, so you'll be wanting to get to sleep before long."

Annabelle tried to push aside all memories of Shelley. "How many miles do you travel in a day?"

"About fifteen. Sometimes twenty," Suzanne answered.

Annabelle bit her tongue. Fifteen or twenty miles! She and Shelley had always traveled two or three times that distance in a day. It would take forever to get to San Francisco. The news shouldn't have surprised her. The ox-drawn wagons were slow, and would be heavily laden.

She lay awake long after everyone had gone to sleep. When she looked overhead all she saw was darkness, deep and complete. The children slept soundly, occasionally throwing their little bodies about with abundant energy, even in sleep. Eventually, she slipped out of the back of the wagon and sat against a large spoked wheel.

From there, when she lifted her head, she could see the stars, and it was comforting somehow. If Shelley looked up he would see the same stars, no matter where he was. A warm breeze lifted her hair and fanned her face, soft as a lover's kiss.

Shelley was out there somewhere, sleeping with his head propped on his saddle and his ankles crossed, happy to have her out of his life. Poor Shelley. He had never asked for the grief she'd caused him.

Suddenly she knew he wasn't sleeping. He was riding his roan in the dead of night, so anxious to get away from her that he didn't even stop to rest.

What would happen if she didn't go to San Francisco? She could open her own general store in a place so remote no one would ever find her. She'd sell tequila and sunbonnets to the travelers who passed by, and beans and bacon and dried apples. In the evening she would close up and sit in the grass and watch the stars come out, and dance and sing by the light of the moon. She'd pick wildflowers for her dinner table, and when the nights were warm she'd sleep outside, with her head on her saddle and her ankles crossed . . .

Just a dream. Nicky would be worried sick. And sooner or later someone would pass through who would recognize her, and she'd end up being taken to some sheriff, strapped to the back of her own mare. Dead or alive.

Shelley rode all night without stopping. He was determined to put as much distance as possible between himself and Annie Brown, or whatever her name was. Brat. That was an appellation that suited her, and when he thought of her, if he ever thought of her again, he would think of her only as Brat. A spoiled, overgrown child.

Why had she insisted on making it difficult for him to leave her? Standing there with the light of the fire behind her, her perfect figure, the cloud of hair around her head. He had wanted to see her face, just one more time, but it had remained in shadows . . . and he *had* been able to turn his back on her. He could and would ride away from that woman.

Kansas could wait. There was a saloon in Cheyenne that he was particularly fond of. There was a dark-haired girl who worked there . . . what was her name? Emily? No. Ellie. He couldn't remember what color her eyes were. Maybe they were brown . . . not that it mattered.

Unbidden, his mind flashed back to the campfire. He hadn't liked the way that Butler fella had smiled at Annie, like he knew exactly what was hidden beneath her clothing, like she'd been sitting there at the campfire buck naked. No, he didn't like it at all, and it wasn't the first time that evening that particular unpleasant thought had intruded on his planning.

But she wasn't his problem anymore. She was armed, she was wary, and she was on her own.

He turned his thoughts back to Ellie, the dark-haired girl who would be happy to see him in Cheyenne. Yes, she would be happy to see him, would do whatever he asked, and when he left her the next morning she would send him on his way with a smile, because she'd expect nothing else.

No regrets.

Brat.

"Good heavens, did you sleep out here?" Suzanne's words woke her, and Annabelle jumped up.

"I couldn't sleep, so I came out to look at the stars. I guess I fell asleep."

Suzanne laughed brightly. "I guess you did. Let's get busy. We'll have a quick breakfast, load the wagons, and hit the trail."

As hard as the traveling was, Annabelle could see that Suzanne looked forward to the day ahead, to the fifteen or twenty miles they would progress that day.

She helped where she could, but the routine was so well orchestrated that she sometimes found herself getting in the way. So she sat by the wagon and plaited her hair. The Castletons' little girl, Penny, watched her closely, never taking her eyes from Annabelle's hair. When Annabelle was almost finished, Penny disappeared into the wagon, crawling like a monkey over crates and boxes, emerging moments later with a red ribbon clutched in her hand. She presented it to Annabelle with trepidation.

"For me?" Annabelle took the offered ribbon with a smile. "Are you going to let me borrow your ribbon?"

The five-year-old smiled and nodded. "You have pretty hair, and the ribbon matches your boots."

Annabelle secured the ribbon at the tail end of her long, heavy braid that hung almost to her waist. "Thank you, Penny." She hugged the shy girl. "I think I'm going to like traveling with you and your family."

Penny gave her a smile, not quite so shy, and ran off to play before she had to climb into the wagon and take to the trail.

The morning would have been a good start for Annabelle's first day with the wagon train if Jim Butler hadn't decided to pay her a visit.

"You look awful pretty this fine mornin', Mrs. Brown."

It would have been a perfectly harmless comment from anyone else, but she didn't like the way Jim Butler raked his eyes over her with undisguised interest, his gaze lingering too long on her breasts.

She jumped up and turned away from him, making the excuse that her help was needed. Butler grabbed her arm before she could escape. She looked all around her. Everyone else was occupied, and on the other side of the covered wagon that shielded them from view. She could hear their laughter, their grunts and sighs as they loaded the last of the wagons.

She looked with cold disdain at the hand that held her. "Remove your hand from my arm, Mr. Butler," she said icily, never letting him see that he frightened her.

"Call me Jim, honey." He didn't release her. "I'm just trying to be friendly."

"I don't need another friend, Mr. Butler. And if you don't take your hand off me this instant I'm going to scream so loud"—she actually grinned as she remembered Shelley's words—"I'll split your goddamn eardrums."

Butler released her with a frown. "No call to be so uppity. I was just being neighborly, bein' as how we're going to be spending the next couple of months together."

She left him standing there, aware that she had made an enemy she didn't need, aware that she would have to watch Butler every minute. Shelley had been right about what waited for her between where he'd left her and California. He just didn't realize she would be riding next to one of the dangers he'd warned her about . . . for the next couple of months. It seemed like an interminably long time.

As the day wore on she realized that the next couple of months might drive her insane.

She rode her mare beside the Castletons' wagon that Suzanne drove. No wonder her arms were so well muscled. It was hard work controlling the oxen. They plodded along at a snail's pace, and Annabelle decided that twenty miles would be a very good day. Very good indeed.

Jim Butler stayed well away from her during the day, driving his own wagon and seeing to his own family when the entire procession came to a halt for a noontime break and a cold meal. His worn-looking wife drove their other wagon. Only the newlyweds rode side by side, their meager belongings barely fill-ing their single conveyance.

They stopped for the day much too early in the afternoon for Annabelle. They couldn't have gone much more than ten miles! The fires were started, a few things washed and hung to dry, the wagons partially unloaded so the women could prepare the beds. It seemed like such a waste of time to her. Shelley had spoiled her.

It was such a pleasant night that she didn't even attempt to sleep in the wagon. She laid out her bedroll beside the wagon the children slept in, used her saddle as a pillow, and admired the stars. They were brighter in the black night sky than any jewels she'd ever seen. Even brighter than the diamond earrings Henri had given her, more brilliant than the sapphire and diamond pendant Nicky had given her, the one that had belonged to his mother. The stars were more precious than all the jewels she'd left behind. The very idea made her laugh softly. A thought like that would have been completely foreign to her a few months ago, even a few weeks ago. Shelley had made her look at the whole world differently.

"What's so funny?" a voice whispered.

She rose quickly and saw Butler leaning against the wagon.

"How long have you been standing there?" she asked indignantly.

"Not very long. Just thought I'd stop by and see if you were feeling . . . lonely. Maybe a bit friendlier than you were this morning."

She sized him up quickly. He was a small man, but wiry and well muscled. His dark hair was slicked back, giving him an oily look that was decidedly unappealing. She turned her back on him, determined to escape from his unwanted attentions. She had no intention of even speaking to the man.

He grabbed her by her long braid and pulled her back. She collided with his chest, and he trapped her with his arm, knocking the breath out of her. "You be nice to me and I'll take care of you."

"I don't need anyone to take care of me," she seethed. And as she said the words, she knew they were true.

"Mrs. Brown." She felt his breath, hot and unpleasant, on her neck. "Annie, honey. You do. I know you want me. I knew it the first time our eyes met over the campfire."

She relaxed and he loosened his grip. She brought her elbow straight back into his gut with all the strength she could muster. Then she brought the heel of her right boot down on top of his foot.

When she spun around and stepped back, Butler was holding his stomach and standing on one bare foot, a look of fury on his face.

"I keep a gun on my person at all times, Mr. Butler," she said coolly. "I was told not to display it unless I intend to use it, and I've found that to be excellent advice." She decided it would be a good idea to let him believe she knew more about defending herself than she really did, as though this sort of thing happened all the time.

"If you touch me again, you'll see it." She couldn't believe that her voice was so calm. "Do you understand?" she prodded as Butler continued to stand there, dumbfounded.

After a moment he turned and walked away without a word, and she gathered her gear and crawled into the wagon. It wouldn't be safe for her to sleep outdoors, not with Jim Butler around.

But she was through running from Butler and men like him. From whatever awaited her in San Francisco. If she hadn't run in the first place . . .

She looked out the opening in the rear of the wagon, back toward the east where Shelley had ridden away from her. She didn't feel very generous toward him at the moment, and she scowled into the night as if he could see her.

"I hate you, Shelley." She whispered, so as not to wake the children. "When I get out of this I'm going to eradicate you from my memory. Forget you exist. I'm going to leave you here by the side of the trail where you belong. Bury your memory in the dust."

There was an unspoken thought that plagued her. Perhaps she could leave him in the dust, but she could never see the night sky and not be reminded, however briefly, that for a moment she had loved him. Deeply, completely, with her heart, her soul, her body. No one else would ever make her feel what Shelley had, and he had walked away from her as if she meant nothing to him . . . because she did mean nothing to him. At least, nothing more than countless other women. Women like Cherry Red.

She pushed away the ugly image that assaulted her. "I hate you, Shelley," she repeated as she turned away from the memories of him, and dreamed of days long past.

Chapter Twelve

Wendell had never claimed patience as one of his traits, and in fact viewed that particular virtue as a weakness in other people. Patience was simply another word for laziness. When you were patient, you weren't getting anything accomplished.

Mordecai had the patience of a saint, and it was driving Wendell to distraction. They'd combed the northeast corner of Colorado Territory and southeast Wyoming Territory. Shelley was a popular fella. Most everybody they'd talked to knew him, or of him, but Wendell didn't know any more about the man than he had when he'd left the Silver Palace. Worse, no one had seen him in the past couple of weeks.

"We've lost them, goddammit," Wendell snapped at his imperturbable partner.

Mordecai turned his head and gave him a disapproving look. "If he has her, and if they're traveling overland, we'll find them. If they catch the rail, Eugene and Dawson will find them," Mordecai said calmly.

They were approaching yet another settlement, but Wendell had almost lost hope that they might find Annabelle St. Clair. If that bounty hunter knew who she was, she was as good as dead. "Dawson's as dumb as a fence post, and he's the smart brother!" Wendell frowned. He couldn't stand the thought of being outdone by the Walsh brothers.

" 'Pride goeth before destruction, and a haughty spirit before a fall.' " Mordecai kept his eyes straight ahead. He had ridden with the same stiff, righteous posture atop his sorrel since they'd left Denver, seemingly unaffected by the growing fruitlessness of their search.

Wendell scowled at his partner, an occurrence that was becoming all too common. "Shut up, Mordecai."

The old man behind the counter in the general store wore spectacles so thick, Wendell almost turned and walked away. It would be a miracle if the old coot could tell what his own reflection looked like in the mirror, much less what he'd seen in the past few weeks.

He leaned over the counter and snapped, "You know a fella by the name of Shelley? Bounty hunter?"

A smile crossed the old man's face. "Course I do. You two friends of his?" He was apparently oblivious to Wendell's impatience.

Mordecai stood behind Wendell. "Have you seen Shelley lately?" he asked, his voice somber.

"Couple of weeks ago . . . or was it three?" The old

man scratched a beardless chin. "Coulda been a week and a half or so."

Wendell shook his head. Lot of help this old coot was. "Was he alone, mister?"

"Malloy. Harry Malloy." The old man paused. "It's funny that you should ask about that. Shelley always come through here alone, before. But he had a woman with him this last time."

Wendell smiled. He wanted to shout Hallelujah. "What did she look like?" A wasted question, given Malloy's near blindness, but maybe he'd seen something.

"Pretty young girl," Malloy said with a smile. "I figured she was a widow, on accounta she was wearing all black even though it was some hot when they passed through. Dark hair, I remember." His grin widened. "Pretty young girl," he repeated.

Wendell turned back to his partner. "It's her. She was dressed all in black at the Silver Palace."

"Did Shelley say where they were going?" Mordecai asked solemnly.

"I can't remember that he did. Bought more supplies than usual, and bought the lady a pretty yellow sunbonnet. Course, he took a bottle of tequila, and . . ." Malloy stared over their heads, his eyes squinting. "Took a wanted poster right off the wall."

Wendell cursed under his breath. "Whose poster was it?" He already knew.

"Well, my eyes ain't so good no more," Malloy admitted. "But Beans cursed up and down about Shelley taking that poster. Elsewise I never woulda missed it, much less known whose it was. It was that woman . . . Annabelle something or another."

"St. Clair," Mordecai said in a grave tone.

Malloy grinned. "That's it! Annabelle St. Clair. Killed a man, what Beans said. Musta been an important fella to get a thousand dollars on her head."

Wendell leaned over the counter. "Shelley didn't say where they were headed?"

Malloy shook his head. "Nope. But they lit outa here headed toward the western trail."

Wendell stormed out of the general store, Mordecai following him.

"Hell, she's probably already dead," Wendell snapped, mounting his own blood bay.

"I don't think so." Mordecai's voice was still and deep, disturbing in its emotionless calm. "At least not yet."

"Why not?"

"Even though we must assume that Shelley knows who she is, and is taking her to San Francisco to collect the reward her surviving victim has posted . . ." Mordecai's gray eyes bored into his. "Think of what we know of this man. He's a womanizer. He bought a bottle of tequila in this store and bought his 'prisoner' a bonnet."

Wendell grinned. "So you figure he's having fun with her while he goes to collect his reward."

"Wouldn't you?"

"Hell, Mordecai, every man I know but you would."

Mordecai mounted his sorrel stiffly. Wendell knew that the man didn't take kindly to ribbing about his religion.

"That's where you're wrong, Yates," he said stonily. "You see," he continued as they turned toward the western trail and started down the dusty street, "women are my . . . my weakness."

"Didn't know you had a weakness."

A stiff breeze came out of the west and lifted Mordecai's thin, pale hair.

" 'Watch and pray, that ye enter not into temptation: The spirit indeed is willing, but the flesh is weak.' "

Wendell studied his fellow agent for several minutes, stunned. Mordecai Butterfield, the man who didn't smoke, drink, or curse . . . the man who looked down his nose at the common men who did . . . was a skirt chaser. He burst into laughter. Mordecai Butterfield?

"My shame is no cause for your amusement," Mordecai said solemnly.

He forced himself to stop laughing. He might be in Butterfield's company for several more weeks, and he couldn't afford to alienate the man. "I'm just glad to find out you're human, like the rest of us."

The dark clouds that rolled in from the west became thicker and darker. They could always spend the night in the settlement, Wendell thought. Malloy would probably put them up, let them wait out the storm . . . but every minute they delayed, Shelley and his prisoner got farther ahead.

"So." He prodded his mount forward. "What do you figure? Promontory?"

"Yes. If we don't catch them by then we take the rail to Virginia City . . . wait for them there." Mordecai shouted to be heard above the rising wind. They both knew that a man of Shelley's reputation couldn't resist a stop in Virginia City, especially after crossing the desert.

A broad grin crossed Wendell's face. "So you don't think they'll take the rail?"

Mordecai shook his head.

"Hey, Butterfield." Wendell looked above his head

127

to the black clouds that threatened them. "I was thinking. Maybe you could use your influence to get this storm to pass us by. What do you say?"

Mordecai shook his head. "Blasphemy," he said flatly. "We're going to get wet." As he finished speaking, the first large drop landed on Wendell's face.

Chapter Thirteen

"Come on, Shelley." The dark-haired Ellie ran her fingers up and down his arm. "Give me a smile. Just an itsy bitsy one." She talked baby talk half the time, and it irritated the hell out of him. His memory of her had been vague, and her voice was one detail he hadn't recalled.

"I don't suppose you can sing." He stared at the pale golden tequila in the shot glass on the bar. All he had to do was pick it up, toss back the fiery liquid, and he'd be well on his way to forgetting he'd ever met Annie Brown. But he continued to stare at the liquor. Hell, he couldn't even enjoy a simple drink, all because of her.

Ellie giggled. "Of course I can sing." She started an off-key rendition of a cowboy song, something about dogies, the words squeaking as she sang in her shrill baby voice. When she hit a high note, he felt as if she were stabbing at his brain with a thin, sharp knife. One eye closed, all on its own.

"Never mind," he snapped, stopping her before she could finish the first verse.

He ignored her pout and the whining protest at his elbow. Ruined. Annie Brown had ruined him.

The bartender leaned forward and shooed Ellie away. "Let me talk to him," he said.

Shelley didn't say a word as Ellie moved away. The barkeep placed one elbow on the bar and shook his head back and forth slowly.

"Women," he said in a low voice that retained a deep Southern accent even after all his years in Cheyenne.

Shelley lifted his head. "What about them, Gil?"

"Damned nuisances." He continued to shake his head, and Shelley resisted the urge to reach out and grab the man's head between his hands and make him be still.

"You can't let a woman get you in the dumps. Men like us, Shelley, we know the truth."

Shelley never would have lumped himself in with the increasingly irritating bartender, but he pretended to be interested anyway. "What makes you think I'm having trouble with a woman, and what is the truth?"

Gil grinned. "I just know. I've been there myself." He leaned closer, divulging his secrets. "And we both know that women are fickle deceivers . . . all of them." Gil's eyes gleamed with a touch of madness, and Shelley wondered what woman had done that to him. Some sweet Southern belle?

"I know about broken hearts. I turned away from the woman who rejected me and I never looked back. Look at me now. My own place. Women . . ." He gestured with a casual hand to Ellie and a new blonde

130

who were socializing on the opposite side of the room. "Women like these are all we need. They ask for nothing but money. They're honest, in their own way. A whore will never break your heart."

Shelley at last took the shot glass and emptied it. Gil's half-mad thoughts were too close to his own.

"Nobody broke my heart," he assured the man. "I don't have one. You can't do what I do for a livin' and have a heart."

Gil nodded his head. "Then you're a lucky man."

Shelley emptied another glass as soon as Gil filled it, and turned away from the ignorant man. Lucky?

"Ellie!" he called to the dark-haired girl, who smiled and hurried across the room to him. When she stood directly in front of him he lifted her face by the chin and looked into her eyes. Gray eyes. Very nice, very pretty. But he wished they were dark brown.

"Let's go upstairs, darlin'." He grinned at her, and she tilted her head to one side coquettishly.

She took his arm and led him to the stairs. "Ellie and Shelley. Shelley and Ellie." She giggled and bumped her hip against his as they climbed the stairs, her arm wrapped possessively through his. "Isn't that cute?"

"Cute, darlin'," he agreed unenthusiastically. Annie was not his responsibility. Charles Castleton had promised to take good care of her, and Shelley was certain he would.

"You know, Shelley," Ellie squeaked, "you could stay with me all night. It'll cost a little extra . . ."

"Huh?" He looked down at her upturned face. "Oh, yeah. Maybe."

"Maybe?"

It hadn't been his fault Annie was a goddamn virgin.

He never would've touched her if he'd known. Never.

It was a lie, and he knew it. He'd wanted her too bad. Hell, he still did.

"I missed you so much, Shelley," Ellie cooed, and he knew she said that to every customer who walked up these stairs with her. Whether it had been a year or a month or a couple of days. He didn't care. Not really. That was the beauty of a relationship like this. He could come and go as he pleased, and never feel a moment of regret. Ellie would be happy to see him, if he came back tomorrow or six months from now, and if he decided never to come back, she wouldn't care.

Ellie would never try to kick him in the balls, and she would never accuse him of deserting her.

She would never look up at him with tears in her eyes, and Ellie would certainly never tell him, with her heart in her voice, how beautiful the night sky was.

Ellie pulled him to her door and pushed it open. "Here we are," she said in a voice that promised a night he wouldn't forget.

"I can't do it," he whispered, not believing the words as they came out of his mouth. "I can't leave her there."

Ellie's smile faded quickly. "What are you talking about?"

He spun away from her, a smile growing on his face. He went down the stairs much more quickly than he'd climbed them, an anxious bounce in his step.

"Can't leave who where?" Ellie shouted harshly from the top of the stairs. "You sonofabitch, where do you think you're going?"

He raised his hands, palms upward in total supplication. "Goddamn San Francisco," he shouted before he spun back around and strode through the swinging doors.

Chapter Fourteen

As friendly as Suzanne and the other members of the wagon train were, there were times Annabelle was reminded pointedly that she was an outsider. When the party rolled to a stop in the afternoon, the couples talked over their plans for the next day. Suzanne's hand often clasped Charles's, their heads close as they discussed the day's events. Tate and Elizabeth Manley were almost inseparable, and managed to distance themselves from the others. Sometimes Annabelle caught them looking at one another so lovingly she felt like an intruder. A jealous one.

Even the Butlers sat together, though Jim did almost all the talking. He gave his wife none of the attention or loving looks that Annabelle saw pass between the other married couples. Looks that made her feel more alone than she ever had in her life.

She wandered away from the camp, not so far that

she couldn't see or hear her fellow travelers, but at a distance that allowed her to breathe a bit easier, and to feel less like an interloper. She sat at the crest of a hill and looked west, at tomorrow's trail before her. There was nothing . . . nothing but tall grass and rolling hills and the quiet, dusty trail they would follow in the morning. Desolate, but somehow beautiful. Wild, but willing to be tamed. Open, as vast and endless as the blue skies above her.

She leaned back in the grass and studied the white, fluffy clouds that drifted across the azure sky. They danced, driven by a gentle wind, their shapes changing rapidly as she searched for the faces and animals and scattered images that formed and quickly disappeared. No matter how hard she tried to drive thoughts of Shelley from her mind, he was always there. Had he ever rested with his head upon his saddle and watched the clouds drift by? It was the sort of thing she could imagine him doing, in one of his mellower moods.

"Do you like boys?"

She started and sat up, turning to look at Penny, the deliverer of that strange question. Penny was frowning, and over the little girl's shoulder Annabelle could see Charlie and Little Jim playing roughly, wrestling on the ground in a game that obviously excluded little girls.

"Well." She patted the ground beside her, and Penny obediently joined her. "Sometimes I do and sometimes I don't. What about you?"

Penny nodded solemnly. "Me, too. Sometimes boys are mean." She turned a tragic face to Annabelle. "Do you have any kids?"

She shook her head. "I'm afraid I don't."

Penny sighed, maintaining her melancholy. "Well, f you ever do, I hope it's a girl and not a nasty old boy."

Annabelle wondered, and not for the first time, what t would be like to carry Shelley's child. In a way, it vould be wonderful to know she would always have omething of him with her, but it would be scandalous as well. As if her situation wasn't perilous enough. Fortunately, or unfortunately, she was not pregnant. She'd discovered that fact just days into her journey vith the Castletons, and to her amazement she had cried . . . briefly, but so hard that she'd given herself a headache that had lasted two days.

"I hope one day I have a little girl just like you, Penny." Her statement drove away Penny's disgust, and the child smiled sunnily.

"Really?"

"Absolutely." She leaned back in the grass. "Do you see the horse in that cloud?" She pointed to the heavens above.

Penny lay down beside her, her hands behind her head. She frowned for a moment, and then laughed lightly. "There! Now it's turning into a dog . . . a man's face!"

They got lost in their simple game, and Annabelle found herself laughing out loud. The clouds shifted and parted, changing rapidly. Once, for a split second, she was certain she saw Shelley's face in a cloud, watching over her as he had since they'd met. Until now.

In two weeks they'd passed close to several small settlements, but they never stopped. The three families and Annabelle had all they needed. In the towns were only temptations to spend money they didn't have. And wanted posters. Annabelle was afraid of finding her likeness everywhere. More newspapers and false accusations. Each time the wagons rolled past yet another small town, she felt her heart start beating faster, until it was racing, and in her mind she saw the rising dust of approaching riders who would point a finger at her and shout to the world that she was a wanted woman. A cold-blooded murderess.

But that never happened, and her heartbeat returned to normal as they left each settlement behind them.

She was also relieved that Jim Butler no longer spoke to her, so her days and nights were more comfortable. He had limped slightly for a week after their late-night encounter, telling everyone that he had tripped over a rock and broken a toe. Even though he ignored her, she was afraid to sleep in the open. Butler continued to look at her with a frightening mixture of hate and desire. It was the threat of the derringer Shelley had given her that kept him at bay.

If only the dreams would stop. Sometimes she couldn't remember what woke her in a cold sweat, the blood pounding through her veins like icy water. Other times she wasn't so lucky. Parts of the dream were hazy, undecipherable, but sometimes she saw Henri's body as if it were real, blood covering his fine linen shirt, his face still and white. Dead. That image stayed with her long after she'd awakened. Refused to be driven from her mind's eye. Poor Henri.

Fortunately, her nightmares didn't disturb the children, even when she tossed and turned and woke with tears in her eyes. They rested soundly, lost in the sweet dreams of innocence.

Annabelle sometimes felt as if she might as well be crawling to San Francisco on her hands and knees, their progress was so slow. She enjoyed her evening talks with Suzanne, and they discussed children, Suzanne's and little ones in general, the country they traversed, harsh and beautiful. The luxuries they missed the most. Pretty dresses, fancy hats, scented bath oils. Unfortunately, there had been no chance to use the small tub Annabelle had seen on her first night with the party. There had been no rain, and the streams they passed were shallow and muddy, sufficient for the animals but unsuitable for bathing, with or without the tub.

It surprised her that Suzanne never asked any personal questions. Not that she minded not having to lie. Suzanne never even asked about Shelley, or the tears Annabelle had shed that night when he rode away and left her there. But then, Suzanne also offered no information about her own personal life before the journey had begun. It was a given that they were all looking forward, not back.

When they did at last camp by a clear stream that ran deep and rushed gently over smooth rocks, everyone was ecstatic. Especially the women. Annabelle didn't have to wonder for long how such a large party handled bathing, when Suzanne grabbed a handful of towels, shouted "Women first," and every woman in the camp except Annabelle ran for the creek while the men thoughtfully gathered on the other side of a covered wagon, allowing the females their privacy.

Annabelle didn't hesitate long before rushing after the other women.

Suzanne was merrily stripping off her dress, and before long all the women, Penny included, had stripped to their underwear and splashed cheerily in the water. Annabelle left her britches and shirt and red boots on the bank, and waded in. The cool water washed over her legs, and she bent to splash her dusty face. She waded farther into the stream and immersed herself slowly and luxuriantly. There had never been a hot, scented bath that refreshed her as much or felt as good as the creek water washing over her body. She stood, the water coming barely to her waist, and unbraided her hair.

Suzanne passed her a bar of soap, tossing it through the air. Annabelle had to leap into the air to catch it, laughing at her newfound ability. She soaped her hair and rinsed it clean. She lathered every inch of her body, over and around her underthings, until she finally felt clean for the first time in weeks.

She joined Suzanne and Judith Butler on the bank where they sat in the sun to dry, and watched Penny and the young newlywed Elizabeth as they splashed and swam.

Annabelle leaned back on her elbows. "This is just heavenly."

Suzanne purred like a kitten. "Isn't it, though?"

Judith sat rigidly and stared at the water with a slight frown on her face.

"What's wrong, Judith?" Suzanne placed a comforting hand on Jim Butler's wife's back, and the woman tensed.

Judith turned to look at Annabelle. She had a thin face and pale reddish hair that might have been strawberry-blonde at one time but was mixed with premature gray. "I love my husband."

The simple declaration shocked Suzanne and Annabelle, but it was Annabelle who found her voice first. "That's as it should be, Mrs. Butler."

The look on Judith's face was sad, just short of desperate. "I know he looks at you when he thinks I'm not watching."

"Annie's a beautiful girl. I'm sure all the men have given her the once-over, even my Charles," Suzanne said, defending Annabelle.

Judith ignored Suzanne. "I know women find Jim attractive. He's a handsome man. Sometimes I worry . . . that he'll find a younger, prettier woman and leave me behind."

Judith was so intent on her fears that she didn't catch the quick glance that passed between Suzanne and Annabelle. Jim Butler? Attractive? Annabelle found the man oily and repulsive, but she couldn't tell his wife that.

Instead, she laid her hand on Judith's knee. "Perhaps I should tell you two a secret."

She had the women's full attention. "I am hopelessly in love with another man. It's impossible. He hates me, or at least he doesn't like me very much, but I can't seem to stop loving him. Even if your husband was . . . paying me any improper attentions, which he isn't, you wouldn't have anything to fear from me. No other man interests me but . . ."

Suzanne grinned. "The man who left you with us," she said, proud of her deduction. "Shelley? Is that his name?"

Annabelle nodded. "Shelley." She found herself telling Suzanne and Judith things about herself and Shelley that she'd mulled over during the past two weeks. She stopped short of telling them who she really was, or about their last night together, but she was somehow certain that they knew her intimacies with

139

Shelley hadn't stopped with a couple of passionate kisses.

She ended her story with the night she'd watched Shelley ride away from her and Suzanne had found her crying.

"I can't believe he doesn't love you," Judith said, her voice and her face more relaxed than it had been before Annabelle's confession.

Suzanne gave them a naughty smile. "But he does."

Annabelle shook her head. "No. He's a different kind of man. He's . . ."

She was stopped by Judith's and Suzanne's mingled raucous laughter.

"What's so funny?"

Suzanne gave her a knowing look. "All men are the same. No matter how they try to deny it, they're all cut from the same cloth."

Annabelle shook her head. "Not Shelley. He's not like other men."

"He's different to you because you love him," Suzanne explained tenderly. "Believe me when I tell you that he loves you. I saw it in his face that night he was here. He didn't want to leave you."

"Then why did he? Why didn't he take me to San Francisco himself?" she asked helplessly. "I don't understand."

"Annie, honey." Suzanne lay back in the grass. "If we understood men, this would be a much saner world to live in. Duller, but saner. It's my guess that Shelley was hurt, and he's afraid of getting hurt again."

"It doesn't matter." She spread her hair with her fingers, trying to dry it before she braided it. "I'll never see him again."

Suzanne smiled. "That's not necessarily true," she said knowingly. "Do you believe in fate?"

She shrugged. "I suppose I do."

"When I first met Charles he was married to his first wife. He was friendly, but nothing more. After all, he was married, and I was barely sixteen at the time, but I was smitten."

"Even though he was married?" Judith asked, shocked.

"I just thought he was a strong, handsome man, different from anyone I'd ever known." She smiled at Annabelle.

"Anyway, his wife died soon after that. He had no children, so he sold his farm and left town. I figured I'd never see him again . . . but three years later my pa sent me to stay with his sister, my mean old Aunt Millie, who wasn't nearly as sick as she tried to make out. She just wanted me around to do all her chores for her. She lived nearly a hundred miles away from my home . . . that seemed like such a long way at the time. Anyway, when I went to town to check her mail and pick up some supplies, who do you think I ran into?"

Judith looked puzzled, but Annabelle answered, "Charles."

Suzanne nodded. "Right there by the penny candy. He looked at me, and I looked at him, and it was love at first sight. Well, second sight, I reckon." She looked dreamily to the blue sky. "That was nine years ago. The luckiest day of my life."

Annabelle looked over the water. The sun glistened off the surface, momentarily blinding her. "Fate," she said, shielding her eyes with the palms of her hands. "I don't know. I'm afraid I'll never see Shelley again, and if I did, he'd probably turn and run the other way."

"Well, then . . . you and I will have to have a long talk about . . . how you might convince him not to turn away." Suzanne grinned, but Judith blushed, obviously disapproving.

Suzanne jumped to her feet. "Let's get dressed before the menfolk get tired of waiting."

While the men were bathing, an Indian party appeared riding slowly over a small rise to the west, the afternoon sun behind their backs silhouetting them against a blue sky. Annabelle counted half a dozen . . . six half-naked redmen riding toward their camp.

Suzanne took charge, sending Judith down to the creek to fetch the men. She produced a rifle from under the seat of her wagon, and on seeing that, Annabelle grabbed the derringer from her saddlebag and stuck it in the waistband of her britches.

"They probably just want something for allowing us to pass through their land. This has happened before." Suzanne tried to reassure Annabelle, but there was an unnatural brightness in Suzanne's pale eyes . . . she was terrified.

Annabelle had never seen an Indian, and she was mesmerized by their presence. They were powerful physical specimens. Dark and muscled, naked to the waist, adorned with paint and feathers and necklaces made with long sharp teeth and claws. She knew she should have been as terrified as Suzanne and the others, but she had the sense to know that hysteria would hurt them more than a strong and assured stance.

By the time the Indians were in the camp, the men had returned, still wet and half frantic. Charles was by far the calmest of the bunch, and it was he who approached the savages.

"Welcome to our camp." He nodded respectfully. "You are welcome to stay and share our food with us tonight."

This greeting seemed to please the Indians, and one member of the party slid from his pony and approached Charles boldly, but unthreateningly.

"You are passing through land that belongs to the Cheyenne. Bathing in our water, sleeping on our grass." His voice was deep and sonorous. "You must pay."

Charles frowned. "We have little, but we will gladly share what we have."

Well armed, with long rifles and knives, and wicked-looking tomahawks hanging from their belts, the Indians dismounted and wandered around the camp, making themselves at home as the women bcgan to cook. They looked inside each wagon while the men watched warily, and one bold warrior gently caressed the braid that hung down Annabelle's back.

After a while they gathered, talking in their own language, pointing and arguing. Finally the Indian who had initially spoken to Charles stepped forward.

"We will take tobacco, sugar, and red boots, and that pony." He pointed to Annabelle's mare.

"No." She rushcd to her horse. "Plcase. Don't take her. Shelley bought her for me." She couldn't stand the thought of being confined to one of the wagons for the remainder of the trip. She sat on the ground and started unlacing the red boots. "You can have these boots. Just please, leave me my horse."

He began to laugh, the arrogant savage who had demanded her boots and her horse. She looked up, wondering what was happening to make the redman laugh. He was looking at her. Two of the Cheyennes jumped on their ponies and rode away, over a small hill.

"No." The Indian who spoke English so well pointed to her. "You are Red Boots," he said, and she finally realized that they were calling *her* Red Boots, and intended to take her captive.

Charles stepped forward. "You cannot take the young lady! Take everything you want, but none of our people."

The Cheyenne warrior looked at him with expressionless eyes. "She is your woman?"

"No. But she is my responsibility," Charles said sternly.

Jim Butler stepped forward and whispered loudly. "Let them have her. They might kill us all!"

The Indian ignored him. "Which of you is her man?"

Butler spoke up quickly. "She has no man. She's traveling alone."

"Then we will take her." The Indian smiled.

Annabelle stood and backed away, coming to a halt with her back to a wagon. The Indian planted himself in front of her and offered his hand. His black eyes pierced her, untouched by the smile that still graced his rugged face. He would have been a fine-looking man, with his strong straight nose and smooth bronzed skin, if not for the utter coldness in his eyes.

"Come. You will like Swift Eagle. Swift Eagle is good to his squaws. You will be well cared for, and will not need to work. You will have your own tepee."

She refused to take his hand. She thought about the derringer stuck in her waistband. Two shots. Even if she killed two of the Indians, that would still leave four. She might get everyone else killed, even the children.

144

"Who is Swift Eagle?" she asked, trying to disguise the fear in her voice.

The Indian pointed to his chest with pride, and she saw numerous scars there, marring his dark skin. "I am Swift Eagle."

She smiled faintly, trying to appear confident. "I'm very flattered, Swift Eagle, really I am, but even though my man isn't here right now, I am promised to another."

Swift Eagle shrugged. His smile vanished. "White man break all promises."

She shook her head. "I don't. I have a man, and I need no other."

Swift Eagle was becoming agitated. His eyes blazed at her, and that was much more frightening than the coldness she had seen there before. "Where is this man? What man leaves his woman to travel with those who would give her away?" He gave Jim Butler a look of disgust.

She opened her mouth to reply, but Shelley's voice, as calm as if he'd been asking for a sip of water said, "This man."

She ran past Swift Eagle. Shelley was flanked on either side by the two Indians who had ridden away, but his smile was easy.

"Shelley!" She was waiting for him when he dismounted, and practically threw herself at him. "They want to take me with them."

"I know, darlin'." He faced Swift Eagle with her at his side, his arm possessively over her shoulder.

Swift Eagle scowled. "He-Who-Follows," he said, staring at Shelley. "If she is your woman, why do you stay so far back from the others?"

Shelley shrugged. "We had a fight."

Swift Eagle raised his eyebrow. "You hit little Red Boots?" It was clear he did not approve.

"No. Not that kind of fight." Shelley extricated himself from her arms. "An argument." He gestured wildly.

Swift Eagle looked confused, and it became clear to Annabelle that the Indian was not as fluent in English as she had first thought.

Shelley pointed to her. "Red Boots says, 'Shelley' "— he raised his voice an octave—" 'I hate beans. Shelley, it's too hot. Shelley, it's too cold. Shelley, you snore too loud.' "

The other five Indians were laughing, pointing at Shelley and her. Only Swift Eagle remained stony-faced.

"Snore?" he asked.

Shelley demonstrated loudly, and the Indians' laughter increased in intensity.

"Shelley, please." She moved closer to him. "I never said . . ."

Shelley turned to face her, and when his back was to the Indians his smile disappeared. "Shut up, Annie," he whispered in a low voice that only she could hear. "Or do you want to be a squaw?"

She snapped her mouth shut, and when Shelley turned back around he was grinning again.

"See what I mean? She even tried to kick me in the balls." He was looking to the Indian for sympathy.

Swift Eagle looked momentarily distressed. "Then you won't mind if I take her."

"But I do mind."

Swift Eagle scowled. "I will give you four ponies for her," he offered.

Shelley shook his head.

"Six," Swift Eagle said, more loudly.

Shelley turned to look at her, made a despairing face, and whispered, "He wants you bad, darlin'."

"That's a lot?"

Shelley nodded and faced Swift Eagle again. "No. I won't give up my woman."

Swift Eagle shook his head, and Annabelle sighed with relief. Shelley had saved her again. Then the nightmare began anew when Swift Eagle insisted in a loud voice, "We will fight for Red Boots."

Shelley groaned almost silently. Only she heard it. "All right, but here are the rules—"

"No rules," Swift Eagle interrupted.

Shelley looked pained. "I don't want to have to kill you over a woman . . . even this one."

Shelley's confidence unnerved the savage briefly. She could see it in his face.

Shelley continued, "No weapons. We fight until you can't get up or else you say, 'You can have her, Shelley.' "

Swift Eagle grinned. He looked Shelley up and down. "You are big white man, but you are no match for Swift Eagle. We will fight until you can't get up or you say, 'You can have her, Swift Eagle.' "

Annabelle grabbed Shelley's shoulder as he unstrapped his six-shooter. His grin was in place until he turned to her, and no one else could see his face.

"If I lose—" he whispered.

"Don't say that." She grasped the front of his shirt with both hands as he began to unbutton it.

"If I lose, don't run. If you run it'll just make Swift Eagle mad, and he's likely to pass you around the campfire like a bottle of tequila."

She trembled, and Shelley tried to give her a reassuring grin, apparently regretting his choice of words.

"He seems to like you well enough, and as long as I'm still alive . . . I'll come after you. I promise."

"Be careful," she whispered.

Shelley leaned down and held her face between his big hands. "How about a kiss for luck?" He'd barely finished the sentence when his lips were over hers, and she threw her arms around his neck.

He released her reluctantly and turned toward Swift Eagle, who waited impatiently. With no warning, Shelley turned back to her. "One more, darlin'." When he kissed her again, the other Indians howled with laughter. But Swift Eagle was clearly not amused.

Chapter Fifteen

Swift Eagle and Shelley sized one another up first, feinting and pulling back, practically dancing around in a circle. The Indians who watched from a distance thought it great entertainment, but Annabelle and the three families who surrounded her were terrified.

What if Shelley lost?

Shelley got in the first real blow, a jab that would have flattened any other man. Swift Eagle's head snapped back, and he grinned appreciatively at his opponent. Standing beside Annabelle, Charles cursed under his breath. Suzanne, on her other side, tightened her grip on Annabelle's shoulder.

Within minutes the two fighters were covered with sweat, their bare chests glistening, their faces beaded with it. They glared at each other with such intensity, as if nothing but the two of them existed.

The first time Swift Eagle's fist connected with Shel-

149

ley's jaw, Annabelle was certain she could feel it. She wasn't alone. Every man in the crowd flinched as Shelley landed in the dirt, only to jump back up again. He quickly delivered a punch to Swift Eagle's face that laid open the skin above the Indian's eye, but Swift Eagle never slowed down or made an attempt to wipe the blood away.

Soon they were both bloody. One of Swift Eagle's eyes was swollen shut, and Shelley's mouth and a cut on his forehead bled badly. Their hands were covered with blood, their own and their opponent's. Suzanne was having more and more difficulty holding Annabelle back as she tried to rush between them.

And then came the blow that knocked Shelley to the ground. He didn't move for a few long moments. There was absolute silence. Then the Indians cheered, certain their warrior had won.

Swift Eagle turned to Annabelle, the proud look on his face displaying his arrogance and his certainty that she should be flattered. He frowned at the tears on her face.

"I have fought for you, Red Boots. Are you not pleased?"

If not for the shouted warnings from his companions, Swift Eagle might not have known that Shelley had risen behind him.

Swift Eagle knocked Shelley to the ground again, swinging his arm with all his force and striking Shelley across the face with the back of his hand.

"Stop it! You're killing him!" She was finally able to break away from Suzanne and rush to Shelley.

"Shelley." She knelt down beside him and brushed the hair from his face. His blood was on her fingers, but she ignored it. "Don't," she whispered when he tried to rise again.

Shelley pushed her away and rose to his feet. His movements were slow, and the blood that ran from his forehead partially blinded him. He was barely on his feet before Swift Eagle felled him again.

"I said stop it!" She stood toe to toe with the Indian and glared at him defiantly. She was no longer afraid of Swift Eagle . . . she was only afraid that Shelley might never be able to get up. "You're going to kill him!"

Swift Eagle grinned. "He need only remain on the ground or say, 'You can have her, Swift Eagle.' "

Shelley rose silently as the Cheyenne warrior stood nose to nose with her. He spun Swift Eagle around and delivered a punch.

The warrior, furious to be caught off guard, knocked Shelley to the ground, and then drew a knife that had been concealed in his tall moccasin. His intent was evident in the rage in his black eyes.

Swift Eagle stood over Shelley, ready to plunge the knife into his chest, when Annabelle threw herself over his target. She felt the rise and fall of Shelley's chest, but he made no effort to move. In his condition, that would have been impossible.

"No," she said as calmly as she could, turning her face so that she could see Swift Eagle lowering his knife. "I'll go with you, but don't kill him."

She stood slowly. As she did, Shelley made an effort to rise again. "Like hell you will," he muttered.

Swift Eagle raised his knife.

Never let them know what's coming. Don't hesitate, she told herself, letting her foot fly, putting all her strength into the kick. Her blow caught Swift Eagle right between his legs, which at first stunned him and then brought him to his knees. She picked up the knife he had dropped, and left the two moaning men lying inches apart.

She walked boldly toward the Indians and studied each one closely. They were not all the same, as she had first thought. There was the young warrior who had touched her hair, two even younger, and a man about the same age as Swift Eagle. It was the sixth Indian she approached. He was the oldest, and wore the most feathers and decorations. There were streaks of gray in his black hair, and his weather-beaten skin appeared to be as tough as leather. More than that, there was a spark of intelligence in his eyes that drew her to him.

"Do you speak English?" She looked directly at him, meeting his gaze. He didn't smile, but his eyes sparkled.

He nodded. "A little."

"I apologize for striking Swift Eagle, but he did promise no weapons," she explained sensibly. "I couldn't let him kill Shelley."

"So you throw yourself in the path of Swift Eagle's knife?" The older Cheyenne gave in to the smile that his eyes had only hinted at. His face became a mass of deep wrinkles when he grinned. "It would be a shame to see such a pretty white woman die for He-Who-Follows."

She froze. She had never doubted that Swift Eagle would stop when she threw herself over Shelley. The thought that he might not had never occurred to her. Would it have made any difference? No, she decided quickly.

"I owe Shelley . . . everything," she said in a low

voice. And then she found herself telling the old man about the false accusations, her attempts to run and hide, how Shelley had spirited her away from the Pinkerton agent. It was so easy to look into those eyes and tell him the truth . . . the truth she had been trying so hard to avoid for the past several months.

The old man nodded and listened intently.

"It is Swift Eagle's folly that he desires a white wife," he said, his voice almost apologetic. "He believes a white squaw will make him a powerful warrior." The old Indian shook his head. "He has begun to think too much like a white man, claiming that we own the land you travel over. No man owns the earth. We are a part of it. It can belong to no man."

"It is very flattering that Swift Eagle wants me as his wife, but I won't go with him."

She lifted her chin defiantly as she stared at the majestic leader who stood, his arms crossed, no more than three feet away. He showed no signs that he'd understood her confession . . . that it had moved him in any way. He wasn't very fluent. Perhaps he hadn't understood her.

"If you make me go, I'll scream until I drive you all mad, and no one screams like I do. I have great lungs."

"Show Red Wolf how you scream." She could tell he was amused with her threat and was downplaying his concerns about Swift Eagle to humor her as he might a demanding child.

She took a deep breath and looked the old Indian in the eye. Years of training had given her a powerful voice, and she let loose with everything she had. Her scream split the early evening air, and caused the old man to step back in surprise. The Indians' ponies whinnied and stomped their hooves, and her own mare snorted and shook her head.

Annabelle's scream continued unbroken, long after another woman would have run out of breath, and the expression on Red Wolf's face changed from amusement to consternation, to one of pain. When she finally stopped, not winding down but coming to a sudden, silent halt, all eyes were on her.

"I can scream like that all night, and all day, until you let me go or kill me."

Red Wolf looked at her with a measure of respect. "No good to kill white man. Kill one, and ten come to take his place."

She nodded. "I believe Swift Eagle will listen to you. That he respects your wishes. I offer Swift Eagle my horse, and she's a fine mare, strong and sure-footed, and everything else that I own . . . if he will allow Shelley and me to go."

Red Wolf wrinkled his brow and nodded slightly. "Perhaps if Swift Eagle comes away with gifts, he will not feel shamed. Let me see this fine animal."

She ran to the wagon and unhitched her mare. She didn't spare a glance for her fellow travelers as she led the horse back to Red Wolf. He waited, his arms crossed, and his countenance severe.

It wasn't until she reached Red Wolf that she turned around and saw Shelley and Swift Eagle sitting up, their blood-covered faces turned to her as they sat inches apart in the dirt. She had never seen two more battered men.

She first offered the knife she had plucked from the ground, handle first, to Red Wolf. "Please return this to Swift Eagle . . . later."

Red Wolf refused to take the knife. "Swift Eagle will not want to fight again with a weapon that was taken from him in battle by a woman."

She frowned. "I just didn't want him to stab Shelley."

Red Wolf's hand closed over hers, wrapping her fingers around the handle. "You keep, Red Boots."

She carefully slipped the blade into her boot. Then she reached into the saddlebag and withdrew her black dress.

"Are you married, Red Wolf?" she asked as she held up the gown. "This is a fine dress, well made, good material. It will keep your wife warm in the winter." The dress had not weathered her attempt at laundering very well. It was spotted and wrinkled, but it was in one piece.

Red Wolf fingered the material. "These gifts will be for Swift Eagle. One of his wives will take it."

She lowered the dress slightly. "One of his wives? How many does he have?"

Red Wolf grinned and leaned closer to her. "Three. That's one too many."

She took her sunbonnet, which was badly crushed, and shaped it in her hands as she presented it. "One of his wives will love this hat. It's very fashionable."

Red Wolf wrinkled his nose in distaste at the headwear. He took it from her and turned it over in his hands, fingering the yellow satin ribbons. "Yes. What else do you have in there?"

She pulled out the bottle of tequila she and Shelley had opened the night before he'd left her with the Castletons. The night he'd made love to her under the stars. "Tequila. Shelley's favorite drink."

Red Wolf took the bottle and uncapped it, sniffing deeply before he gave it back to her. "Firewater. No good for my people. Makes them act like crazy white men. You keep."

Annabelle presented every item she owned. Her satchel, the coins inside, her mirror and comb. The dried apples she still had in her saddlebag. Red Wolf looked with interest at each item.

When she was finished he pointed to her waist. "Your pistol?"

She had been hoping he wouldn't ask about the derringer. What if she gave it to him and Swift Eagle used it to kill someone?

With a sigh, she presented the weapon. "Very pretty grip," she said. "But only two shots."

Red Wolf looked with undisguised disgust at the pistol. "No good for hunting. Only good for killing man."

She held the derringer in her open hand.

"Red Boots keep little gun," the Indian said finally. "She might need it if bad man tries to stop her before end of journey."

So he had been listening, and understood.

"Swift Eagle will accept gifts," Red Wolf continued, "and allow Red Boots and He-Who-Follows to go."

She smiled, but when she looked over her shoulder, Swift Eagle's scowl stole her brief moment of happiness. She turned back to Red Wolf, finding comfort in the leader's stern calmness.

"Are you certain he'll agree?" She whispered, leaning close to Red Wolf. "He looks so angry."

Red Wolf smiled, talking in a low voice that only she could hear. "Swift Eagle is my youngest son. He is bitter, and hungers for many things he cannot possess. I pray that one day he will come to accept what is, and find peace in his heart." The Indian pounded a fist against his chest. "That day will not come for a long time, but he is a good son, and will listen today to the wise words of his father."

She breathed a sigh of relief. "Thank you, Red Wolf."

His dark eyes glinted as he continued to whisper. "You are a brave woman, Red Boots. I have never before seen a white warrior woman who would go into battle unarmed. But I am glad not to be taking you to Swift Eagle's tepee. He has too many wives already, and they would not like him bringing home another one."

Annabelle had almost forgotten everyone else in the camp, and when she turned around she saw that no one had moved. They stared at her and Red Wolf, and Suzanne's face was white as a sheet. Penny clung to her mother's skirts, her eyes wide with wonder and fear. To assuage their fears, she smiled at them warmly, then turned back to Red Wolf as a thought struck her.

"You and Swift Eagle called Shelley 'He-Who-Follows.' Why? How long has he been following the wagon train?"

Red Wolf shrugged. "We have been watching for three days. The man you call Shelley has always been there."

She frowned as she turned away from Red Wolf, and the older man called, in his native tongue, to his son. Swift Eagle came slowly to his feet, and gave her a wide berth, scowling and watching her closely.

"Shelley." She knelt beside him, laying the bottle of tequila in the dirt.

"What in the hell do you think you're doing?" Shelley asked, in obvious pain, through swollen lips. There was more than a little anger in his voice.

She tilted her head so she could see his face better. "Making a deal." She brushed the hair from his forehead and frowned at the cut there. "We'll need to take care of that right away."

Shelley slapped her hand away. "What kind of a deal?"

Behind her, she heard Red Wolf and Swift Eagle arguing, but Swift Eagle's angry words were overshadowed by his father's authority, and she ignored them.

"Swift Eagle gets my mare and everything else I own but the clothes on my back, we get to ride away from here alive, and I don't end up as Mrs. Swift Eagle the Fourth," she snapped. Why was he looking at her like that?

"You gave away your horse? And your thirty-six dollars? And that ugly damn black dress?"

She nodded. "Well, I didn't have the entire thirty-six dollars." She held up the bottle of tequila. "He didn't want this, though."

"Great," Shelley moaned.

"Or this." She drew her derringer. "And he let me keep this." She drew the knife from her boot with the same hand that held the derringer. For the first time she noticed that the smooth wooden handle was set with polished stones. "It's very pretty, isn't it?"

Shelley shook his head. "Very pretty, darlin'," he said somberly.

She looked over her shoulder at the Indian party as they mounted their ponies, securing their booty on her mare and leading it away. Red Wolf turned to face the camp, and raised a hand to her.

She heard Shelley groan as she lifted her hand and waved, a smile on her face while she watched the old Indian ride away.

Chapter Sixteen

Shelley leaned back in the grass by the stream as Annabelle bathed his face, washing the blood from his skin in the dying daylight, cleaning the evidence of the battle from his beard. But he protested when she started washing his shoulders and chest.

"What the hell do you think you're doing?" he asked gruffly, grabbing her wrist.

She sighed. How could he be so stubborn, even now? She was so grateful that he was alive she felt the need to touch him, to assure herself that he was real.

"You've made a mess of yourself, Shelley. 'What's the matter, darlin'?'" she mimicked. "'Are you modest?'"

He opened one eye narrowly. "Get me my shirt. It's up in the camp . . . unless you gave that away, too."

She called to Penny and her big brother Charlie, as the two children watched from several feet away. She

160

sent them to fetch Shelley's shirt and continued to wash the blood, his and Swift Eagle's, from his chest.

"You needn't be so cranky," she said almost primly.

"Darlin', I'm way beyond cranky. I've passed vexed and piqued and indignant and gone all the way to pissed," he practically growled at her.

She leaned back from him and sat on her heels. She couldn't understand why he was so angry. They were both alive. They were together. An hour ago she wouldn't have bet on either of those situations happening.

"I don't understand you at all. Why are you mad at me? I didn't ask you and Swift Eagle to beat one another to a pulp. That's not my fault. Why are you even here? It's been two weeks since you left me . . ."

"You know why I'm here." He sat up slowly. "Just listen to yourself. Since I left you. You make it sound like I deserted you."

"Didn't you?"

They stared at one another wordlessly as Penny ran down the gentle slope, Shelley's white shirt clutched in her hand. She threw it to him and ran back up the bank.

"No, I didn't, dammit." Shelley waved her away when she tried to help. "I can still dress myself."

"Then what are you doing here . . . He-Who-Follows?"

She remembered what Suzanne had said that very afternoon. "He loves you, Annie. I could tell." There was no love in his eyes at the moment, and she suspected there was none in his heart, either.

He shook his head as he buttoned his shirt. "You know why I'm here. You called me back. You refused to let me rest. You . . . like an itch in the middle of my back that I couldn't quite reach. You preyed on my mind like a bug in a bedroll . . ."

"I did none of those things," she defended herself angrily.

"You did all of those things. I know I'll never get another moment of peace until I see you safe in San Francisco." He narrowed his eyes and glared at her. "I can't even enjoy a simple drink anymore . . . can't even . . ." He stopped abruptly.

"Can't even what?" she snapped.

"Nothing," he growled. "So that's where we're going. San Francisco." He forced himself to his feet. "I just wish you hadn't given away your horse."

"We can both ride on yours," she said. "We've done it before."

He pointed a finger at her and stared hard, looking down at her upturned face. "We've done a lot of things before that we're not going to do again. Understand?"

She nodded.

"Say it, Annie," he demanded.

"I understand." She frowned. "No. I don't understand. You kissed me—."

"For Swift Eagle's benefit," he interrupted.

"And you fought for me—"

"How could I live with myself if I let that happen . . . to any woman?"

She looked at the ground. She'd been right all along, and Suzanne had been wrong. He didn't love her. He felt a grudging responsibility for her, and that was all. Well, she did have her pride. She could never let him know how much she loved him.

"Then, if you don't mind, I'll continue to travel with the Castletons," she said softly.

"Well, I do mind," he drawled. "They travel too goddamn slow. It's driving me crazy."

She wanted to look at him, but she didn't dare. "You don't need to follow me anymore. I don't want you to. You claim I called you back . . . well, I didn't, but I can certainly send you away."

She waited what seemed like a long while for his response, and when he finally answered his voice was calmer. "No, you can't, Annie. What if Swift Eagle decides to come back?"

"He won't."

"You can't be certain, and if he does come back he's gonna be none too happy. You'll be risking the lives of every man, woman, and child in this wagon train."

She stood and turned away from him quickly, striding up the hill so he couldn't see her face. "Then I guess I have no choice."

Shelley followed her, mumbling under his breath about choices and women and dark braids . . .

She tried to ignore his muffled curses as she strode toward the camp.

Shelley stared into the fire as everyone tried to talk at once. The Castletons, the Butlers, and the Manlcys—men and women and children alike—chattered in high and excited voices until it all became an irritating buzz around him. Only he and Annie were silent.

Everyone wanted to know what she'd said to the old Indian. Red Wolf, she'd said his name was, but she didn't seem willing to share much else.

He'd had a little of the meal the women had prepared, but for once in his life he couldn't eat much. He hurt all over, though he didn't utter a word of complaint.

His mouth was cut and swollen, and Annie had told him—with little sympathy in her voice—that he had a tremendous black eye. Her words, not his. There were several small cuts on his face, stinging but not deep, and one gash above his eye. Even his hands were battered.

At last there was a lull in the chaotic conversation. It had been a long day for them all, and Shelley was sure that exhaustion was catching up with them.

Tate Manley spoke up, and for once the rest of the crowd was silent. "I can't believe you were so quick to offer Annie up to that Indian, Jim," he blurted. "Makes me wonder what you would have done if it had been Elizabeth, or any of the other women." Tate's voice was condemning, and no one jumped to Jim Butler's defense.

Shelley lifted his eyes from the fire and found Butler staring at him. "What's this?"

"I was thinking of the other women and the children," Butler answered, quick to justify his actions.

"You were thinkin' of your own hide, I reckon," Shelley said so casually that Butler relaxed.

The welcomed silence grew cumbersome, and one by one the women made their excuses and left the fireside. Suzanne and Judith held their children close as they led the little ones to their beds. Tired as they were, Shelley was certain no one would fall asleep too quickly on this night. Visions of the Indians would still be too vivid.

Annabelle left soon after Suzanne, making a quick and unnecessary excuse.

Tate left the fireside with his wife, his arm around her waist, their fair heads together. Butler was looking with apparent avid interest at his feet, and when he lifted his head and saw Charles Castleton walking away from the fire—and realized that he was alone with Shelley—he jumped to his feet.

"I'd best get on to—"

"You'd best sit down," Shelley said in a gruff voice that left no room for argument.

Butler did as he was ordered.

"It truly distresses me that you, as Tate said, offered Annie up to the Indian."

Butler began to sweat, beads popping up on his shiny forehead. "I explained that. I was thinking of the other women and the kids—"

"I know damn well what you were thinkin' of." He rose, ignoring the pain that seemed to be everywhere, and moved to stand directly behind Butler. "Damned cowardly thing to do."

"Hell, the woman can take care of herself," Butler snapped nervously.

He laid his hand on Butler's shoulder. "And exactly how would you know that?" He remembered the way Butler had looked at Annie that first night, the way he stared at her tonight, his eyes widening at the sight of her derringer.

"I think she broke my baby toe, and she elbowed me . . ." he stopped as Shelley's hand tightened on his shoulder.

"Now, why would she do that?" Shelley's voice was surprisingly calm, given that he wanted to kill the man beneath his hand.

Butler squirmed, but Shelley didn't let up the pressure on the man's shoulder. "I didn't mean no harm, I swear." His voice rose half an octave as Shelley grabbed him by his collar and lifted him to his feet.

He turned the man around so he could see his

pinched face, and he sighed tiredly. "You messed with the wrong woman, Butler," he said as he clipped him under the jaw, sending the weak, spineless man to the ground.

Shelley groaned and cradled his right hand. That had hurt like hell. He stared down at the unconscious man in the dirt by the fire. If only Swift Eagle had been so easy.

A few moments later Annie and the Castletons joined him by the fire. They all looked at Butler.

"Jim fell asleep by the fire?" Suzanne shook her head. "He's never done that before."

Only Annie frowned. He knew she had guessed what had happened.

"Annie says you'll be taking her with you in the morning," Charles said.

He shook his head slowly, and the other three stared at him. "Tonight," he said. "The sooner we're out of Swift Eagle's territory, the safer we'll all be."

Charles nodded his gray head and reached into his pocket. "I feel I must return this." He handed Shelley a huge folded wad of money, which Shelley refused.

"We didn't see her all the way to California, as agreed," Charles insisted. "I wouldn't feel right—"

"You paid them to take me?" Annie stepped forward, and Shelley groaned. "You paid them? How much?"

"Later, Annie," he said in a low voice.

"No. Right now. How much?" She placed her face close to his and narrowed her dark eyes.

"Three hundred dollars," he growled. "And it would have been worth every penny."

"To be rid of me?"

"Yep. It was a small price . . ." He stopped when Annie drew back her hand as if to slap him.

She hesitated, her eyes softening just a little as she studied his face. "If Swift Eagle hadn't done such a good job . . ."

Shelley didn't pull away, didn't even flinch. "Go ahead. Might make you feel better."

Charles, his guilt written on his face, leaned warily between them and placed the money in Shelley's vest pocket. "Sorry," he whispered.

Shelley brushed off his apology and turned away. "Let's go, Annie," he called without looking back.

He knew in a heartbeat that she wasn't behind him, and he turned impatiently to watch her hugging Suzanne Castleton. The married woman was whispering urgently in Annie's ear, and Annie was shaking her head furiously. The only words of their parting conversation he heard were Annie's final words to Suzanne, called over her shoulder as she approached him. "You couldn't be more wrong, Suzanne."

The other woman wore a sly smile as she waved good-bye to Annie.

"I don't suppose you'd like to tell me what that was all about?" he asked as he started to assist Annie into the saddle.

She slapped his hands away and put a red-booted foot in the stirrup. "I don't suppose I would."

Chapter Seventeen

Annie rode astride, perched stiffly in front of Shelley as they rode on well into the night.

"You might as well lean back and relax." When he spoke, Annie jumped, apparently startled that he would bother to talk to her. "We'll ride for a while longer. Put some distance between us and the wagon train."

"I'm not tired, thank you," she answered him crisply.

Shelley smiled, studying her stubborn spine and the dark braid that fell down her back. So she was still angry. That was good. In fact, it would be a good idea to keep her that way all the way to California.

"It's no wonder Swift Eagle was smitten. Look at this." He lifted her braid, unwilling to admit to himself how wonderful it felt, silky and soft. "You're even beginning to look like an Indian."

Annie reached back and jerked the braid from his hand, pulling it forward so it fell over her shoulder. "You don't like it? Good. I'll keep it this way."

He cursed his foolishness. For eleven years he'd managed to avoid the kind of attachment he felt for Annie. She was nothing but trouble. Since his first look into her wide brown eyes he'd had to lay out the Pinkerton agent, a man who was probably just doing his job; Jim Butler, a man who certainly deserved what he got; and he'd gotten himself beaten to the point where he could barely hold his body straight in the saddle. Not that he'd ever complain to Annie about that. And he was riding west when he should be in Kansas, hunting down those outlaws Vaughan and Blount.

Aggravation. Still, he couldn't forget how she'd felt in his arms. Like she belonged there. Like she was a part of him, and when he let her go he would again be incomplete . . . dangerous thoughts best kept buried until they could be completely forgotten.

When he finally stopped in a protected clearing with stone walls on three sides, he managed to dismount without groaning aloud. He even managed to lift his arms to help Annie down, but she ignored him and dismounted on her own.

Just as well.

There was a nearly full moon in a cloudless sky illuminating Shelley's face, showing Annabelle more than she wanted to see. His battered face, his eye swollen almost shut, the stiffness of his normally graceful body . . . all reminded her that she was indebted to him.

Three hundred dollars! She didn't know what

bothered her most, his willingness to pay the Castletons so much to be rid of her, or her doubts about where he had gotten so much cash. He seemed to have nothing. Was it possible that he was an outlaw? That the 300 dollars was part of his takings from a bank robbery or a stage holdup?

It made perfect sense. He disdained hard work, spent all his times in saloons, and had never mentioned his profession. Given the numerous people they had met along the way who knew Shelley, it was obvious that he didn't stay in one place too long. Shelley, with his easy smile and his quick fists . . . an outlaw.

Their campsite was so secluded she decided that he must have know it was there. Had probably spent many nights there, hiding from a posse. Three hundred dollars!

He laid out his bedroll and placed the saddle at the head. "You first," he said, motioning graciously. "We'll keep a cold camp and sleep in shifts for a few days, just to be safe."

"I'll stay up for a while. I couldn't sleep right now anyway, and you look terrible." She could have said it more kindly, but she managed to make it sound like an insult. The moonlight cast eerie shadows on his battered face, and in spite of herself she felt a tugging at her heart. He was in that condition because of her.

Shelley dropped to the makeshift bed and closed his eyes. "So I'm supposed to trust you to watch over me?" He smiled ever so slightly.

She pulled the derringer from her waistband and Swift Eagle's long knife from her boot. "I don't suppose you have any choice."

He was asleep in minutes, and she lost the grim

frown that she'd worn since leaving the Castletons' camp. She sat beside Shelley, a weapon clutched in each hand as if an enemy might appear at any moment. He slept as deeply and soundly as the Castleton children. How did he do that? How could a man like him, an outlaw, sleep the sleep of the innocent?

She had tried all day, ever since she'd sat beside him and washed the blood from his face, to convince herself that she didn't really love him. He was arrogant, demanding, short-tempered, sometimes downright mean where she was concerned, and in her opinion he was much too free with his affections. With the moonlight on his face he was nothing special to look at, all bumps and bruises. Still, she wanted nothing more than to kiss him, and to have him kiss her back. To love him, and to have him love her back. She wanted him to sit up and grin at her and make love to her the way he had before . . . but he'd already said that wouldn't happen. Not ever again.

His breathing was deep and even, and she watched the rise and fall of his chest. She knew if she pressed her ear to that chest she would hear the gentle, steady pounding of his heart, the constant, staid beating that could comfort her and fill her with a peace that was so precious, so rare.

He would never know, she thought as she laid her head gently against his chest. She wouldn't sleep, she would simply rest for a few moments, perhaps close her eyes and listen to the tender thumping in her ear . . .

Her performance had come off perfectly and Annabelle left the stage to appreciative applause. She wore her lovely low-cut green silk costume, which revealed more of her ample bosom than she would have liked, and flared becomingly at the waist. Lisette had had to let the seams out a bit. She was gaining weight, her face was becoming too round and her hips too wide. Lisette and Pierre were feeding her too well, insisting that she needed lots of strength for her vocation. More than a vocation . . . a calling, a God-given gift. Her only passion.

She knew Henri was waiting for her in her dressing room. Dear, sweet Henri. It was his first trip to America. She couldn't wait to introduce him to Nicky. In a few weeks they would leave New York and take the rail to San Francisco. She wanted Nicky to approve of Henri. What was there not to approve of? Henri was tender, cultured, and his family was far wealthier than Nicky, and Nicky was quite well off. But more than that, Henri cared for her, and she for him. Theirs was a deep friendship. The perfect basis for a good marriage.

If only Albert wasn't being so difficult.

She didn't know why Albert disliked Henri so much. Albert would always be the one to manage her finances, would always be a part of her professional life. True, he had expressed an interest in marrying her once, but that had been long ago, and she'd let him know that she had no interest in him, other than as her business manager.

He'd accepted that all these years, but he openly detested Henri, whom he insisted on referring to as "that damned Frenchman." But Henri was her fiance, and her best friend.

She opened the door. Henri was slumped on the floor, blood soaking his shirt, his throat, the floor around him. So much blood. Albert was standing over Henri's body, a knife in his hand, a distorted look of rage on his face. That look changed to surprise when he looked up and

172

*saw her. Their eyes met, and for a moment there was
complete silence. They were both terrified, but it was
Albert who recovered his wits first.*

*She watched as Albert grimaced and raised the knife.
She wanted to run, but couldn't. It was as if her legs
were made of led. She was forced to watch as Albert
brought the knife swinging across into his own shoulder, wincing as the blade drove in and he withdrew it,
only to toss the weapon at her feet.*

*He yelled then, and she screamed, and moments later
the room was filled with people. Other singers, Pierre
and Lisette, the manager of the theater. They all looked
at her as though she were mad.*

*The knife was at the hem of her gown. Henri was
dead, and Albert was on his knees, clutching a bleeding
shoulder.*

*"Why, Annabelle?" Albert whispered loudly before he
collapsed.*

*She turned to the crowd behind her. Every pair of eyes
accused her. Every pair. She opened her mouth to protest her innocence, but she could make no sound. At
last she ran from the room, brushing past the accusers
who crowded the doorway, shoving them all aside as
she ran, and ran, and ran . . .*

"Annie."

The strange voice pulled her from the nightmare. It
was not Albert, not Henri, not Lisette. There was no
accusation in this voice, but a gentle kindness.

"Annie."

She felt a warm hand on her face, and she jerked
up, coming instantly awake and moving away from
the hand.

Her breathing was coming fast and heavy as she

173

jumped away from Shelley. In the soft light of a new morning's sun she stared, transfixed, at the wound on his forehead. It had come slightly open in the night, and there was a thin trickle of fresh blood.

There was a frown on Shelley's face as he looked from her to the derringer in the dirt, and then to the knife still clutched in her hand.

She followed his gaze down to the knife, and dropped it as if it were burning her palm. Slowly, her breathing and her heartbeat returned to normal as she sat in the dirt and tried to push the dream away.

"If you were tired you should've given me a shove and a holler so I could keep watch," Shelley said in a low voice.

"I didn't intend to fall asleep," she said, her voice small, unsure.

"If you're gonna fall asleep using my body as a pillow, please discard the weapons first," he pleaded, rising to his knees on the bedroll. "It's a goddamn miracle you didn't stab me with that very pretty knife you took from Swift Eagle."

She couldn't help it. She burst into tears at the words he spoke so casually.

"Come here." He pulled her into his arms. "It was just a dream, darlin'. No reason to cry."

She let him hold her, nestling her face against his shoulder, and took several deep breaths.

If only he knew. She'd decided that he was an outlaw, so perhaps he would understand what had happened. Maybe he wouldn't judge her too harshly. She was beginning to realize that Shelley was the one person she could tell anything to. Anything.

But what if he didn't believe her? What if he decided

to turn her in for the thousand-dollar reward that had been posted for her?

"Shelley. " She sniffled and pulled her head away from his shoulder. She looked deep into his hazel eyes, eyes that looked into her very soul. "You don't know anything about me. I'm not . . . I'm not who you think I am."

"Darlin', I decided a long time ago that I'd never figure you out. Widow Brown, bootmaker's widow from St. Louis." He gave her a grim smile. "Doesn't matter what you're runnin' from, or what you're runnin' to." He tapped his finger under her chin. "It's not like you killed anybody."

Her chin quivered. "No. Nothing like that."

Shelley saddled his horse. His face looked even worse than it had the night before, but if it was bothering him, she knew he wouldn't tell her. He kept his pain to himself, and she would have to do the same.

She couldn't tell him that it wasn't just a dream. It was a horrible memory.

Chapter Eighteen

Early the next afternoon, when Shelley brought the roan to a halt by a stream of running water that barely qualified as a creek, Annie turned her face to him, craning her neck.

"Why are we stopping?"

He ignored her as they dismounted and he led the roan to the clear water. Annie's fear had passed, and her eyes were bright and clear, her cheeks pink, her lips like roses. She had no right to look so good.

"I said," she repeated, "why are we stopping?"

He turned to her exasperated. "Do you want to kill my goddamn horse? Do you suppose the two of us can race the poor thing all the way to goddamn San Francisco?" He couldn't tell her that he hurt all over. His face hurt, his hands hurt, his stomach and his back ached. Swift Eagle had managed to leave no muscle undamaged.

Annie sat in a shady spot and sighed almost wistfully. "I apologize. I don't mean to be unreasonable, but do you think it would be possible for you to utter a sentence without the word 'goddamn' in it?" She was evidently trying to sound reasonable, but to Shelley she sounded petulant.

He grabbed some dry meat from his saddlebag and tossed her a piece. She took a bite of the tough nourishment and turned to him. "I don't suppose you have a hairbrush in that saddlebag of yours?"

He grinned at her wishful notion. "No, darlin', I certainly don't."

Annie unbraided her hair and tried to comb it with her fingers, before she began to plait it again. He sat in the grass behind her and watched, the simple pleasure making him forget his aching muscles for a while.

She was, for all her lies and mystery, a fine woman. Not only beautiful, but sweet and strong and passionate. Even though he knew the words she'd spoken to him in a moment of passion weren't true, could never be true, he would never forget the moment she'd looked straight into his eyes, through his eyes to his soul, and said that she loved him. Damnation, those simple words had scared him! Perhaps she'd meant it, at the moment, with the blood thrumming through her veins and her heart pounding against his, but he knew a woman like her would never really love him. She was headed for a world he had fled long ago, and he had no intention of going back. Yes, she was headed for a better life in San Francisco. Maybe a life with Icky.

That thought made him frown, and his pains returned with a vengeance.

She must have realized that he was watching her, because she started to talk to him as if he were sitting right beside her instead of several feet away, glaring at her back.

"I've been thinking, and I've decided that what we need is a treaty."

"A what?"

"If we're going to travel all the way to San Francisco together we need some sort of pact. A peace agreement, if you will."

"I know what a treaty is, darlin'," he drawled.

Annie kept her back to him, didn't attempt to turn and watch his face. "We can each make a list of what we don't want the other person to do, and that will make our journey much more enjoyable."

Enjoyable? Journey? Sounded like she thought they were on some sort of pleasurable grand tour.

"You first, darlin'."

"I would appreciate it if you didn't swear quite so much," she said politely. "I realize it would be impossible for you to stop entirely, but a little restraint—"

"I've got it," he interrupted sharply. "And you've got to stop using my chest like it was your personal pillow . . . no . . . change that. Just don't touch me at all. That should cover everything."

Annie looked over her shoulder, raising her eyebrows slightly and pursing her lush lips. "Until we arrange for another mount that will be difficult, but I'll do my very best."

She continued to stare at him. "Is it possible that you might arrange an occasional meal that doesn't consist entirely of beans, bacon, and dried meat?"

He gave her his most disgusted grimace. "I'll do what I can, but once we start crossing the desert you'll be damn . . . pardon me . . . extremely glad to get that." He scratched his beard. "I wish we still had that

178

ugly da . . . that ugly black dress. I'd make you wear it now and again."

"That's one possession I don't miss," she said.

He folded his hands under his chin. "No more sleeping with deadly weapons in your hands. I don't want to wake up dead one morning."

"Very funny," Annie snapped. "You'll get me my own horse as soon as possible."

He nodded. He would have done that anyway, and Annie certainly knew it, but he wouldn't protest. Her request allowed him to make one more demand. "Sing to me at night, like you said you would when I first agreed to this fool's errand."

She nodded curtly. "All you had to do was ask. I guess that's enough, for now."

"Yep. Well, if I think of anything else, I'll let you know." He rose slowly from the grass.

"So will I," she said primly, rising as she spoke. She lifted her chin and gave him a properly distant smile, and he tried his best to return it.

A cold camp, Annabelle learned, meant no campfire, so there was no coffee, no beans, and no amount of talking had changed Shelley's mind about making a fire. She had tried to convince him that Red Wolf would not allow his son to bother her again, but Shelley was not convinced. No man likes to be beaten when he's fighting for a woman, he had told her, especially if that woman brings him down as she had.

She had offered Shelley a bottle of tequila, and he had refused it so ardently that she returned it to his saddlebag without uncapping it. She had sat on the blanket Shelley had provided for her for hours after he had fallen asleep. But now she needed rest, even

179

though she was afraid the nightmare would return. Yet when sleep finally came she was so exhausted that she didn't dream at all.

"Wake up, Annie." Shelley's stern voice roused her from a restful slumber that she was reluctant to leave behind.

"Not yet," she murmured. It was still dark, just a hint of the morning sun turning the sky gray.

"Goddamn it, Annie," he whispered, and she sat up tiredly.

"You're not supposed to curse at me," she chastised, but when she saw the worried look on his face she lost her irritation. "Is something wrong?"

He leaned over and reached behind her ear. His hand came away holding a single feather, a long eagle feather with a horsehair tuft at the tip.

"That was in my hair?" She raised a hand to her ear. "Did someone . . . put it there?" Her voice was weak, fading softly. While she slept someone had placed the feather behind her ear, and she'd felt nothing.

"That's not all." He turned from her, and she jumped to her feet to follow him. Tethered next to his roan was her own horse, the mare that had been a gift to Swift Eagle. Her saddle was still on its back.

She smiled with relief. It had been Red Wolf, she was certain, who had placed the feather in her hair and returned her mare.

"Isn't that sweet?" she said, sighing. The daylight was approaching quickly, and she saw Shelley scowl.

"Sweet? They could've slit our throats while we slept."

"But they didn't," she answered reasonably. "I told you Red Wolf wouldn't allow it."

Shelley shook his head. "You're too damn trusting,

Annie. Dammit, I didn't hear a thing!"

She decided that was the reason he was so gruff, so angry. He'd slept through the Indians' visit.

"Check the saddlebags," he snapped.

One side of the saddlebags held her hairbrush and mirror. She crossed to the other side and tossed back the leather flap. For a moment she just stared at the contents.

"Shelley? What are these?"

He took the items she placed in his hand. "Well I'll be goddamned."

She didn't even attempt to remind him of their agreement. "What are they?"

He held aloft a leather bag attached to a thong. "This is a medicine bag. The Indians believe if you wear it, it will protect you."

"And this?" She held up what looked like a man-made spider web, a crude circle made with a supple twig, and laced with fine strings that crisscrossed in a symmetrical web across the opening that was not much larger than the span of her hand.

"Dreamcatcher," he said, the anger in his voice gone, replaced with wonder.

"What's it for?" She held it up to the brightening sky and watched the sunrise play through the web.

"It's a child's toy . . . to stop bad dreams," he whispered, and Annabelle lowered the dreamcatcher slowly. "Do you know what this means?"

She bit her lower lip. "That they were watching us that first night?"

He nodded. "And yesterday afternoon you asked for a hairbrush. I'll bet that black dress isn't in there."

She shook her head.

"You said you didn't mind losing that black dress,"

he reminded her. "And look at this." He held the last item in his hand, a beaded belt with a buckskin sheath for the knife she had taken from Swift Eagle.

She gave the belt a cursory glance, then turned her eyes back to the dreamcatcher in her hand. A toy? She studied the crudely crafted article with wonder. Was it the reason she'd slept peacefully for once?

"What in the hell did you say to that old Indian?"

She shrugged her shoulders, trying to appear nonchalant. "Not much. We just . . . made a deal."

"Well, you must have said something," he snapped. He held the feather in front of her face. "See this horsehair at the end? Do you know what this means?"

"Of course I don't."

"Your first coup." Shelley placed the feather back where he had found it, behind her ear. "For bringing Swift Eagle down."

"Red Wolf is a nice old man, and he just feels . . . protective toward me," she insisted. "That's all."

"Protective, hell," he whispered, as if he were afraid the Indians might be listening. "The Cheyenne don't feel protective toward white women."

She turned away from him, and he grabbed her arm to stop her.

"No touching, remember?" she reminded him.

She was tired of avoiding his glare, of hiding from him the way she'd hidden from every difficult moment in her life. She lifted her face and stared into his eyes. "It's your rule," she said as he dropped her arm.

"Perhaps he admired your bravery."

She would have expected sarcasm to drip from such a statement, but he sounded sincere. "He said I was a white warrior woman, but I'm not brave. Not at all," she insisted. "I'm afraid of everything. I run from my fear because I can't stand to face it."

"You were brave with Red Wolf, and the Cheyenne respect bravery more than anything else." He smiled too easily. "It was brave to kick Swift Eagle in the . . . well, where it hurts the most."

"That was different," she said. "He was going to kill you."

Shelley shrugged. "Maybe."

"What do you mean, maybe?"

"I've been in worse situations and come out just fine," he declared.

She rolled her eyes. "Men."

"And you walked right over to those Indians and singled out the leader and made your own peace treaty."

"I just asked myself"—she hesitated—"what would Shelley do?"

He raised his eyebrows. "Is that a fact?"

"Well, you were no help, lying on the ground bleeding to . . ." She stopped, and a tremor ran through her body. She'd been about to say "bleeding to death" when a vision of Henri entered her mind. "I did what I had to do to get us out of there alive," she said simply. "That's all."

Shelley hung the medicine bag around her neck. "It was very brave. Red Wolf thinks so, and so do I."

"Do you really, Shelley?" She looked up at him. "Do you really think I'm brave?"

He nodded, but she still felt, deep inside, like a coward.

Chapter Nineteen

Their pact and the presence of her own horse seemed to ease the tensions of their journey during the following week. Annabelle placed the feather securely in the headband of her hat, wore the medicine bag around her neck, and tied the beaded belt at her waist. Swift Eagle's knife hung in its sheath at her hip. She wasn't sure why she felt so much comfort from the objects she was certain Red Wolf had left for her, but she did. At night she slept with the dreamcatcher propped up close by, and the dream, the nightmare that had haunted her for months, disappeared.

At night she sang for Shelley, often singing him to sleep, but she fell asleep a long while later after watching the stars. Sometimes she could persuade Shelley to recite a limerick he had written, but she noticed that he rejected the bawdier ones for those that were simply tasteless.

He was actually pleasant to her, most of the time, as they traveled westward toward the desert that would be their toughest challenge. He had adopted an almost businesslike attitude toward her. Once again she was the employer and he her hired hand. Sometimes she caught him staring at her with a look that bordered on distaste, but when he noticed her looking his way he smiled, that quick grin that was his trademark.

They camped by a gently flowing creek that Shelley promised would be the last decent water they'd see for a while. He explained that though they would follow the Humboldt River across the desert, the water was so heavily alkaline it was too dangerous to drink.

Annabelle couldn't find two trees close enough together to string a rope between, so she devised her own barrier. She drove two sticks firmly into the ground and hung the blanket over them. It was a makeshift tent that provided a small amount of privacy on the bank of the creek, but it was sufficient. She knew Shelley wouldn't bother her as she bathed.

Since it would be their last chance for a real bath for a while, she stripped to her skin. She would wash out her underthings as best she could and let them dry in the sun. They were becoming so thin she didn't think it would take them long to dry.

She stepped into the water slowly. It was cool, but pleasantly so. She missed the fun she'd had when all the women from the wagon train bathed together, splashing and playing. She immersed herself in the water and came up slowly, her face lifted to the blue sky, so that her hair fell straight down her back, slick and clinging to her head. The sunlight on her face felt warm and wonderful, and she wondered if she would ever enjoy a tub bath so much.

She saw it when she opened her eyes, black and twisted and slithering across the top of the water.

"Shelley," she whispered. "Snake."

He didn't come. Of course he didn't come. He couldn't hear her because she couldn't find her voice. So she screamed. When all else failed, she knew how to scream.

She heard him behind her, splashing into the water, and she raised her arm to point straight ahead. It was the only movement she was capable of.

"Snake." Her voice was still a whisper, but Shelley was there to hear her, and soon he was at her side.

She stared at the reptile, and before she knew what was happening Shelley took a few splashing steps forward, the water at waist level, and picked up the offending snake.

He was furious when he turned to her, holding in his hand the "snake" that had frightened her. It was nothing more than a length of twisted limb, water-soaked and bobbing across the surface of the water.

Realizing that her breasts were exposed, she bent her knees and sunk until the water touched her chin.

He waved the "snake" in front of her face. "Is this some sort of joke?"

She shook her head. "I thought it was a snake, really I did."

He didn't believe her, that much was clear. She had never seen him more furious, had never seen so much rage in his eyes.

"I don't suppose you're trying to seduce me?"

She choked on her disbelief. How dare he! "You conceited oaf. I'm not like Cherry Red and the other women you choose to associate with. They may throw themselves at you, but I will not, I assure you. I would never throw myself at a man who obviously finds me unattractive."

He scowled and tossed the "snake" to the other side of the creek. "For God's sake, the next time you scream make sure the danger is real. I almost had a goddamn heart attack."

She smiled. "You're breaking our treaty."

He took another step toward her, headed for the bank. "Am I now? That's a goddamn shame."

He stepped again, splashing water all around him. "Snake my ass," he muttered under his breath when he was right beside her.

She rose slowly, the water reaching just above her waist, and as she turned to face him, Shelley jumped as if he'd been shot. Impulsively she reached out and brushed her fingers gently across his neck.

"I guarantee," she said, her voice throatier than usual, "that if I ever try to seduce you, you'll know exactly what I'm doing."

He reached down and wrapped his hands around her waist. He returned her seductive grin, lifted her into the air, and then threw her farther into the water.

She landed with a loud splash in the middle of the creek, and her first reaction was to feel with her toes for the mud at the bottom. There was nothing there, and she sank, kicking and flailing her arms, panic-stricken.

Shelley watched his tormentor hit the water with a mixture of pride and revengeful satisfaction. He'd be damned if she'd get the best of him, standing there in the creek like a water sprite . . . And she knew exactly what she was doing to him.

As he headed toward the bank, he waited for her

screams of protest, but it was ominously quiet. Turning around, he saw her head break the surface of the water and he heard a brief scream before she sank again. She couldn't swim.

He swam to the spot where he had seen her. He was positive it was the right place, as he dove under the water and reached out for her. She wasn't there. The water was too murky for him to see his own hand in front of his face, and he had no idea how deep this spot was. He rose out of the water for a deep breath of air and then dove again. He would not be responsible for her death.

Finally his hand closed over flesh—an arm, a hand—and he pulled her to the surface coughing and sputtering. He held her head above the water as he swam toward the shore, and when he could stand he lifted her into his arms and carried her to the bank, where he lay her gently on the grass.

"Why didn't you tell me you couldn't swim?" he demanded angrily, even as he rolled her onto her stomach and pounded on her back until she coughed up the water she had swallowed.

Annie lay with her face buried in the grass. "You never asked. I'm fine now, if you would please hand me the blanket." She was trying to sound dignified, but it was difficult, lying there completely naked while he pounded on her back.

Assured that she was all right, he gave her a swift slap to her bare behind before he complied and yanked the blanket from her tent. Annie wrapped herself in the blanket, refusing to look at him. He knew he should walk away and leave her alone, but he sat beside her and removed his boots.

"I hope these aren't ruined," he said almost conversationally as he set his soaked boots aside.

Annie didn't even give him a sideways glance. She stared out over the creek, now so serene, where she had nearly drowned. All because she'd mistaken a twig for a snake.

"You tried to drown me," she accused.

He stretched out his legs. "Darlin', if I'd wanted to drown you, you'd still be out there."

"I know it's all my fault. It seems I can't do anything right anymore." She pouted, pursing her lips and refusing still to look at him. "I'm sorry I got you into this. You should have let me drown."

"Then you'd never get to San Francisco." He kept his voice light. He could never let her see, ever, how scared he'd been.

"Maybe I'd be better off if I never saw San Francisco again. I should have become the fourth Mrs. Swift Eagle and disappeared."

"Don't say that," he rasped.

Annie finally turned her face to him and gave him a daunting look. "Then you'd have six ponies, and you wouldn't have to worry about crossing the desert or being forced to spend the next few weeks with someone you can't stand the sight of."

"That's not true."

"I'm not so insensitive that I can't tell how much you dislike me. Oh, you tolerate my presence well enough, I'll give you that. I don't mind. I'd just like to know why."

He tried to think of a flippant answer, something that would keep her at a distance, but when he looked at her face he couldn't do it. Her brown eyes looked huge in her delicate face with that perfect nose, her inviting lips. He looked for the timid girl he had seen at the Silver Palace, but she wasn't there. This Annie had a sun-kissed face, and hair like silk, and a body he had to force himself not to reach out for every night as she lay just across the campfire from him. A woman who had discarded her "widow's" attire for form-fitting clothes, a hat with an eagle feather in it, a medicine bag, a knife, and those damn red boots. And she was still looking at him, waiting for an answer.

He sighed. "Ah, Annie. Sometimes you're so goddamn dense. It's not that I don't . . . like you. I've lived on my own for a long time, and I like it that way."

"Well, I didn't ask you to marry me," she replied sharply. "I thought we were friends once. Can't we at least be friends again?"

"Hell, I don't think so."

"You're breaking our pact again," she accused.

"Yes I am, goddamn it. Hellfire, damnation . . ."

Annie cocked her head and frowned at him. "What are you doing?"

"I'm breaking the goddamn pact." He offered his hand to her. He would show her why they couldn't be friends. "Your turn."

"I don't know what you mean."

He slid across the grass and put his arms around her shoulder. "I'm breaking the pact. Now it's your turn. I want you to touch me."

She held the blanket under her chin with both hands. "I don't—"

"Just do it."

Annabelle didn't want to release her hold on the blanket, so she turned her head and kissed him on the side of his neck. His skin was warm, and somehow comforting against her lips. She had barely moved away when he pressed her back into the grass and covered her lips with his. It wasn't a gentle kiss, but one that vented all his rage and frustration, and when her shock subsided she returned his kiss with all the fire he lit within her. Her hands found their way from underneath the blanket to his throat, his face, the back of his neck.

He pulled his lips away from hers and stared into her eyes. "Do you see what I mean, Annie? You think I don't like you. But the truth is I like you too goddamn much. It's easier for me to keep my distance than to get too close knowing we can never—"

"Why can't we?" She interrupted him.

"Because I'm the worst thing that could happen to you, Annie." Her lips were mere inches away, and in spite of his words he kissed her again, but this time it was tender.

"Shouldn't I have something to say about that?" She held him close, her hands clasped together at the back of his neck.

"You don't know what's best for you. I do."

She stared at him, this man who was as much a part of the untamed country as the mountains, the plains, the desert itself. "Look who's talking," she whispered. "Let yourself get beaten nearly to death for a woman you don't even want." She knew it was a lie. His eyes told her how much he wanted her. His eyes and his lips.

He rolled away from her and spread the blanket that had gotten twisted around her legs and her torso beneath her. His browned hand looked strong and dark as he rested it against her stomach. She didn't try to cover herself or hide from him as he began to slide his hands over her body.

She watched those dark hands against her breasts

191

and her legs. This was what she'd wanted, what she'd craved for weeks. When he kissed her again, she spread her legs, and he rested his hand between her thighs, there where she wanted him so much. She sighed and wrapped her arms around his neck.

"This isn't fair," she whispered when he moved his lips from hers to burn her throat and her breasts with their touch.

"What's not fair, darlin'?"

"Don't you think you should . . . get out of those wet things?"

She tugged at his damp shirt. Their eyes locked as he moved away from her to undress. She helped, pulling his sleeves down his arms, impatient for his touch.

"Shelley, I . . ." She stopped. She knew how much she loved him, with everything she had to give. But she didn't want to scare him away.

"What is it, Annie?"

"I don't love you, I swear," she whispered, and he smiled down at her.

"That's good, darlin'."

Chapter Twenty

"We broke our treaty," Annabelle whispered into Shelley's ear.

It had been dark for a while and still they hadn't moved from the gently sloping grass by the creek. Annabelle didn't know how much time had passed. Didn't care. It might be midnight, it might be almost dawn. They'd made love three times there on the blanket that was now wrapped around them, cocooning them against the night air.

Shelley lay on his back, one arm holding her snugly. He gave her a low, affirmative murmur, showing little concern for their pact at the moment.

"We need another one," she insisted gently.

He grinned and rolled onto his side to face her, his chest pressing against her breasts, his lips close to hers. "You can touch me anytime you want."

She ran her fingers along his spine. She loved the

feel of his skin, the softness of his lips against hers. "And you can touch me anytime."

He took advantage of her addition to their new treaty and ran his hands down her sides, across her hips, coming to rest there. "You'll sing to me every night."

"You can write poems and recite them to me by the fire."

His smile faded. "Sure, until I leave you at the ferry to San Francisco, then that's it. Look, Annie I'm not a romantic. This is lust, pure and simple. It doesn't mean—"

"I understand," she said, not letting her disappointment come through in her voice. If this was all she could have, then it was enough. "No questions," she added. "I don't care what you did before we met or what you'll do after we part. No questions about the past. I'm just Annie, you're just Shelley. I want you; you want me. That's all we need to know."

He pulled her on top of him and wrapped his arms around her. "I want you right now," he whispered huskily, seeking her lips with abandon.

She held his face in her hands and returned his kiss hungrily, her mouth open, her tongue learning how to drive him wild. "Just one more small demand," she whispered, her lips a heartbeat away from his.

"Anything."

"Don't call it lust. I don't like that word." She settled her lips over his briefly, then pulled them away again. "Passion," she whispered. "You're my passion, Shelley."

"Passion. If you say so darlin'."

He rolled her onto her back, throwing the blanket off their legs despite the cool air. He locked his lips to hers, drawing her very soul into him with his mouth. He rested his hand on her breast, massaging her taut nipple before his hand moved lower, over her belly to rest between her thighs. She arched her back when he touched her.

"Shelley," she whispered his name as he moved his lips to the base of her neck. "It hurts." Her voice was so low she wasn't certain if he could hear her.

"What hurts, darlin'?" He was very still as he waited for her answer.

"I want you so much it hurts."

She took his hair in her hands and pulled his lips to hers, lifting her hips to him as he entered her. How was it that the feel of him inside her was more wonderful, more exciting every time? That with every meeting of their bodies the release he brought her was more powerful than the time before?

He felt it, too, she was certain, the wonder they created. She saw the knowledge in his hooded eyes as he languidly studied her, she felt it in his touch. His appetite for her was as insatiable as hers for him.

The culmination of their joining came almost too quickly, and she dug her fingernails into his back and screamed his name as he whispered hers again and again.

He rolled over and brought her with him, wrapping the blanket around her.

She was breathless, feeling as if Shelley had sucked her very spirit from her. She felt cheated out of the nights they'd spent denying themselves the pleasure they found in making love.

"How long will it take to get to San Francisco?" she whispered when she could speak again.

He thought about her question for a few seconds.

"Three weeks, give or take a few days."

She laid her head on his chest, listening to the beating of his heart. "Is that all? Can't we go . . . by way of Canada?"

He brushed her hair from her face. "Are you trying to kill me, darlin'?" His tone of voice was light.

She propped her chin on his chest and looked into his eyes. "Is what we've been doing life-threatening?"

"Not normally."

She gave him a satisfied smile and laid her head down again, her ear against his heart. For the next three weeks . . . her heart.

They slept long into the morning, and when they woke Shelley carried Annabelle to the creek and they bathed, Shelley washing her hair, Annabelle volunteering to wash his back. She saw the scratches she had inflicted the night before and laid her lips against each one.

"What are you doing?" he asked, motionless as she kissed his shoulders and his back.

"Kissing away the hurt," she murmured into his spine.

When she stopped, he turned to her. "What about this?" He pointed a long finger at the healing cut on his forehead, and leaned forward while she obediently kissed him there. "And this." He pointed to a fading bruise on his shoulder, and she laid her lips against his wet skin, finishing with a fast flick of her tongue. "And this." He pointed to his lips.

She wrapped her arms around his neck and lifted her face to his. She didn't kiss him, but studied his perfect lips. "They look fine to me."

"You bit me last night." He wrapped his arms

around her waist and pulled her close. "Remember?"

"But I didn't bite very hard." She smiled, her lips almost touching his. "You on the other hand . . ."

He kissed her lightly. "I'm sorry. Where else did I hurt you?"

She pointed to her earlobe, and Shelley kissed her lightly there. She placed a finger at the base of her throat, and he kissed her there, letting his lips linger against her skin. He lowered his head when she pointed first to one breast and then the other, licking droplets of water from her skin before he lifted her and carried her to the grassy bank. She pressed her face against his neck and rained feathery kisses on his damp skin.

"Goddamn it," he swore as he lowered her to the blanket.

She ran her hands over his wet skin, slick and smooth. "What's wrong?"

"We'll never get to San Francisco this way," he said, resigned as he lowered himself to her.

The ache in the pit of her belly was so strong she didn't want to talk. She wanted Shelley, her passion, to kiss her and touch her and she never wanted to leave the bank of their little creek.

"Maybe that wouldn't be so bad," she whispered as his lips closed over hers.

They made barely ten miles that afternoon, but neither of them seemed to care. They had plenty of water and food, simple as it was, and the weather was agreeable. They had the warm sun in their faces, and there was a cooling breeze in the air. Annabelle rode her mare just behind Shelley, so close she could almost reach out and touch him.

Every so often he smiled at her, that easy grin, his eyes sparkling when they lit on her. It was almost as if he were checking to make certain she was really there, that she wasn't a dream. His smile warmed her heart, though she knew it was a smile he gave generously. Did she feel this way because she felt so safe in his presence? Was it, as he claimed, a purely physical attraction? Lust? Passion?

She pushed her questions to the back of her mind. Three weeks, maybe more, maybe less, was all she would have of him, and she wasn't going to spoil it by thinking too hard. If she did she'd be forced to think about life after Shelley. Prison, death, or, if she were lucky, a return to the life she'd led before that horrifying night in New York. Even that wasn't very appealing at the moment.

They camped for the night away from the worn trail, in a green spot not nearly as enchanting as their campsite by the creek. But a thick copse of trees and a natural L-shaped cluster of cool gray boulders afforded them some semblance of privacy. They silently went about their chores, Shelley unsaddling and unpacking the horses, Annabelle making coffee and heating beans over the fire he had started.

They ate not side by side, but across the fire from one another. The firelight flickered on their faces, in their eyes. Annabelle knew she should be starving, but she could barely eat the all too familiar beans. She was growing more and more nervous. Last night they had fallen together so naturally that there had been no time for thought. But now . . . would he come to her or did he expect her to go to him? Would it be possible to recreate the magic that had brought them together like thunder and lightning?

"Not hungry?" He tossed down his own empty plate and nodded to her almost full one.

She shrugged. "Not really."

She offered her plate to him, but he declined, shaking his head and running his hand over his beard. If she didn't know better, she would have sworn that he was as nervous as she.

"No complaints about the cuisine tonight?" he teased.

She found a leaf in her hair and plucked it out, deciding to unbraid her hair there by the fire. "No complaints, but I'd sell my soul for a fresh peach."

"A fresh peach," he repeated. "Canned peaches won't do? I might manage that."

She licked her lips. "No. In exchange for my soul it would have to be a fresh peach."

Shelley was entranced, watching the simple act of Annie unplaiting her hair. She held her head to one side and slowly loosened each strand, sending her dark hair free to fall over her shoulder and down her back.

"What could I get for a can of peaches?"

She smiled at him across the fire. "Anything else."

The air between them was charged with their newfound sexual energy, but they didn't move. He rested his chin in his hands, and Annie brushed her hair as he watched.

"Sing to me," he demanded moments later when she laid down her hairbrush.

"Your wish is my command, master." She mocked his authoritative tone. "What do you want to hear?"

He shrugged. "You choose."

Annie looked at him thoughtfully for a moment.

"Something new. Something I haven't sung for you before."

She began to sing a tender ballad, but she didn't get far before he stopped her. "Not that," he said gruffly. "Anything else."

She looked at him oddly, but began again, with "I'll Take You Home Again, Kathleen," and this time he didn't stop her. Eventually his frown eased, and he smiled at the woman across the fire.

Though he didn't show it, that moment of remembrance that had begun when she'd started to sing had not disappeared, but he hid his pain, as he always had.

That song, "Home, Sweet Home," that damn song that had haunted him for four years, as he'd served with the Union Army. It was a ballad much requested of entertainers and military bands, and usually left not a dry eye in the camp. The song had resounded in his head a thousand times as he'd finally gone home . . . weary, tired of the stink of death . . . wanting only to resume something resembling a normal life.

He hadn't allowed himself to remember his homecoming in so many years that the memories that assaulted him were freshly painful. He almost didn't hear Annie when she leaned expectantly toward the fire and said, almost seductively, "Your turn."

"I don't sing."

"No, silly. My poem. You're supposed to recite me a new poem. Our treaty, remember?" She grinned as he gave her a look of consternation.

"Every night?"

"Whenever I ask."

He pondered, his hand massaging his bearded chin, his eyes on the vision across the fire. Then he said:

"The Widow Brown twittered and fussed
When I called what I felt for her lust.
    She called me her passion,
    After a fashion,
And left my poor heart in the dust."

"I thought you didn't have a heart," Annabelle answered.

"Poetic license." His voice was almost a whisper. "Your turn."

She leaned closer to the fire, unafraid of the heat that threatened to burn her. Beads of sweat broke out on her forehead, but she didn't back away.

She began to quote the Percy Shelley poem "Love's Philosophy" as she watched her Shelley. She spoke from her heart . . . and she did believe that her soul and his were mingling, as surely as the rivers and the ocean, as surely as the winds of heaven. But as the words flowed from her mouth, unwanted doubts assailed her.

She stopped suddenly and backed away from the intense fire.

"Forget the rest?"

Shelley rose from his seat and crossed to her. He offered her his hand, and she laid hers in his, shuddering as he closed it over hers. That was all it took, his hand on hers, to make her anxious for his kiss.

She nodded her head, unable to speak.

"What was that?" he asked as he pulled her gently to her feet to face him. "More of the 'real' Shelley?"

She nodded again and lifted her face to his. She had told a lie, of course, but a small one. She never forgot a line of a song, or a verse from a poem. She was too well trained for that. But she couldn't let Shelley see

201

how much she really cared for him, or know that if she could she would keep him with her forever. If she had finished the poem that had sprung into her mind as she'd watched him across the fire, he would have known. She would never forget the first time she had realized her love for Shelley, and had made the mistake of telling him. He had pushed her away and run from her angrily. She couldn't . . . wouldn't do that again.

"You are my passion, Shelley," she whispered as he lowered his head to kiss her. She had been afraid it would be awkward, but it was the most natural act in the world to have him take her in his arms and carry her to their secluded corner of the world.

Chapter Twenty-one

For nearly a week they traveled west, the weather continuing to bless them with cloudless blue skies and cool nights. It was as if they were charmed, for a short time. At night Annabelle sang to Shelley as they sat by the fire, and when she demanded a limerick he quickly provided one.

She felt wanton as she anxiously waited for Shelley to take her in his arms each night. Some nights they made love only once, and then slept intertwined beneath the stars. Other nights they barely slept at all, reveling in the intimacy that neither tired of.

In one way they were truly blessed. Annabelle pushed her fears about what awaited her in San Francisco out of her mind. She took her life one day at a time, and with Shelley at her side they were happy days. He didn't mention again that what they shared was a physical attraction that he would dismiss when they reached San Francisco . . . that it was nothing more than simple lust that drew them together.

Annabelle watched Shelley across a low fire. Each night he found them a beautiful campsite, off the trail and usually buffered on two or even three sides. Private. Quiet. In her heart she knew that anywhere they stopped would be beautiful as long as she was with him. He lifted his head and grinned at her, and she couldn't stop the wide smile that spread across her face as he leaned forward and began to recite in an almost melodious voice:

> "Now, Annie's a lovely young lass
> With poise, and bearing, and class.
>   Her face, oh how fair,
>   Her lustrous brown hair,
> But nothing compares to her ass."

"Shelley!" She laughed. "That's terrible."

He frowned, but his eyes still sparkled with laughter. "You don't like my poetry anymore."

"I do."

She rose and sauntered around the fire to stand behind Shelley. She laid her hands on his shoulders and dug her fingers gently into his muscles, kneading as he rolled his head forward.

"But must a limerick always be so . . . so disgraceful?"

"Um-humm," he answered with a contented murmur. "Always, darlin'."

She felt the muscles in his back tighten seconds before he stood, shaking off her hands. "Where's your derringer?"

She put her hands on her hips and glared at him. "In my saddlebag."

"Get it," he ordered as he removed his rifle from its sheath and set it near the flat rock where he had been sitting.

There was no trace of a smile on his face as she removed the derringer from her saddlebag and stuck it in the waistband of her pants. She had moved to stand beside him, near the fire, before she heard what he had heard moments earlier. Riders.

He turned to her and placed his big hands on her shoulders. "Stay close to me. It's probably just travelers like us, but there are three of them . . ."

"Hello, the camp."

They turned to face the friendly call. Shelley had been correct. There were three of them, three dusty, bearded men riding slowly toward the camp.

"Got any coffee?" the man in the lead asked, smiling as if to an old friend.

"Nearly a full pot." Shelley was smiling once again, but it didn't touch his eyes. She knew he was tense, but he didn't convey his tension to the intruders. "Bring your cups and sit with us for a spell."

If there was any truth to intuition, Annabelle knew they were in trouble. The three men made her so nervous she could barely speak. Shelley introduced himself as Travis Johnson, and she as his wife Annie. He told the three men with a grin that they were headed to Salt Lake City for a visit with relatives. When asked if they were Mormon, Shelley laughed and told them one wife was plenty enough for him. All three of the intruders laughed a bit too loudly at this, and Annabelle stood close to Shelley as the strangers helped themselves to coffee.

All three men wore six-shooters at their hips, slung low. They'd introduced themselves by name, but she couldn't remember even one of them. In her mind they were The Fat One, The Skinny One, and The Ugly One. And The Ugly One was truly ugly. His nose had been smashed almost flat, and his face was scarred and pitted. One eye was set slightly higher than the other, so that one had to study his face for a moment to figure out what was wrong with it.

Those skewed eyes had lit on Shelley's pistol more than once.

It was The Ugly One who spoke directly to her. "What's that around your neck, Mrs. Johnson?" he asked almost too politely.

She gave him a poor smile. "This?" She lifted the medicine bag Red Wolf had given her with a slightly trembling hand. "This was a gift."

"Looks Injun to me," The Ugly One said with disgust. "Looks like one of them magic doohickeys."

"Medicine bag," Shelley said shortly. He didn't like the intruders any more than she did, but he was much better at hiding his feelings. "It's a good luck charm."

The Ugly One gulped his coffee and wiped his wet mouth with the back of his hand. "Mighty good coffee, ma'am. Hit the spot."

She tried to smile in response, but she couldn't maintain it.

"So," Shelley said as he refilled his own cup. "Where you boys headed?"

"Headed for Cheyenne," The Ugly One answered.

His companions sat directly behind him, sipping hot coffee. He was obviously the leader of their small group, and the only one who cared to open his mouth.

His eyes kept lighting on her, making her even more uncomfortable.

Shelley stood and paced in front of the fire, never turning his back on the three men. "We've just come from that way. Good traveling weather."

The Ugly One nodded his head as if this were important information.

Shelley was trying to place himself between the man and her, she decided, as he took small steps in front of the fire. His senses were sharper than hers, and it scared her to think that he considered these men a threat.

Her hope that the men would move on when they'd finished their coffee was shattered when The Ugly One stood and stretched his arms over his head. "You wouldn't mind if we bedded down close by, would you? I'm bushed."

Shelley smiled and assured him that it would be just fine to have some company nearby. As the fire died he led her to their bedrolls, side by side a short distance from the fire, and they watched the three men prepare for the night in a similar way.

"Don't worry," Shelley whispered in her ear as he lay down beside her. "I'll keep an eye on them."

"All night?" She looked across the dying fire to the three perfectly still men. "Why didn't you tell them to leave? What if you fall asleep?"

"If I'd told them to leave we'd have to worry about them approaching from all sides. This way, I have all three of them in sight." He kissed her on the forehead. "And I won't fall asleep, but you can."

She couldn't. Even knowing that Shelley was beside her wide awake, she couldn't close her eyes. Long after the fire had died and they were surrounded by darkness, she lay there, her heart pounding, the blood rushing through her veins. Fear.

Sleep finally overtook her when she least expected it, her exhaustion and Shelley's presence allowing her to drift into a dreamless sleep that was all too short before she felt Shelley's hand on her arm. She saw nothing when she opened her eyes but darkness, the black of the night complete.

Shelley drew his gun and palmed it. His right hand rested between them, and he nudged her gently with his elbow to make certain she was awake. She very slowly laid her hand over the derringer at her waist and slid it free. Still she heard nothing.

Then there was a shuffling sound, a man's boot sliding across the dirt, and as her eyes adjusted to the dark she saw the three forms approaching them from the other side of the camp. Shelley kept a stilling hand on her arm, making no sound until the men were almost upon them.

Shelley rolled away from her, shoving her in the opposite direction. He rolled up on one knee and took aim at the outlaws. Two guns were pointed toward him. One man was coming after her.

The outlaws' pistols blazed wildly, but Shelley fired only two shots. Two silent shadows fell, one after the other.

The Ugly One snatched Annabelle to her feet and held her in his grasp, his strong arm around her waist pulling her to his side. She held the derringer in her hand, but she couldn't pull the trigger. Her hands were shaking, her palms sweaty, and her knees felt as if they might buckle if The Ugly One released his firm hold on her.

They stood there, the three survivors. Shelley was

on one knee, his Colt aimed at The Ugly One. But he didn't fire, and she knew it was because the outlaw held her so close that Shelley was afraid he would hit her instead.

She held the derringer pointed into The Ugly One's side. His own pistol was at her head.

"You wasn't asleep after all. That's not exactly fair, now is it?" He chuckled, low and menacing, and swung the pistol toward Shelley.

"Shoot him, Annie," Shelley commanded.

"If you do, Annie, I'll shoot your husband," The Ugly One promised, cocking the pistol that was aimed at Shelley. They stood like that for several minutes, at a stalemate.

If she had been hesitant to fire before, she was now incapable of pulling the trigger. If she shot The Ugly One, he would shoot Shelley.

His arm at her waist tightened. "You drop your little toy pistol, sweetie, and I'll think about letting you live."

"Don't lie to her, Winston," Shelley said, no emotion evident in his voice. His aim never wavered. He was like a statue lit by pale moonlight, calm and motionless.

"How do you know who I am?"

"Let's just say I'm observant, and an ugly mug like yours is hard to forget." There was no fear in Shelley's voice, and that unnerved Winston a little as Annabelle felt a tremor shoot through his arm.

She refused to drop the pistol. Even she knew that the threat of the derringer was all that was keeping Winston from firing at Shelley. She wanted to push herself away from the ugly, stinking man who held her so close, but she was afraid a struggle would cause him to shoot.

Finally, after an interminably long time, Shelley broke the strained silence. "Snake!"

Annabelle dropped down just as Shelley and Winston fired almost simultaneously. She screamed, loud and long, to drown out the sounds that reverberated around her. She didn't stop until Shelley was beside her, pulling her to her feet and wrapping his arms around her. She sobbed into his chest, and he smoothed her hair until she pulled away from his embrace.

"Snake?" she shouted. "Is that all you could think of?"

"Yes, actually," he said tiredly. He looked down at the body at his feet, and she followed his gaze. The round hole in the center of Winston's forehead was black in the moonlight, and his eyes were open as he stared blankly at the heavens.

The Fat One and The Skinny One had fared no better. The Fat One had a hole in his forehead similar to Winston's, and The Skinny One had a hole in his chest. Also dead center.

She stared at the carnage around her and started to cry again. The sky was a shade lighter . . . morning would soon be upon them. She didn't want to see . . . didn't want to see what remained of their campsite by the light of day. She turned and started for her mare.

"Why didn't you shoot him when you had the chance?" Shelley followed her, irritation in his voice. "Jesus! He could have killed us both."

"I couldn't," she whispered.

"What?" He almost had to run to keep up with her.

"I couldn't!" She shouted. "I couldn't pull the trigger." She handed the derringer to him. "You keep this. I can't fire it . . . ever." She didn't think she would ever forget the sight of those three dead bodies, dispatched so quickly and easily by the man she thought she knew. "Can we leave here . . . now?"

"Not just yet. We've got to have our gear, and . . . I need you to help me with something."

"Now?" She shouted. "You need me to help you with what?"

She could see his face more clearly as the sun's promised light appeared on the horizon. He was pale, his eyes were narrowed slightly, and he was holding his hand over his left arm. "I was hit. I need you to . . ."

Her anger dissolved. "Hit?" She peeled his fingers away from a spreading bloodstain. The sleeve of his shirt was torn, and blood, still black in the meager light, was spreading.

"Don't look so terrified," he admonished her as if she'd done something wrong. "It's just a scratch."

"Just a scratch?" She led him as if he were mortally wounded to sit on the flat rock near the remnants of last night's fire. "Shelley . . . it could've . . . he could've . . . It's all my fault."

"No . . . it's not all your fault. But you should've shot the sonofabitch when you had the chance," he said as he ripped away his sleeve. He allowed her to bind the deep furrow tightly, her horror over the events that had left three men dead in their camp forgotten for the moment.

They were on the trail before full morning, as Annabelle couldn't bear to remain in the camp, and Shelley had assured her they could be in Salt Lake City before dark. There a doctor could clean and bandage his arm properly, and they could stock up on supplies for their trip across the desert.

He led her through a narrow pass, and when they emerged Annabelle fixed her eyes upon what she was certain was the most marvelous sight she had ever seen. The Great Salt Lake shimmered beneath them so majestically that it took her breath away.

As he led her toward Salt Lake City, she watched Shelley closely. If his wound bothered him, he didn't show it. For her benefit? She didn't think so. The outlaws had fired several shots at him and only inflicted one scratch. He had fired three shots, and left three dead men behind. How many men had he killed with that Colt?

The intruders had done more than injure Shelley or steal a night she should have spent in his arms. They had stolen a bit of the magic that allowed her to stop time, to suspend the reality that was so frightening.

"Shelley." She prodded her horse forward until she rode alongside him. Most of the day had passed in silence. "How did you recognize that man? How did you know who he was?"

He grinned easily. "With a face like that? Who could forget—"

"You'd met him before?"

He shook his head. "Saw his picture on a wanted poster."

His answer silenced her.

"Manfred Winston. Wanted for . . . hell, just about everything. A five hundred dollar bounty on his head. Think we should've trussed him up and collected the reward?" he asked, looking straight ahead.

"No," she answered quickly. "Not even for five thousand dollars." The thought of leading the dead man's horse to town with a body strapped to its back was repulsive, and she shuddered as Shelley turned to her, his face betraying no emotion.

He looked away, his countenance impassive. "That's what I thought."

Chapter Twenty-two

In Salt Lake City a solicitous doctor cleaned and bandaged Shelley's arm, the gray-haired man clucking like an old woman over the nasty-looking wound.

Shelley never flinched, never made a sound as Annabelle observed silently. She knew it had to be terribly painful. It hurt her just to watch. She grimaced when she thought the doctor was too rough, winced when he cleaned the wound, and sighed with relief when he was finished.

As they walked along the boardwalk, she held onto Shelley's arm and let her gaze wander from building to building. Salt Lake City was a quaint and beautiful oasis, adobe houses surrounded by well-tended gardens, the magnificent white houses of the Mormon leaders veritable mansions compared to the poor housing she had seen thus far in the West. Plain and poorly dressed women glared maliciously at her in her britches and red boots. She would have been shocked herself a few months ago, but her attire seemed natural to her after all this time.

A small group of women of various ages, from eleven or twelve to about forty, passed close by, their scorching gazes riveted on her. They were dressed, each and every one, in black dresses, high-necked and long-sleeved in spite of the heat. Annabelle couldn't help but sympathize with their obvious discomfort, but frowned at their equally obvious dislike of her.

"Don't you worry none, darlin'." Shelley patted her hand reassuringly. "They're probably just afraid their husbands will get one look at you and decide to take another wife."

"You don't mean all those women are married to the same man?" She glanced back over her shoulder at the retreating women.

"Could be," he said casually.

She shook her head in disgust. "First Swift Eagle, and now this. Why would a man possibly need more than one wife?"

Shelley said nothing.

"Oh, I know what you think. A man doesn't need a wife at all." Her voice was lightly teasing.

"Now, I didn't say that, darlin'."

"No, but you were thinking it," she insisted, her voice still casual. "I suppose you'd rather we all go through life single . . . free as the west wind that blows the sand across the desert."

"That's not for everybody, Annie." His voice was losing its humor. "Just for me."

She kept her hand on his arm, her touch feathery as they walked through the town. He shortened his stride to accommodate her, and their booted steps thudded against the shaded boardwalk. There was nothing else for her to say.

Shelley stopped outside a simple boardinghouse. "We might as well spend the night here. Can't put many more miles behind us today anyway."

"Do you mean it?" she asked, her eyes widening with excitement. "We can sleep in a real bed, with pillows and sheets and . . . and . . ."

He looked down at her and clucked her chin with his brown finger. "Is that all you think about?"

"Shelley!" She felt the heat rising in her cheeks.

He gave her a crooked grin. "You're blushin', darlin'."

Shelley rented a room, ordered a hot bath for his "wife," and left her alone in the small room. She didn't want to let him go. She never would've admitted it to him but she was still scared. The wound he had dismissed as a scratch horrified her, and she was haunted by the faces of the three dead men they had left behind in their camp. The last thing she wanted was to be left alone.

As long as Shelley was with her she was fine. Her heart beat as steadily as his, her mind was clear and free of doubts about the future. When she was alone she wondered if she had any future at all.

Scared or not, she sank into the hot water of the too small tin bathtub slowly. It was delicious. There was a bar of scented soap, and she lathered her hair, her face, her neck . . . every inch of her body that had been subjected to dust and sand and pesky insects.

Nearly an hour later she was still in the small bathtub, her knees drawn up and her hair floating on the sudsy water. She was facing the door and looked up with a start when the key turned in the lock and the door opened.

"Shelley." She stood as he closed the door and locked it. "You're gorgeous."

"No one's ever called me gorgeous before." He grinned at her, tossing his packages on the bed.

She grabbed up the white towel that lay folded on the floor beside the tub and wrapped it around her, ignoring the water that ran down her legs and through her hair to the floor, puddling at her feet. She touched Shelley's smooth jaw.

"You shaved your beard." Her fingers danced along his jaw and over his clean-shaven cheeks. "It makes you look younger . . . absolutely gorgeous." She smiled and leaned toward him to kiss his smooth cheeks, then his top lip. Even his moustache was gone.

"Well, there was a barber shop next to the general store, and I was long overdue—" Her kisses silenced him, and he wrapped his arms around her, loosening her towel and dropping it to the floor.

"You need a bath," she whispered, unbuttoning his torn shirt, unbuckling his belt.

She made no move to replace the towel he had removed as she stripped him and led him into the tub, careful not to get his bandage wet. He simply sat in the already cooled water while she soaped his chest leaning over him. Her hair fell across his body as she bathed him slowly, her hands dipping boldly beneath the surface of the water. Once, when she leaned over so she could reach deeper into the tub, she made the mistake of kissing him, just a light brush against his lips, and he grabbed her without warning and pulled her on top of him. The soap went flying and she landed in his lap.

She settled herself comfortably, her knees drawn up and pressed to his hips, and she pouted seductively. "Now look what you've done." She wrapped her arms around his neck and kissed him again, more thoroughly this time. "This tub is too small for both of us."

He pulled her close. "Seems just right to me."

They stood, Shelley keeping his good arm around her. "But I'll be damned if I finally get you into a room with a real honest-to-God bed and we end up in a goddamn tin bathtub."

She stepped out of the tub as he held her hand, and she led him across the room. She was still worried about his injury, careful not to bump his left arm at all, her eyes occasionally drifting to the bandage on his upper arm.

"Don't worry about that, darlin'."

He moved her toward the bed, kissing her lightly, drying her half-heartedly with the damp towel, pushing his parcels to the floor. One package landed with a loud thud, and she jerked her head around.

"What was that?"

"Later."

He pushed her onto the waiting bed and lowered himself gingerly beside her.

She forgot about the parcels. "Your arm does bother you, doesn't it?"

"A little," he conceded.

"I don't want to hurt you."

She kissed him softly, his face, his neck . . . there where a vein throbbed . . . his lips again.

"You won't."

He rolled onto his back and brought her with him, his hands on her waist guiding her.

She followed his lead and straddled him. "You want

218

me on top?" She smiled and bit his lower lip lightly. "This is so decadent."

Her smile broadened as she ran her hands over his body, coming back to his face. He really was handsome without his beard. Strong jaw, full, firm lips. Smooth cheeks she loved to kiss.

"I should've shaved a long time ago."

He caressed one breast and then the other, and she rained kisses over his body, until neither of them could find words anymore.

She lowered herself slowly, taking in every silken inch of him. She raised herself gradually, every nerve in her body exposed, on fire. When she and Shelley were together nothing else mattered. Not the past, not the future. Not his other women, not her uncertain fate.

She forgot everything but Shelley as she moved faster and faster, raising and lowering herself with gradually increasing rhythm.

Shelley raised to meet her, his own breathing as heavy as hers, his eyes open to watch her. Her breasts bounced gently. Her head was tilted back, and her eyes were closed. When she reached her climax she ground her hips against his and bit back a scream, and then he shared that release with her, the release he'd been holding back from the moment she'd lowered herself onto him.

He brushed back a dark lock of her hair that hid one brown eye from him. How had he allowed this to happen? Jesus, he was like an eighteen-year-old kid when she touched him. He should have tired of her by now, but he only wanted her more.

"Shelley," she whispered as she lowered her face to

his and kissed him ardently. "I . . ." She hesitated, kissed him again.

"What, darlin'?" He wrapped his good arm around her and she rested her head against his right shoulder.

"I'm glad you're all right, and I'm glad you shaved your beard." She didn't look at him as she whispered into his neck.

"I should get shot and shaved more often," he teased.

She lifted her head then and looked right into his eyes. "At least for the next couple of weeks, right?"

He dismissed her reminder of their limited time together. "I bought you something." He grinned and kissed her forehead as he gently set her beside him and reached to the floor where his packages had been scattered. "Let's see . . ."

The first item he showed her was a brand-new shirt to replace the one that had been destroyed. He threw everything on the bed . . . coffee, beef jerky, dried apples, beans . . . Finally he grinned and asked her to close her eyes. As soon as they were shut he began dropping heavy things between her spread legs, one after another, ordering her to keep her eyes closed until he said she could open them. Finally he told her she could look.

Canned peaches, a dozen cans, were piled on the bed between her legs. Annie squealed and grabbed one can and then another. Finally he tossed a can opener into the middle of the pile.

"You're the most wonderful man I've ever known." She gave him a girlish smile that threatened to break the heart he claimed not to possess.

"I seem to remember you said a can of peaches would buy me anything I wanted," he said as casually as he could manage. "I did wonder what a dozen cans would purchase."

Annie wrapped her arms around his neck. "Everything you want. All you have to do is ask."

He smoothed her still-damp hair with his hands. This was getting dangerous. Two weeks—maybe a day or two more, maybe a day or two less. She was working her way into his heart, with her voice and her heartfelt smiles, with her innocent blushes and her bold advances. He'd shielded his heart from the feelings she threatened to stir for too long to relent now. He remembered their pact. Just Shelley and Annie. Just two more weeks.

"Ummm," he mused. "I think I'd like you to rub my back and feed me a can of those peaches."

Annabelle obliged him with a smile, feeding him peaches and dutifully kissing away the syrup from his lips. In spite of the contented smile she gave him, she wished he would ask for something more—her heart, her love, her body by his side forever. But those were wishes he would never make, for those were the very burdens he didn't want. It should have made her love him less, but it didn't.

And it was becoming harder and harder not to tell him how she felt.

Leaving him when they reached San Francisco would break her heart, so she pushed that vision out of her mind. There was only here and now. Shelley and Annie.

Two more weeks.

Chapter Twenty-three

The nights were cool, the stars bright in a cloudless sky as Shelley and Annabelle followed the Humboldt River across Nevada. They did much of their traveling at night, preferring cool moonlight to the blistering sun.

Shelley filled her head with stories of the wonders of Virginia City, that rollicking town that waited for them before the Sierra Nevada Mountains. Of course, his tales were primarily of saloon brawls and dancing girls, but Annabelle didn't mind. She loved the sound of his voice, his soothing timbre, the easy drawl that made everything he said a balm to her spirit.

The nights were pleasant, but the days were brutal. The blistering sun beat down on them unmercifully, with no relief in the form of shade or rain. Even the wind was painful, pelting their faces with sand and alkali dust. They rested during the hottest part of the day, Shelley constructing a crude shelter from two sturdy poles he'd purchased as they left Salt Lake City, and a blanket, much as she had that day by the creek. Even then, the heat was unlike anything she could have imagined. When the wind was too harsh, Shelley enveloped her in his arms, her face to his chest, his arms around her head.

They slept in the shelter in spite of the heat, exhaustion ruling their bodies. Annabelle knew that if she had attempted to cross the desert alone she never would have made it. Shelley's strength was her strength. When it seemed that the barren land was endless, he sensed her desolation and began another tale of Virginia City . . . reminding her of what waited for them at the end of the trail. He promised her a scented bath, a hot meal, and a clean bed in the finest hotel in town.

The trail was marked with reminders of its harshness. Crudely marked graves lined the trail, and the bleached bones of animals were littered among the dust and sand. Wagon wheels, dried and cracked, broken beyond repair, had been abandoned. Annabelle wondered how the Castletons and the rest of the wagon train would fare during this part of their journey.

Near the end of the fifth day, Shelley pulled up his horse and pointed west. The dust had settled over him in a fine coat. "Do you see it?"

She halted her mare beside him. "I don't see anything but more dust and barren godforsaken land."

The long days, the heat, the alkali dust had all worn her to the bone. She was wearier than she had ever been, and tried to be perturbed that Shelley wasn't nearly as affected as she was. When she looked at him, with his dark blond hair and his hazel eyes, his browned skin and his tan britches, he looked as if he might have been part of the landscape, part of the desert itself.

"You'll see it soon enough." He grinned at her, and that only irritated her more.

"What?" she asked sharply. "If there's anything out there that's not identical to the dusty land I've looked at for the past five days, I'd like to know about it."

They hadn't been traveling long. They'd slept through the hottest part of the afternoon, but several hours of daylight remained. Sometimes she felt Shelley was pushing her too hard, but she knew his objective was to cross the desert safely, and as quickly as possible.

"Green." He looked away from her and prodded his horse forward. "Wonderful, marvelous, water-fed green."

She followed him skeptically. She saw nothing different from what they'd traveled across for the most eternally long five days of her life. It was almost half an hour later when she saw just a hint of what Shelley had seen.

There was, remarkably, a neat-looking farmhouse in the middle of nowhere. In the distance, still far away and misty blue, were the Sierra Nevada Mountains. The green they had seen was a huge garden to one side of the farmhouse. On the other side was a large barn and a smokehouse. They stared at the site as if it were a mirage.

Before long a man appeared on the porch, and he waved to them grandly, as if he'd been expecting them and was waving them in. Shelley approached slowly, Annabelle shyly behind him.

"Afternoon," the smiling man greeted them heartily. "Traveling to California?"

"Yep. You wouldn't have any water to spare, would you? The horses have been drinking out of the Humboldt for five days, and our canteens are low," Shelley said.

"More than enough." The man introduced himself as Jacob Filmore, and explained to Shelley, as they led the horses around back, where he came by his abundance of water.

The railroad had tapped into the mountains and piped out water to their work crews and later to the stations. For a fee, and after much wangling, Filmore had convinced them to let him tap into their source, just enough for his animals, his family, and his garden.

It became clear after a short time that the man, though friendly, was as suspicious of them as they had been of the intruders who had ridden into their camp—Manfred Winston and his gang. Annabelle couldn't blame him, not after what she had seen that night.

It didn't take long for Shelley and Jacob to hit it off. Shelley's open grin was almost as effective on men as it was on women. He was easy to trust, and to like. Jacob fetched his wife and children from where they'd been hiding in the barn.

There were three boys, not one of them over eight, gathered around the skirts of a woman who smiled widely at her husband.

"I told you they looked all right, Jacob." She shook Shelley's hand and turned to Annabelle with her hands folded primly in front of her. "Good heavens. It's been so long since I conversed with a woman I feel like I'm looking at a long-lost sister. Do you mind if I give you a hug?"

Annabelle wasn't certain exactly how she should respond to such a request from a stranger, but the woman seemed so sincere, so warm, that Annabelle opened her arms. "Why not?" And the woman gave her a warm but gentle embrace before she introduced herself.

Mary Beth Filmore set Annabelle away from her. "Jacob, they must stay for supper . . . and for the night. This poor girl is exhausted. I remember that awful trek across Nevada. What a nightmare! We don't get many folks this way anymore. Most everybody takes the rail, unless they're hauling wagons and such."

Without waiting for a reply from her husband, Mary Beth placed an arm around Annabelle's shoulders and led her to the house. "You look like you could use a nice, warm bath. I've got some clothes you can borrow while we wash out your things. Jacob!" she yelled over her shoulder. "Put those younguns of ours to work and stay out of the house for a spell. Oh, and have Matthew fill the tub first," she said as she reached the back door that opened into the kitchen. "I'll do up some chicken fixin's, and we'll have a grand old time."

Mary Beth had taken over, and Annabelle was delighted. She gave one last look over her shoulder at Shelley. He was grinning at her, and shrugged in surrender as the woman led her into the house.

When Matthew, the oldest boy, had filled the tub with water, Mary Beth heated some of it on the stove to warm the bath. Annabelle bathed in the kitchen while Mary Beth began preparing dinner, chattering

constantly, obviously starved for female companion-
ship.

She was, it turned out, Jacob's third wife. He had
grown children spread across the West, sons and
daughters of his first two marriages. Life with a twice-
widowed man several years older than herself seemed
to agree with the pleasant woman.

Jacob was a circuit rider, a traveling preacher
whose congregation was small and scattered. He'd
spend a few days at home, then travel for several days
from settlement to settlement before returning home.
When he was on the farm, he tended the cows and
chickens and the garden. While he was away, those
chores fell to Mary Beth and the children.

Annabelle was surprised to learn that Mary Beth
was only five years older than herself. She was a little
heavy, pleasantly rounded, and her face was brown
and showing signs of wrinkling. Too many days in the
hot sun and too many hours being pounded by alkali
dust had taken its toll. But Mary Beth was warm and
friendly, and by the time Annabelle stepped from the
tub, she felt as if she'd known the woman all her life.

Annabelle had never had any real women friends
before. Her vocal training had begun at the age of
twelve, just after her parents had died in a freak carriage accident. The musical conservatories in Paris
were fiercely competitive, and no one developed close
friendships. The women she met after she left the conservatory were still competitors, singers vying for the
same parts, rivals of a sort. But Suzanne Castleton had
quickly become a friend, and now Mary Beth, a
woman she'd just met, was beginning to seem like the
sister she'd never had.

Maybe running had been the right decision after all.

Maybe a short life lived with love and friendship and excitement was better than a long and lonely life. If only Henri hadn't had to die for her to discover that fact.

Mary Beth behaved as if they were having a grand dinner party. She presented Annabelle with a white dress, eyelet over linen, a young-looking dress that Mary Beth swore she hadn't been able to fit into since her first child had been born. It was with a comically dismal face that she surveyed Annabelle's tiny waist, and then her own.

They fiddled with one another's hair, putting it up and taking it down, giggling at the absurd styles they created. Finally, they piled their hair atop their heads, and crowned themselves with a few simple flowers from Mary Beth's garden. Annabelle felt as light and free as the feather in the band of her hat. She giggled as she set the table for seven, and filled a vase with flowers like the ones she and Mary Beth wore in their hair.

Annabelle smoothed her dress, the snug waist and the flowing skirt. It had a simple collar trimmed with lace, and she had a difficult time deciding whether to wear her medicine bag. She finally removed it and placed it with her hat, grudgingly parting with her good luck charm.

She even polished her red boots until they shone again, and when she walked they peeked out from under her skirts. She wondered what Shelley would think of her now, with her white dress and pink flowers in her hair.

Mary Beth called the men to the table and placed Shelley not at Annabelle's side, but directly across from her. Jacob sat at one end of the table and Mary

Beth at the other, her three boys nearby.

Shelley was clean-shaven and had put on a fresh shirt with a string tie, the tie borrowed from Jacob, no doubt. His face was so brown the white shirt was striking against his skin, and Annabelle wondered if the same was true of her. She knew her skin was not as brown as his, but it was darker than it had ever been, browned by the sun.

He stared at her across the table, a sly smile on his face. She couldn't help but return his smile. There was a fire in his eyes that only she could extinguish. A hunger only she could satisfy.

"You look lovely tonight, Annie," he said finally.

"So do you." She couldn't wait to finish their delicious supper and retire to the barn, where Mary Beth had said they would spend the night. For a while the voices around her faded and there were just the two of them. Shelley and Annie. She barely tasted the chicken, even after all her complaints about their limited menu on the trail. Shelley didn't take his eyes off her. Not as he ate, not as he answered Jacob Filmore's questions.

She was a vision. How did she manage to be more beautiful every time he saw her? It wasn't just the dress, or the hair, though they were lovely. Her face was radiant, alive, pink-cheeked and lightly browned. Her lips were the color of fresh plums, her hair as shiny as silk.

Jacob cleared his throat. "I'm quite a fiddler, you know."

"What?" Shelley turned to him, pulling himself away from his daydream.

"Mary Beth suggested you might like to hear a little

music this evening," Jacob repeated. "I play the fiddle."

Shelley grinned. "Maybe you could do a song with Annie. She's a fine singer. Prettiest voice in the world, I bet."

Jacob and Mary Beth dismissed his praise as prejudiced, but Annie and the preacher huddled together until they decided on a song they both knew.

First Jacob fetched his fiddle and warmed up for a few minutes, tuning, listening with a practiced ear. He was, Shelley decided, a musician at heart. He was lost in his own world, heard nothing of their chatter as he tuned his instrument, his eyes closed and his body relaxed.

Annie smiled at Shelley when Jacob asked her to join him. She stood next to the fiddler in front of the fireplace, her back erect, her head high. The tips of her red boots were peeking from under her white skirt as she folded her hands at her waist and began to sing, Jacob accompanying her.

She sang "Amazing Grace," her voice strong and rich and rapturous, her eyes fixed somewhere beyond Shelley's shoulder as she poured her heart into the song. It was powerful, literally and emotionally. Jacob closed his eyes. Mary Beth ignored the tears that fell from hers. The three boys, completely quiet for the first time that day, stared at her with open mouths, awed.

Shelley's face revealed nothing, but deep inside there was a sickening gut-churning.

She stood there, poised and regal, singing from her very soul. Near the end of the hymn her eyes met his and she smiled. Just for him. But she wasn't his Annie anymore.

She was Annabelle St. Clair, and he still carried her wanted poster in his saddlebag.

Chapter Twenty-four

The room was silent for a few seconds after Annabelle and Jacob finished "Amazing Grace." The boys were the first to break the silence, their whoops and hollers enthusiastic. Mary Beth wiped away her tears and then applauded loudly. Only Shelley remained evidently unmoved.

Annabelle turned to Jacob with a pleased smile. "I never expected to find such a fine violinist out here in the middle of nowhere."

Jacob blushed. "Just a fiddler, ma'am."

She turned to Shelley. She wanted him to be proud of her, and she looked for some reaction. There was nothing. His eyes were unreadable, but they held none of the warmth she had seen earlier.

"Your wife sings like an angel," Jacob said to Shelley.

Shelley never took his guarded eyes of her. "She's

not my wife," he said emotionlessly. "I'm just escorting her to San Francisco."

"Oh." Their host frowned slightly. "We'll need to change our arrangements in that case. The boys can sleep on pallets in our room, and Annie can sleep in the loft. I just assumed . . ."

"I should have made our situation clear," Shelley said sharply.

Annabelle pursed her lips slightly. What was wrong with Shelley? He could have lied and claimed she was his wife, as he had in Salt Lake City, or at the very least kept his mouth shut and let the Filmores assume that was true. Instead, he had coldly dismissed her, and now they would be forced to spend the night apart.

He didn't even say good night as he and Jacob left the house to smoke their cigars, leaving her and Mary Beth to clear away the dishes and put the boys to bed.

"How embarrassing," Mary Beth said as she straightened and cleaned. "I must admit, I assumed the same as Jacob. You two just look . . ." She quieted suddenly. "Jacob would never allow an unmarried couple to sleep in his barn. It's just not proper." She spun around and rested her eyes on Annabelle. "I know. You two are going to be married in California, aren't you? Why don't you two stay around here for a few days and let Jacob perform the cermony. A barn might not make a very romantic honeymoon spot, but—"

"Shelley and I aren't going to be married. He's simply escorting me to California, as he said." She gave Mary Beth a tired smile. "Is there anything else I can do?"

Mary Beth shook her head, a confused frown on her

233

face. She looked as baffled as Annabelle felt. The change had come over Shelley so unexpectedly, so quickly. She couldn't even muster any anger, just yet.

"I'm really exhausted," Annabelle claimed. "Would you mind . . ."

"I've got a nightgown you can borrow." Mary Beth walked her to the ladder that led to the loft where the boys normally slept. "Your things will be dry by morning, and I'll fix you up a big breakfast before you go on your way."

"Thank you." She impulsively hugged Mary Beth enthusiastically. "For the dress, and the bath, and the dinner . . . for everything." She pulled back, suddenly remembering something very important.

The dreamcatcher was in her saddlebag. In the barn. She excused herself and stepped into the cool night air, the normally blustery winds still for once. Not a night had gone by that she hadn't slept with the dreamcatcher at her side, and her nightmare hadn't returned. She marched past Jacob and Shelley as they talked in low voices, and she ignored both of them coolly. Ungrateful, unfeeling men. She marched past them moments later, the dreamcatcher in her hand, with a curt good night for both of them.

Shelley and Jacob watched her strut by, her head held high, her dark hair falling from its pinned capture, her hips swinging as she returned to the house as quickly as she could without seeming to hurry. Shelley remembered his hands around that tiny waist more clearly than was comfortable, and watched wordlessly as she entered the house and slammed the door behind her.

"She don't seem none too pleased with the two of

us this evenin'." Jacob offered.

"I'm none too pleased with her myself at the moment," he answered sharply.

Jacob expertly flicked ashes to the dirt and studied the burning end of his cigar. Shelley recognized the look. Thoughtful, reflective, wondering if opening his mouth would get him flattened.

"Son," Jacob began, "I've been married three times. I've got six grown daughters and five daughters-in-law. All of 'em fine-lookin' women. And I was quite a ladies man in my younger days, before I found the Lord."

He glared at the man, unable to hide his growing impatience. "This goin' somewhere?"

Jacob caught his eye. "I ain't never seen a woman prettier than that one."

"Annie?" he asked casually. "She's not bad-lookin', I guess."

Jacob laughed, a sincere and hearty laugh that disturbed the quiet night air. "Son, you don't fool me. You can fool her, and you can fool yourself, but don't try to fool me. I'm going to give you some advice," he added, his voice controlled, calm.

"Don't want it."

"Gonna get it anyway," Jacob insisted kindly. "Marry her."

Shelley rolled the cigar between his fingers. "Nope. Can't do that."

"Why not? You already married?"

"Nope."

"She married?"

"Nope."

Jacob tossed his cigar into the dirt and ground the stub with the tip of his plain work boot. "Shame," he muttered. "If you don't, somebody else will."

Shelley looked toward the window of the loft. "Most likely."

Jacob tried to convince him that he should marry the girl he was so obviously smitten with, and who obviously cared for him, but all of Jacob's reasoning fell on deaf ears. Shelley displayed no anger, but the more Jacob talked, the more withdrawn he became. He didn't argue, didn't agree. He just didn't listen. Jacob finally gave up and retired for the night. He left Shelley standing in the open doorway to the barn, lighting another cigar.

Shelley lifted his eyes to the window of the loft again. The moonlight was bright, and he saw her hands as she placed the dreamcatcher in the windowsill, propping it against the pane. He thought she had gone to bed, but then he saw her palm pressed against the glass. Beyond the dreamcatcher and her hand, all was dark, but he knew she was there, watching him.

She'd played him as expertly as Jacob had played his fiddle. She'd gotten what she wanted, Annabelle St. Clair had. Wrapped him around her little finger and steered him halfway across the country.

Once a fool, always a fool.

Chapter Twenty-five

"I don't think they're coming," Mordecai said, unusually tense. "We've been in this Godless town for nearly a week—"

"They'll be here," Wendell assured his partner calmly. "I feel it in my bones."

Their hotel room was adequate, but it was cramped and less than clean. The noise never seemed to stop, not even in the dead of night. In the street beneath their window there had been three shootings since their arrival, and the screams of revelers were constant.

Mordecai had told Wendell again and again how he hated Virginia City—the sin, the sinners. Wendell was sick to death of hearing Mordecai complain.

"They might have decided to pass Virginia City by," Mordecai reasoned. "If that's the case, we can only hope the Walsh brothers catch up with them before they reach San Francisco . . . if it's not too late."

Wendell stood in the window and looked down at the street. The location was the reason they had requested this particular room, why they tolerated the small space and the dirty floor and the bugs that had lived there long before his and Mordecai's arrival and would be there long after they left.

He could see the main street from one end nearly to the other. If . . . when Shelley and Annabelle St. Clair rode into town, he would know it.

"She's still alive," he insisted.

Mordecai shook his head. "Do you feel that in your bones, too?"

He turned to Mordecai and smiled. "Common sense. Easier to guide a live woman through the Sierra Nevada than to carry a body. No. She's still alive."

The search for Annabelle St. Clair had changed for him in the past few weeks. He began to forget about their assignment, and to concentrate on the man who had punched him out in the alley in Brayton. Had tricked him. Had taken the woman out of his reach. As his hate for Shelley grew, his mission changed, though he never mentioned it to Mordecai. Wendell no longer cared if they returned Annabelle St. Clair to her uncle, or if she was turned in for the reward by some bounty hunter. She was a killer, after all.

"We may have to kill Shelley." He broached the subject carefully, casually. He was never certain how Mordecai would react to such ideas.

"That shouldn't be necessary," Mordecai said coldly. "If he becomes a problem, he can be taken out with a bullet in the foot or the leg. There's no reason to—"

"How in hell did you end up in this line of work, Mordecai?" he snapped. "You ain't got the stomach for it. Why? I'd really like to know."

Mordecai stared at him with those pale eyes, sad and self-condemning. "I found myself unsuited for my true calling, and 'Blessed are the peacemakers, for they shall sit at the hand of God.' "

He laughed harshly. "Is that what you think we are? Peacemakers? You're deluding yourself, Butterfield. We're not peacemakers. We're executioners."

Mordecai drew himself to his full height and stared at Wendell through narrowed eyes. "I'm leaving, Wendell," he said softly, turning away to gather his hat, his holster, and his Bible.

"Well, don't be too long," he snapped. "I'm going out for a bite to eat later on, and I haven't slept in twenty hours, so you'll have to keep watch."

"You don't understand," Mordecai replied calmly. "I'm not coming back."

Wendell turned a stern face to Mordecai Butterfield, a man he was beginning to consider weak and ineffectual. He didn't need him. He could take Shelley alone.

He turned back to the window. He had no farewells for his partner. Even after the door was closed and he was alone, he felt no trepidation. This was the way it was meant to be. Shelley and Annabelle St. Clair would come riding down the street sooner or later . . . and he would be ready.

Shelley was going to have to die. With Mordecai out of the picture, that would be simple. An ambush would work just fine. And if the St. Clair woman got in the way . . . that was too bad. She was secondary, now, and her death would be meaningless.

Virginia City was little more than half a day's ride from the Filmores. It was, as Shelley had described, a bustling town, with saloons lining the streets. The tinkling of poorly tuned and poorly played piano keys drifted from one open door, squeals of laughter from another. As they rode down the dusty street a man flew through the swinging doors of one saloon followed by a burly man twice his size, angry and redfaced.

Shelley had been silent throughout the day, and Annabelle was afraid to question him directly. He rode slightly ahead of her, his stance relaxed as usual. When he slid from his horse in front of the general store at the end of the street he instructed her, without actually looking at her, to wait for him there. His curt words were the first he had spoken to her all day.

She eased herself from the mare's back and stretched her aching arms over her head. She would never ride with the same ease Shelley did. Though she never complained, some days were longer than others, and her rear end and her back screamed at her to stop.

"Howdy."

Annabelle jumped. The greeting came from directly behind her, from a thin little man wearing a ten-gallon hat that overpowered him and made him look even thinner.

"Hello," she greeted the strange-looking little man coolly.

He smiled and shook a crooked finger at her. "You rode in with Shelley, didn't ya?"

She simply nodded.

"What's your name? You look mighty familiar to me." He narrowed his eyes and studied her much too boldly.

"I'm certain we've never met." Her voice was icy.

The filthy man made her skin crawl. Didn't men in the West bathe at all?

She removed her hat and began to fan her perspiring face, turning away from the annoying man. He followed her movements step for step, still staring inquisitively at her face. She saw his rush of satisfaction as he recognized her.

"I've got it! You're that opera singer! Annabelle St. . . . St. . . . " He searched his memory while shaking his finger at her excitedly.

"St. Clair," Shelley stated.

She swung around to face Shelley, but he was calmly storing supplies in his saddlebags, his broad back to her.

"That's it!" the nosy man cried. "Annabelle St. Clair. The opera singer what slit her man's throat."

"I did not!"

"They always say they're innocent, don't they, Shelley?" The man in the huge hat turned his back on Annabelle. "Hell, I almost didn't recognize her, but they run a new drawin' of her in the San Francisco paper I saw last week. Where you been, anyways? I ain't seen you in a coon's age."

Shelley turned away from his horse, the saddlebags filled and closed, and his eyes met hers. She was looking at him expectantly, waiting for some sort of explanation. "Been busy. Here and there."

"This un's a real gold mine, huh? A thousand bucks. How come she ain't tied up?"

Annabelle's face had lost all its color. Her lips and her cheeks, usually so pink, were pasty white. Her dark eyes looked huge, lost in her delicate face. Shelley held her eyes, never looking away as he spoke to the man.

"Hell, Riley. She knows she can't get away from me."

Riley chuckled. "Yep. How long since you actually turned in a live one for a bounty?"

"A coon's age." Shelley kept his voice cold, emotionless. "This one's going to San Francisco. Private bounty, and that's where the money is."

"Ain't she givin' you no trouble? That's a helluva long way. You better watch your back, Shelley. I been readin' all about her. She's a cold one, she is." Riley seemed to think about this fact a bit, and he moved further away from her.

"She gives me any trouble and I'll shoot her. The reward is for her body . . . dead or alive. Makes no never mind to me." He finally turned his head away from Annie and stared at the unsmiling Riley. "I know you and your mouth. If anybody should even think of taking her away from me . . . they'll get the same."

Riley smiled nervously. "You know me, Shelley. I'm gettin' too old for this game. I stick mostly to Indian scalps and coyote pelts these days."

"That's good, Riley. I like you. I'd hate to have to kill you, but for a thousand dollars, I would."

"Let's go," he ordered as he mounted his roan. He watched as Annie stepped into the stirrups and lifted herself into the saddle. Her hands were trembling, even her knees, encased in the tight britches, shook slightly.

He didn't look back at her as they left town, riding at a moderate pace. They were out of Virginia City and on the trail again before she let the tears start. They were silent, deeply felt tears that tore at her heart.

He had known all along. All this time he had been taking her to San Francisco not because he felt responsible for her, not because he cared for her, but for the money.

He was a bounty hunter, like the despicable Beans and that horrible Riley. He killed people for a living. No wonder he'd been so adept when they were attacked. No wonder he had been carrying so much cash in his pocket.

She realized she'd led a sheltered life, particularly since her parents' deaths. She'd never understood men, not until she'd met Henri. He had been so sweet, so undemanding. They liked the same music, the same foods, autumn better than spring.

It was no wonder she had fallen for a man like Shelley, who made her feel safe, and grinned assuredly, and ignited her newfound passion. But all along he had been using her, playing with her fragile emotions. She wished he had simply shot her and thrown her over the mare. It would have been less painful.

She stared at his stiff back. This was the real Shelley. All his good humor, his tenderness, his feigned desire for her . . . gone. He was a good actor. Belonged on the stage.

To think that she had once felt such comfort in the simple sound of his heartbeat, had ached for his touch as if he were the only man alive. Well, he wasn't. He was a despicable man, no better than Beans or Riley.

She would let him lead her to San Francisco. He could turn her over to the police and collect his reward. She didn't care. She would make her way to Nicky. The one man in the world she could trust.

And Shelley could go to the devil.

*   *   *

Shelley purposely traveled at a monotonous pace, never turning to check on Annie. When he found a suitable campsite late in the afternoon, he silently tethered his horse and waited for her to do the same. He built a fire, started their dinner, tended the animals. All the while he was silent, trying not to look at her. That was too damn hard to do.

Annie sat away from the fire, her knees drawn to her chest. When he approached her with a plate of beans, she shook her head silently.

"You gotta eat," he said in a low, gruff voice.

"No, I don't." She refused with stubborn dignity. Why hadn't he seen it before? Spoiled, pampered, rich little girl . . .

"You've got to keep your strength up."

She looked up at him then, her dark eyes flashing, her full lips pursed. "Why? If I get too weak to keep up with you, you can shoot me and truss me to the back of my mare and take me in. Dead or alive, remember?"

"Jesus!" He flung the tin plate toward the fire, and beans exploded upward when Annie's dinner hit the ground. "I'm not taking you in for the goddamn bounty."

"Why should I believe you?" She rested her head on her knees and looked into her lap. "You lied to me. You knew all along—"

He grabbed her arm and jerked her to her feet. "If we're going to talk about lying here, let's start with you, Widow Brown. Annie. Miss St. Clair. I never lied to you."

His fingers dug into her arm, and he all but growled down at her. Still, she lifted her face and looked up at

244

him. Where was the timid creature he had rescued from Oscar's place?

"You're a bounty hunter," she said calmly. "You kill people and turn in their bodies for money."

"I hunt down killers and thieves," he responded icily. "When they cooperate, I take them in alive. When they don't . . ."

"Is that a threat?" she asked emotionlessly.

He wouldn't answer that.

"You might have told me." It seemed her voice softened just a little, and her eyes were not quite so hard.

And have you look at me the way you looked at Beans? He kept that thought to himself. "You never asked."

He dropped her arm and returned to the fire. "I won't force-feed you, but at least try to get a little sleep."

He sat at the fire with his back to her, sipping coffee and ignoring her presence as best he could. He felt foolish and angry. He should have known from the moment he saw her wanted poster that she was Annabelle St. Clair. Poor resemblance or not, there were too many coincidences to ignore. But he had chosen to ignore them anyway. Because he wanted to? Because he preferred to think of her as a helpless woman running away from overbearing relatives or a relentless suitor?

She'd gotten under his skin, just as she'd planned, knowing that he wouldn't be able to turn her in when the time came. Her innocence, her passion, all an act to capture his loyalty, his unwavering allegiance. His heart.

He would fulfill his end of the agreement. He would put her on the ferry and turn his back on her forever.

*   *   *

Wendell lay on his stomach, motionless, and watched. He had planned to wait until they were asleep . . . but his heart was racing with excitement, and his victims were almost as helpless now as they would be once sound asleep.

They'd been fighting. He couldn't hear their words, but the stiff way Shelley stood, the way he had turned his back on his prisoner . . . and now they both sat silently sulking, with no knowledge of the danger that awaited them.

He was well hidden in a stand of cottonwoods, had been there minutes after Shelley and Annabelle St. Clair had made camp. Wendell had followed them from town, keeping his distance, knowing they would be his before the night was through. He was glad Mordecai had deserted him. The man would have slowed him down, Wendell thought as he left his hiding place.

"Well, well, well," Wendell said casually as he boldly walked into camp, a six-shooter in each hand, one aimed at Shelley, the other at the woman.

"How nice to see you again. Miss St. Clair." He cocked both pistols when Shelley and the woman simultaneously rose and turned to him. He took in her new attire.

"Not a bad disguise. I never would have recognized you if it hadn't been for your partner here." He nodded to Shelley.

"Who are . . ." Annabelle began, looking Wendell up and down.

"How's your jaw?"

Wendell turned his attention to the bounty hunter. "I wouldn't be worrying about my jaw if I were you. You have bigger concerns. Much bigger."

Wendell could see the helplessness in Shelley's eyes. With the pistols trained on him and the woman, going for his own weapon would be suicide . . . and probably get the St. Clair woman killed as well.

"You wanna make a deal? Split the reward?" Shelley asked coldly. "Five hundred dollars is a lot of money. I can give you your half right now. Most of it, anyway." He made a move for his saddlebags.

"Stop right there," Wendell ordered, waving the pistol that was aimed at Shelley. "And you." He motioned to the woman. "Come a little closer."

She took a few tentative steps toward Shelley, and Wendell moved forward as she did.

"What do you want?" she asked. "Is it the money? I can pay you. More than the reward, if—"

"Shut up!" he yelled. "I don't want your money. This is my pride. Pride in a job well done."

The woman sighed. "Then put the guns down. I'll go to San Francisco with you. There's no reason for anyone to get hurt."

"Well, I think there is. Your . . . friend here knocked me out, after he played me for a fool and snatched you out from under my nose. I take offense at that. If I'd wanted to take you from him, I would've done it in Virginia City."

The woman appeared strangely calm. "So you're going to kill us both?"

He smiled. "Smart girl."

She looked at Shelley. He had barely moved.

"I don't suppose you'd be willing to grant a man one last request?" the bounty hunter asked.

Wendell leered at Shelley. What a joke. This was going to be easier than he had anticipated. "What is it?"

Shelley nodded his head in the woman's direction. "Let me give her one last kiss."

So that was how it was. "Drop your gun," he ordered, and Shelley complied, dropping his six-shooter into the grass and turning to face the woman.

"You're insane if you think I'll kiss you now," she snapped.

Giving her a quick grin and shrugging, the bounty hunter appeared so casual, so calm.

"We're about to die, Annie. You wouldn't deny me one last—"

"All right," the woman snapped, and she allowed him to wrap his arms around her and lower his lips to hers. One of the big man's hands was at the back of her head, the other he ran down her back, over her hip, finally coming to rest there.

The St. Clair woman changed her attitude quickly and threw her arms around his neck. She pressed herself against him, and Shelley pulled his mouth away from hers and whispered in her ear.

She hit the ground, and the bounty hunter lunged at Wendell with a knife in his hand. Caught off guard, Wendell dropped one pistol, and the other was knocked aside, firing into the cottonwoods. Wendell landed on his back, and Shelley plunged the knife into his shoulder.

He screamed and released the six-shooter he had managed to keep possession of. It had happened too fast. Shelley had gotten the drop on him again.

Without a word to Annie, Shelley tied the ambusher to one of the cottonwoods that had served as cover earlier. The Pinkerton agent's wound was bleeding badly, but it wasn't fatal. Shelley figured that in a day or two, if the man yelled loud enough when travelers passed by on the trail, someone would find him.

"You're lucky," Shelley whispered to the agent as he secured the knots. "If the woman wasn't here I'd put a bullet between your eyes and leave you for the wolves."

The man's eyes widened. "Wolves?"

He flashed a grin. "As long as you're alive they probably won't bother you . . . unless they're really hungry. You're lucky it's not winter."

When Shelley turned around he saw that Annie had saddled her mare and was starting to saddle his roan. She moved quickly, wasting no movements, and he stopped for a moment to watch her. Just a few weeks ago she'd been unable to ride, and now she lifted the heavy saddle, if not effortlessly, at least steadily.

It stunned him to realize that he didn't care what she had done . . . it wasn't going to make it any easier to let her go. He had to make certain she never realized that.

Annie mounted her sable brown mare and gave the Pinkerton agent a cutting glance. "You bounty hunters are a ruthless lot."

The bound man was too far away to hear her, but Shelley was not.

Chapter Twenty-six

They didn't rest until they'd left the agent far behind, and even then neither of them could sleep. The wind in the trees, the small animals in the forest that surrounded them, these sounds of nature were intrusive, and in every whisper Annabelle heard an intruder.

Shelley was restless all night, and rose with a curse while it was still pitch black. Without a word he saddled the horses, his anger evident in every tense movement, in the set of his jaw. He expected her to follow his lead without instruction, and she did. It was obvious that he was anxious to be rid of her, and how could she blame him?

They traveled at a brisk pace, but she didn't dare complain. She was as anxious as he to reach San Francisco and be done with this nightmare . . . one way or another. The Sierra Nevada Mountain range loomed before them, and she wondered how they'd ever manage to cross that barrier. A few days ago she would've simply asked, and Shelley would have explained to her, in an easy drawl, exactly what they would be doing . . . but today she didn't dare. His silence was absolute, controlled. She didn't want to know what he might say to her if he was forced to speak.

They almost rode past the shack that sat in the distance, surrounded by tall grass bending in the breeze for miles and miles of untended plain. It looked deserted, except for the child who struggled with a shovel that was too large for her to handle.

Annabelle brought her mare to a complete stop and watched the odd scene, her brows knit in a frown. The little girl was small and very thin, wearing a brown dress that was miles too large for her. The skirt of the dress whipped in the wind, as did the child's long, unbound hair. As Annabelle watched, the child stopped her chore and leaned against the shovel, laying her head upon the hands that grasped the handle, and Annabelle turned her mare and led the animal toward the shack and the child.

"Where do you think you're going?" Shelley was beside her before she had a chance to go very far. "We don't need anything from this place. There's a comfortable site up ahead. Plenty of water for the horses, good shade—"

"I think that little girl's in trouble." Annabelle didn't look at Shelley or attempt to turn the mare from its path. "Something's not right."

Shelley looked toward the shack. "Working in the garden, most likely. Most children on these small farms work hard from the time they learn to walk."

Annabelle didn't listen to him. Something about the child was drawing her—the way the child stood, slumped and tired; the desolateness of the tiny cabin itself; the effort the child put into forcing the shovel into the ground.

There were no more words of protest as Shelley followed her.

"Wait here," he instructed flatly as they neared the child, but Annabelle ignored him.

The girl's eyes were huge in a white, drawn face. Her hair flew about her head in sweat-dampened tendrils, and when she lifted her face, Annabelle thought her heart would break.

Near the child was a body wrapped in sheets and lying in the dirt a few feet from the small plot of broken ground. It lay at the end of a furrowed trail, marks obviously made when the little girl had dragged the body from the cabin.

She shielded her eyes as she looked up at Annabelle and then Shelley. She didn't appear to be more than ten years old.

"If you came to see my pa, he's dead." Her voice was weak, watery, and she looked away and drove the shovel into the ground, dislodging a tiny bit of dirt.

Shelley slid from his horse, took the shovel from the child's hands, and took over. "Get on in the house, darlin'," he said, the first hint of kindness Annabelle had heard in days in his voice. "I'll handle this."

The girl turned away tiredly without a word and disappeared into the shack.

Annabelle jumped from her mare and started to follow her, but Shelley grabbed her arm.

"Leave her be."

She shook off his grip. "No. Can't you see she's ill?"

He reached out and grabbed her again. "Can't you see she's got the same fever that killed her pa? You wanna catch it? I'll bury her pa, and then we're out of here. Got it?"

"No." She shook him off again and stepped back. "I won't leave the child like that. I can't believe you would either."

Shelley drove the shovel into the hard ground. "Goddamn it, Annie. I don't suppose you'd agree to wait here and let me see to the kid?"

"No."

"Jesus." He didn't look at her. "Don't touch anything. Don't eat or drink anything in the house. Could be something's tainted. Keep your hands off the kid."

She didn't answer, and she heard Shelley cursing as she pushed open the door to the cabin.

The girl's home consisted of one small room, unglazed windows, a dirt floor. There was a single bed in one corner, a wood stove in another. The room was not particularly clean or well kept, but Annabelle had no way of knowing how long the girl's father had been sick.

The child was lying on the bed, on top of a faded quilt, her eyes closed.

"Hello." Annabelle's call was a whisper as she moved to stand beside the little girl's bed. "What's your name?"

"Pearl." The sick child turned her head toward Annabelle, and her eyes drifted slowly open. Pearl's face was so thin that her eyes looked enormous, lost.

"What a beautiful name." Annabelle placed her hand on the child's forehead. Pearl was burning up with fever.

She found a pitcher of water and a few clean cloths, and began to bathe the feverish child. Pearl barely moved. How long had she been ill? Had there been anyone to care for her at all?

"Are you an angel?" Pearl whispered, looking up at Annabelle through fevered eyes. "My ma's an angel, and Pa said she watches over us."

Annabelle shook her head, keeping the tears from her eyes with great effort. "I'm not an angel, Pearl."

"Oh." The answer seemed to be a disappointment to her. "I hope there really are angels, like Pa said. Do you think I'll go to heaven?"

Annabelle's hands shook slightly at the unexpected question. "You needn't worry about that. You're young. You have a long time to think about heaven."

"But I'm sick, like Pa, and he died. He said if I was bad I wouldn't go to heaven, and I tried to be good all the time . . . but sometimes, when I was supposed to be doing my chores, I'd run to the mountains. It's cool there, and I love the trees and the wildflowers."

"I love those things, too, Pearl. I don't believe God will hold it against us that we took a little time to enjoy the beauty he gave us."

Pearl smiled weakly, satisfied with her answer, and she drifted into an uneasy sleep.

Annabelle heard the door open, heard Shelley close it gently behind him. He would be furious with her for disobeying his instructions, but she continued to hold Pearl's hand and sang a soft lullaby through the tears that streamed down her face.

"It's done," he said simply, his voice tired and free of anger.

It was almost dark, and Shelley lit the single lamp in the cabin and set it near the end of the bed.

Pearl opened her eyes. "Thanks, mister," she said weakly. "That ground was so hard." The girl turned her eyes to Annabelle. "I don't even know your name."

"Annie," she said as clearly as she could, fighting to keep the tears out of her eyes and her voice.

Pearl closed her eyes again. "Sing to me some more, Annie."

Annabelle sang more lullabies, sang all night. Her voice was hoarse and whispery as she watched the child slipping away. Occasionally Pearl would open her eyes and laugh weakly, or speak to someone who wasn't there, and once she called Annabelle "Ma."

It was near dawn when she took her last breath. Annabelle was still holding her hand, and when she felt Pearl's hand go limp she laid her forehead on the bed and cried. She cried long, wracking sobs that tore painfully from her heart. When Shelley touched her shoulder she jumped from her chair and spun around, burying her head against his chest, forgetting for a moment that she hated him.

He must have forgotten, too, because he wrapped his arms around her and comforted her with soothing hands and a low, reassuring voice.

"It's not fair," she whispered huskily, her voice strained and rough.

"I know, darlin'," Shelley said gently. "I know."

Shelley had watched Annie and little Pearl all night, not dozing in the chair as he might have, but studying the accused murderess closely.

His Annie, a killer. He'd learned long ago not to expect too much from people, not to take anything at face value. And still, it was unbelievable. He'd begun the long evening cursing his stupidity, fretting over every clue he had missed.

And then his thoughts had turned to Annie's behavior. She hadn't been able to pull the trigger of the derringer he had given her, even when her life was in danger. She'd panicked when she'd seen the scratch on his arm. She had probably, he grudgingly admitted, saved his life by stopping Swift Eagle's knife. The pretty knife he had returned to her after he stabbed the Pinkerton agent. The pretty knife she still wore strapped to her hip. It had never occurred to him not to return it to her, because he couldn't imagine her using it.

Does a woman who relies on a child's dreamcatcher for a decent night's sleep cut a man's throat? Could a woman who cries her heart out for a little girl she didn't even know take a life so easily?

Shelley buried the child beside her father, while Annabelle fashioned a crudely carved marker. She used Swift Eagle's knife to write PEARL on a scrap of wood she had found, and the wood shavings collected in her lap as she sat on the ground and turned all her attention to the task. There was a deep frown on her face, and an occasional single tear trickled down one cheek.

Her tears were all gone by the time they rode away from the shack, leaving behind two freshly turned mounds of dirt. Shelley was silent again, but not as angry as he had been. That little girl's passing had affected even his stony heart.

Chapter Twenty-seven

Shelley glanced over his shoulder at the woman who rode silently behind him, her face pale and glum.

They'd been following the Truckee River Pass for days, their progress slower than he had anticipated. Alone he could've traveled faster, but he knew Annie's limits, sensed them even though he never let on that he knew or cared how the journey across the Sierra Nevada tired her.

The death of little Pearl had affected her deeply, but he had expected her to shake off her melancholy after a day or two. She hadn't. As they had ridden away from the shack, he'd reassured her tersely that there was nothing more she could have done . . . and she'd agreed with him, her voice little more than a whisper.

After that, Annie hadn't mentioned the child again, or complained to him that life wasn't fair, but her silence was profound. She followed him. She ate. She slept. That was all.

As he set up camp by the river, Annie sat tiredly by the fire. They had taken to sleeping on opposite sides of the campfire, his head in one direction and hers in the other, so if either of them happened to glance to the side they saw nothing more than feet and tan-encased legs. They traveled like two strangers who just happened to be headed in the same direction.

He was more anxious than ever to get her on the ferry and be rid of her. In spite of everything—her lies, her blatant manipulation, the accusations he tried to convince himself were false—he still felt something for her. He wanted to comfort her, he still wanted to touch her. More than anything, he wanted to make love to her just one more time before he sent her on her way, to whatever fate awaited her in San Francisco.

"Shelley?" His name was spoken, a soft question from the other side of the fire where Annie lay. He'd believed she was asleep, she'd been still for so long.

He rolled onto his side and looked at her red boots, crossed at the ankles. "Ummm," he murmured as if he'd been asleep.

"I'm sorry. I didn't mean to wake you." Her voice was like a gentle caress. "There's something I need to tell you."

He twisted around slowly, placing his head on the opposite end of the bedroll so he could see her face. As he moved, she turned her head to the side and looked at him.

"How much longer?" she whispered.

"Couple days." He shrugged noncommittally. That

was all she wanted, to know how soon she would be done with him.

The firelight flickered on her face, soft in the undulating light, strange shadows giving her face an eerie look, reminding him of the woman he had found crouched beneath the stairs behind Oscar's place.

"I'm going to tell you what really happened." There was a dreamlike quality to her voice, and if she hadn't been looking right at him he would have believed she was talking in her sleep. "And I don't want you to interrupt me, no matter what I say."

"All right, darlin', but you don't—"

"Please, Shelley. Just listen. I haven't told anyone what happened that night . . . the night Henri died." She faced him with her head resting childlike on her hands instead of on her saddle. "It's important to me that you know the truth, and it is the truth . . . I swear."

She told him every detail, from the moment she walked off the stage to her dressing room and found Albert Gibson with the knife in his hand, and her fiancé, Henri Cuvier, dead. She told him about the accusing faces of those present at the theater. Even Pierre and Lisette, the couple who looked after her home in Paris, who traveled with her, who had become more than servants, had looked at her with stunned surprise and fear in their eyes.

Annie told him about stealing the black dress from the wardrobe room and the makeup, too. Her expression never changed, her voice never became excited. It was almost as if she were talking about someone else.

"I don't really care anymore if the world believes me or not. But I want you to believe me, Shelley. You do believe me, don't you?" There was a hint of desperation in her voice.

"I do, darlin'," he said quietly. "Why didn't you tell me before?"

Annie gave him a weak smile. "I was scared. I told you I was scared of everything."

"Even me?"

She thought about his question for a moment seriously even though he had delivered it with a smile. "No. I was never frightened of you, Shelley, and I . . . don't regret anything. No matter what happens, I don't want you to think . . ."

She stopped abruptly when he stood and made a move toward her.

"No!" she said sharply. "You stay on your side of the fire, and I'll stay on mine."

He lowered himself slowly, her sharp words stabbing at his fortressed heart. "Sure, darlin'," he said casually. "Now that you've got that off your chest, let's get some sleep."

He stayed where he was, where he could see her across the fire. She watched him unsmilingly for a moment and then turned away, the firelight dancing across her white cotton shirt and her silky hair.

"Let's go, Annie," he called to her as he started breaking camp. She hadn't moved since she'd turned her back on him hours earlier. "Coffee's boiling, and it's time to . . ."

He crossed the camp, stepping over her legs and staring down at her with his fists on his hips. His impatience faded when he saw her face. She was as white as her shirt, and there were dark circles under her eyes. Even in sleep her mouth twitched. He dropped to his knees and laid his hand on her forehead. She was burning up.

"Jesus, Annie." He smoothed back the hair that had fallen over her face and her eyes fluttered then opened.

"No." She weakly slapped his hand away.

He pulled away from her sullenly. "Listen. I know you don't want me to touch you, but you don't have any choice."

He left her, dampened a rag in the river, and then bathed her face, cursing under his breath the entire time.

He didn't know what to do. Only one other time in his life had he felt so helpless. It was a feeling he detested. He had no medicine, no inkling what kind of fever had claimed the little girl and her father, and now attacked Annie. Even if he'd known, he still wouldn't know what to do for her. Should he keep her by the river, cool her fevered skin, and hope for the best? Or should he risk traveling to San Francisco, where a doctor could care for her properly?

But there was no choice at all. If he stayed by the river she would die, just like Pearl and her father. When Annie was a bit cooler he wrapped her in a blanket and set her on his roan, against her weak objections. All their provisions were packed on her mare, which he led behind them. Annie faced him, her cheek against his chest, while his arm held her securely and his other hand controlled the reins.

"I'm cold, Shelley," she said so softly he barely heard her.

He held her tighter, making certain the blanket covered her well. She was burning up, shivering against him.

Annie lifted her hair and weakly pushed it over her shoulder, pressing her ear against his chest. She even smiled, a faint, barely perceptible smile as she closed her eyes and fell asleep.

They stayed in the saddle for most of the next 36 hours, Shelley forcing her to take sips of cool water from his canteen . . . forcing her even as she turned her head away from the offered water. He tried to feed her bites of dried apple, but she wouldn't eat.

At last they arrived at the ferry to San Francisco. He had planned to put her on board and ride away, but all that had changed. It had been five years since he'd been to the city . . . had sworn as he left that he'd never return.

"Annie." He shook her gently. She'd become too still, and he needed the assurance of looking into her eyes. "We're here, darlin'." His voice was little more than a whisper as she opened her eyes slightly.

"San Francisco? We made it?" Every word seemed to be an effort.

"We made it."

"Take me to Nicky's house," she said softly as she closed her eyes again.

He tensed. "Nicky's house?" Icky, no doubt. "I don't know where Nicky lives, darlin'."

"Big white house . . . my room is yellow," she said as she drifted away in his arms.

"Damnation," he muttered as they left the ferry

at Market Street. "A big white house with a yellow room. I guess I could go to every goddamn white house in the city and ask if someone named Nicky lives there, and if they have a yellow room. Dammit." His voice was low, and Annie slept in his arms. He'd already decided on his destination, and hurried toward it. "Wouldn't take more than two or three years."

The real reason for his agitation was her easy request to be taken to Icky . . . to her yellow room in Icky's big white house. Who the hell was he to her, anyway?

Brat.

Shelley stepped quickly up the stairs to the familiar wide front door, Annie's head lolling against his shoulder as he carried her firmly in his arms. He kicked at the heavy door several times, lowered his booted foot for no more than a second, then kicked again. It seemed like a lifetime before the door was opened slowly by Andrew.

The old man lifted his eyes to Shelley, and studied the feverish Annie as her loose hair fell over Shelley's arm. In a flash, the light of recognition came into Andrew's eyes.

"Master Travis," he said primly, opening the door wide as though it were a common occurrence to find Shelley at the entrance with an unconscious woman in his arms.

Shelley strode through the front door and straight for the wide stairway. "Bart here?" he called over his shoulder as if it had been a few days since he'd last been there and not five years.

"Master Bartholomew is out for the evening," the

elderly butler said slowly, tottering behind him.

He took the steps two at a time with Annie in his arms, and he turned when he reached the top of the stairs. He looked down on the old man who was following him up the stairway at a snail's pace.

"What room can I put her in?" He asked sharply.

"Your room is always kept ready for your return, Master Travis."

"I need a doctor, Andrew. A discreet one. And water. Bring me cool water . . . and some broth or something. Ask Rose what's good to feed somebody with a fever."

"Yes, Master Travis." Andrew turned slowly, stopped, and craned his head around. A small grin cracked his face. "And welcome home, sir."

"Thank you, Andrew." He turned toward his room. "Hurry with that water."

His room, the room he had grown up in, was unchanged. The dark blue bedspread and draperies, the forest green rugs scattered across a polished floor. There was not a speck of dust or any other sign that the room had been unoccupied for the better part of 15 years.

Rose was responsible for the impeccable condition of his room, he was certain. He couldn't remember a time when she hadn't been in this house. Cook, housekeeper, a stern woman with a loving hand and a warm heart. She'd lectured him on more than one occasion, and had cried over Sarah's deathbed.

He threw back the bedspread and lay Annie in the center of the big mattress. She was listless and pale, and her hands slid from his arms

imply. He undressed her, trying hard not to dis-
urb her rest. He slipped off the red boots and
ler tan pants, her white cotton shirt. When he
reached for the medicine bag she lifted her hand
o stop him, laying her palm over the bag, so he
eft it against her chest.

He met Andrew at the door and took an ewer of
water and a fluffy white towel, along with Andrew's
assurances that a doctor was on his way and that Rose
was preparing tea and broth.

Shelley bathed Annie, hoping to cool her fever, and
vhen he patted her skin dry he dressed her in one of
his old shirts. He'd found it in a dresser drawer, neatly
olded and ready to wear, along with all the other
clothes he'd left behind.

Annie limply allowed him to bathe and dress her,
and to feed her a spoonful of broth. When he was fin-
shed and had tucked her snugly under the covers, she
ourrowed into the pillow and slept, peacefully enough
or him to sit in the plush chair by the window and
relax for a moment.

She looked as fragile and vulnerable as little Pearl,
with her hair spread across the pillow and her long
lashes resting against her pale cheeks. Soon those eyelashes began to flutter, and she turned her head from
side to side, opening her eyes suddenly and lucidly,
and staring at him.

"Where am I?"

He grinned for the first time since she'd taken sick.
"You're in my room, in my bed."

Annie looked vacantly around the large, well-
furnished room. "I'm so tired."

He carried his chair to her bedside, keeping his

voice and his stance casual. "You just got a little fever that's all."

"The fever that killed Pearl and her father," she said already exhausted. "Don't sit so close to me, Shelley," she snapped when he lowered himself into the chair that was almost touching the bed, ignoring his frown

"Pardon me, Miss St. Clair," he said sarcastically "Should I wait in the hall?"

"Yes," she whispered, already closing her eyes and drifting into a deep sleep. "Wait in the hall."

He settled back into his chair. "Damned if I will Miss St. Clair."

Shelley had been expecting an old gray-haired doctor, one with a store of knowledge and years and year of experience. What Andrew presented to him was a man younger than Shelley, fresh-faced and anxious well dressed and smiling thinly. Dr. John Smith. Shelley had no confidence in the man, none at all.

But Dr. Smith leaned over Annie and examined her professionally, asking Shelley questions about the disease she had been exposed to. When he made a move to take the medicine bag Annie wore around her neck Shelley stopped him with a quick hand over the doctor's wrist.

"It stays," he snapped.

Dr. Smith raised one eyebrow smugly. "Why?"

"Because Annie wants it to stay."

Their eyes met for an instant before Dr. Smith pulled his away. "I don't suppose it will do any harm."

He gave Annie a dose of foul-smelling medicine, left a bottle and instructions with Shelley, assuring him that with proper care the disease should not be fatal in a young, healthy woman. Some sort of bacteria nfection, he speculated as he packed his black bag and prepared to leave.

"Doctor." He stopped the man as he was opening the door. "Annie's had a little trouble. It would be best . . ."

The young doctor smiled. "I know who she is, and you needn't worry. I won't tell a soul."

"You recognized her?" He resumed his seat by the bed. He was suddenly exhausted.

Dr. Smith turned back to him and half closed the door, as if someone might be eavesdropping. "I saw Miss St. Clair perform here in San Francisco three years ago," he whispered. "Magnificent. You don't forget a face like that."

As the doctor closed the door behind him, Shelley laid his head back and slumped in the chair, his legs extended parallel to the bed. The doctor hadn't promised that Annie would recover, but had seemed optimistic . . . and Shelley was able to close his eyes.

At one point in the night, Annie called his name . . . and he took her hand in his. She grasped it tightly, using all the strength she could muster. "Shelley," she gasped. "I don't love you, I promise." Her words were tinged with desperation.

He turned to her. "I know."

"I mean it." She squeezed his hand as tightly as she could. "I don't love you. Don't leave me."

He frowned, puzzled by her words, but too tired to give them much thought. "I'm not going anywhere."

She relaxed after that and fell into a deep sleep, her hand still resting in his. He was too exhausted to spend much time thinking about her odd statement, but it rang in his head. "I don't love you. Don't leave me." He lifted her hand and kissed it. She didn't seem as hot as before . . maybe she would recover after all.

He laid her hand gently on the bed, continued to cradle it as if it were the most fragile porcelain, and slept.

Chapter Twenty-eight

"Jesus, you look old," Shelley said as he opened his eyes to a room filled with morning light. His brother, Bart, stood at the end of the bed, looking down at him with a half smile.

"Me?" Bart grinned, and Shelley knew that anyone who knew him would know that except for their coloring this dark-haired, blue-eyed man was his brother. "You look like shit, Trav. At least I've shaved and had a bath this week."

Shelley glanced over at Annie. She was still pale, but not so hot, and she was sleeping peacefully. He released her hand slowly, allowing it to rest on top of the covers, before he stood and faced his brother.

Bart was four years younger, and Shelley had once towered over him, but now Bart was the same height, and in spite of the fact that he was a city boy his shoulders were just as wide.

Bart advanced toward Shelley, giving him a hearty hug. "Five years is too long, Trav. Why the hell don't you visit, or at the very least write so I'll know you're still alive?

"Sorry," he added casually when Shelley pulled back and glared. "At least when you do come home you do it in style. With a fabulous, wanted opera singer in tow."

He groaned. "You recognized her, too?"

Bart nodded slightly. "Yes. I saw her a few years ago. Who else knows she's here?"

"The doctor. You haven't mentioned . . ."

Bart shook his head. "No one. Rose and Andrew have been instructed to keep quiet, and the other servants have been given an unexpected paid vacation. You certainly don't have to worry about John."

"Who?"

"Dr. Smith." Bart grinned again. "I wasn't kidding. You really do look like shit. Let me have Andrew prepare a bath for you. You've got plenty of clothes here, out of style though they may be. A good meal, a shave . . ."

"Not now." He resumed his seat. "Maybe later."

Bart cocked his head to the side and looked down at Annie. "How on earth did you manage to hook up with Annabelle St. Clair?"

"Long story." He placed his hand on her forehead. She was still warm, but not terribly hot as she had been the night before.

"I don't suppose you'd want to tell me—"

"No," he said abruptly.

Annie rolled over and reached for his hand, and he took it tenderly, weaving his fingers through hers.

Bart made a low humming noise, amusement

mixed with wonder. "I'll bet it's a good one."

"Mind your own business, Bart," he said gruffly, but he had to admit it was nice to be in the same room with his brother, even if only for a short time. The reason he'd left San Francisco had nothing to do with Bart, the only family he had left. There were just some things that were too hard to face. Too hard to remember.

"Dorothea was widowed last year," Bart said without warning, and Shelley lifted his eyes to his meddling brother. Bart couldn't seem to take his eyes off Annie.

"So?"

"She keeps asking about you."

Bart had never liked Thea, and that dislike was evident in his unusually cool voice.

"When she hears that you're home—"

"She won't hear," he said coldly. As if he didn't have troubles enough.

Bart pulled his eyes away from Annie and stared down at Shelley, that infuriating grin in place. "What makes you think she won't find out? She keeps her ear to the ground, our Dorothea does."

"I won't be here that long. As soon as Annie's all right, I'm gone." He leaned back and closed his eyes. He was so damn tired.

He heard his brother's footsteps and opened one eye to look directly up into his too amused face.

"I must admit, I'm a bit envious," Bart confessed.

He closed his eye, shutting out the vision of Bart smiling down at him. "Of what?"

He opened his eyes just enough to see that Bart was staring down at Annie again.

"Let's see," Bart said lightly. "One gorgeous blonde

widow . . . one dark-haired beauty . . ."

"Wanted for murder," he added.

Bart studied Annie's sleeping face intently. "I can't believe she's capable of—"

"She isn't," he interrupted, then his eyes flew open. "Throw me that vest."

He pointed to the leather vest that rested on the dresser, caught it with his free hand when Bart tossed it to him, drew Annie's wanted poster from the pocket, and snapped it open.

Bart peeked at the paper. "Godawful likeness."

"This Albert Gibson she supposedly stabbed . . . the one who survived. He put up the reward. Is he still here in San Francisco?"

Bart shrugged his shoulders. "There were several interviews with him in the newspapers, but I haven't seen anything about him lately. I don't know if he's still—"

"Can you find out?" He looked up at his brother expectantly.

"Sure."

"By this afternoon?" He pushed.

"By noon," Bart said with a grin, leaving the room quietly.

His eyes rested on Annie's face. He could do her one more favor before he left San Francisco. He owed her that much.

Annabelle searched blindly for Shelley's hand, her hand sliding over the covers that warmed her. When she found nothing she opened her eyes narrowly, the soft afternoon light hurting her sensitive eyes, and she saw a shadowy figure at the foot of the bed.

"Shelley?" She tried to lift her head, but it was too

difficult. The man at the end of the bed moved to her side, blocking out the light, and she saw a strange face smiling down at her with a familiar grin.

Annabelle frowned. She could barely remember how she'd come to be in the bed. "Where's Shelley?"

"Who?" The dark-haired man by her bed placed his hands in his pockets and leaned forward slightly. "You just rest. You've been very ill."

He wouldn't leave her here, she knew. "He's sick, isn't he? I told him to stay away from me. I didn't want him to get sick, too." She tried to sit up, propping herself on her elbows before the man laid his hands hesitantly on her shoulders. "Where is he?"

"You mean Travis."

"No." She frowned. "I mean Shelley."

The man grinned. "Sandy hair, shaves once or twice a year, mean as a snake . . ."

She relaxed and slumped back to the pillow. "That's him. He's not sick?"

"No. He'll be back soon, I promise."

"Travis," she said dreamily. She was already ready to fall asleep again. "Is that his real name?"

The man's broad shoulders rose and fell. "Yes. What did you call him? Shelley?"

She looked around the bedroom with its high ceilings and gilt-framed mirrors, polished wood and arched windows. "Like the poet. Where am I?"

"My home. Travis's home, too, though he's rarely here." He took the chair by the bed.

"This is Shelley's home?" She could barely keep her eyes open, and she couldn't believe what she was hearing.

He nodded. "I'll let him tell you all about it when he returns." He tucked the covers tightly around her, and frowned as he touched his hand briefly to her forehead. "Damned if you're not a bit warmer than you were when Travis left. Sleep, my dear."

She was glad to oblige, but before she closed her eyes she asked the stranger with the oddly familiar face one more question. "Who are you?"

There was that grin she knew so well. "I've spent so much time hovering around this bed I forgot that we-'ve never been properly introduced. Pardon my atrocious manners, Miss St. Clair. I'm Travis's brother, Bartholomew Shelton."

It was dark before Shelley returned to the quiet house.

"It's about time," Bart growled when Shelley opened the door to his bedroom.

His smile faded when he saw Bart's consternation. "She's worse?"

"Yes, she's worse," Bart snapped. "And I can't get her to take her medicine, and she slapped my hand when I tried to bathe her face. This is really not my forte, Trav."

He ignored his brother and leaned over Annie. His palm on her forehead made him curse, and he reached for the medicine on the bedside table.

"Come on, darlin'." He measured out the medicine and lifted her head. Annie cooperated and took the medicine he poured down her throat, never even opening her eyes.

"Shelley?" she whispered.

"Right here, darlin'." He dampened a rag and cooled her hot face. Annie was completely relaxed in his arms, and Bart shook his head dismally.

"I thought you'd left me again." Her eyes opened

slightly. "I told you I didn't love you," she admonished.

"You did." He wiped the cool cloth across her throat. "I don't love you, too."

Annie smiled. "Then you don't have to leave."

He rolled up the sleeves of her old shirt and bathed her arms, then dried them tenderly before rolling her sleeves down again. What to tell her, and when?

"I've got some news for you, Annie," he said as he finished bathing her and tucked the covers around her. "That fella who said you stabbed him? Albert Gibson?"

Annie's eyes flew open, and he almost swore at the terror he saw there.

"No. It's all right." He brushed loose tendrils of hair away from her face, unable to keep his hands away from her. "He went to the police and told the truth . . . that he killed your fiancé and stabbed himself, and tried to place the blame on you. He told it all, darlin'. You're no longer a wanted woman."

"I wouldn't exactly say that," Bart said under his breath, and Shelley shot him a piercing glare. "Sorry, Trav," he apologized insincerely.

"You can go, Bart," he said sharply. "Thanks for keeping an eye on her."

"Do I have to go?" his brother asked, rising slowly. "This is just getting interesting."

"Is it true, Shelley?" Annie asked, ignoring Shelley and Bart's exchange. "Albert told the truth?"

He nodded. "Yep. He's in jail . . . right now."

"Why?" Annie was barely lucid, and was having trouble keeping her eyes open. "Why now, after all this time?"

He took her hand in his and caressed it absently. "Guilty conscience?"

Slightly frowning, he watched her fall asleep, her hand resting comfortably in his.

Albert Gibson was lucky to be alive. When Shelley had looked at the little man's smug face he'd wanted to kill him then and there, but that wouldn't have helped Annie.

Guilty conscience? As far as he could see, the man didn't have a conscience at all. The little man who accused Annie of murder and attempted murder also had no guts, no class, and no common sense.

Shelley had grabbed Gibson by the collar and dragged him to the police station, the weasely man protesting the entire time. Gibson had never stopped complaining . . . not until Shelley presented him to the San Francisco police and told Gibson, in a clear and calm voice, that if he used his tongue for anything other than telling the truth he'd find himself without it.

Gibson then told how he'd killed Annie's fiancé when the unfortunate man discovered that Gibson had been syphoning her fortune and earnings for years. As he told the story with Shelley's hand on his neck, he had admitted that the safety of a jail cell now seemed inviting.

Shelley had mixed emotions about the outcome. Annie was free . . . free to return to the stage, to return to Icky. She didn't need him anymore. Didn't want him. Reminded him often enough that she didn't love him.

It was her worst night thus far. She was restless and her fever remained high. Shelley cooled her as best he could, and forced tea and Dr. Smith's medicine down her throat. He talked to her, recited poems, bawdy limericks, to her half the night.

Near dawn her fever broke, and she began to sweat. When she opened her eyes he smiled down at her, and she frowned and jerked her hand away.

"What are you doing here?" she asked ungraciously.

He sat back and crossed his arms over his chest. "Takin' care of your ungrateful ass."

It appeared she would survive after all, and he began to think about leaving. Back across the Sierra Nevada . . . maybe south to Mexico. He hadn't been to Mexico in years.

As he silently made his plans, he became aware of the softening of Annie's face. She smiled weakly, but her eyes sparkled . . . clear for the first time in days.

"I'm not ungrateful, Shelley," she said softly. "I don't want you to get this sickness. I don't want you to die."

He leaned forward and took her hand, the hand he had held for days. "I'm too mean to get sick, and nobody's going to die." He almost wished he could have left believing she hated him, wanted to push him away. If only he could believe that she was as cold-hearted as he had thought for a short time. Knowing that she cared for him, even a little, made it hard to turn his back on her. But he would.

Annie looked around the room. "I remember bits and pieces . . . that this is your room? That your name is really Travis?" She gave him another small smile. "And you took care of me."

A new sparkle lit her eyes. "Was it a dream? Did you tell me that Albert had confessed?"

"Yes I did, darlin'."

She laughed and threw her arms around his neck in a burst of energy he wouldn't have thought her capable of. "Thank heavens. It's over. I never could have made it without you."

"Sure you could have." He held her head against his shoulder. "You're brave, remember? A real white warrior woman."

He was glad she couldn't see his face as she nestled against his chest. Yes, it really was over. She didn't need him anymore.

Chapter Twenty-nine

When Annabelle woke later that morning after a few restful hours of sleep, the first thing she saw were three different San Francisco newspapers spread across the foot of the bed. The headlines were basically the same. "Diva Innocent!," "Annabelle St. Clair Vindicated," "Alleged Victim Confesses." She stared at the newspapers, and a smile grew slowly.

"Good morning, Miss St. Clair," Bartholomew Shelton said cheerily, sitting in a chair, a relaxed grin on his face.

She pulled the covers up around her chin. "Good morning, Mr. Shelton. Where's Shelley?"

He shook his head. "Oh, please, call me Bart. As for my brother I finally convinced him he could take a bath and sleep in a bed for a couple of hours and you wouldn't waste away. You're looking much better, by the way."

"Thank you." He was looking at her so piercingly that it made her nervous. "It's not necessary for you to sit with me. I'm fine, really. A little tired . . ."

"I don't dare leave this room," Bart said seriously. "Travis made me swear that I wouldn't leave you alone."

"Travis." Annabelle smiled. "That sounds so strange."

They stared at one another silently for a moment, and then Bart lifted the paper he had been reading. "You're quite a celebrity. All the papers are speculating on where you're hiding and when you'll reappear."

She sighed. "All I ever wanted to do was sing. I never cared about the money or the fame . . . and I certainly never asked for this." She indicated the papers at her feet with her finger.

Bart dropped the *San Francisco Chronicle* and leaned forward expectantly. "I'd love to hear the entire story."

She shook her head timidly. "I don't think I'll ever be able to talk about what happened."

Obviously disappointed, Bart sat back in his chair. She rolled onto her side and faced him. "I know. Why don't you tell me about Shelley? I don't understand him at all. Why doesn't he live here in San Francisco? Why is he so . . . so stubborn?"

Bart grinned, and it was Shelley's grin, easy and charming. "I have an idea. You tell me about your adventures of the past several months, and I'll tell you everything you ever wanted to know about Travis."

"You are Shelley's brother, aren't you?" she said accusingly. "Always wanting to make a deal, a trade."

Leaning back in his chair, his legs thrust forward, he continued to smile. "I suppose that's true."

She kept her eyes on Shelley's brother. They were so alike, and yet so different. Bart was darkly handsome, and impeccably dressed in black and gray, his suit perfectly fitted, his black boots polished to a high shine. He crossed his feet at his ankles and his arms over his chest just like Shelley. It was eerie.

Bart was happy to relate to her all the transgressions of his brother's youth, proving that Shelley had always been stubborn and willful. Her spirits were lifted as she pictured Shelley as a young boy . . . defying his father at every turn, horrifying his mother with daring feats and bloody accidents. None of them life-threatening . . . all of them unnecessary.

"Are your parents living?" she asked, and Bart lost his smile for the first time.

"No. They both died several years ago."

"Why did Shelley leave all this behind for . . . for the life he leads?"

Bart leaned forward. "Not so fast. Your turn."

She laid her head against the pillows and looked at the ceiling as she told Bart how she had met Shelley . . . how he had pretended to be drunk and punched the Pinkerton agent who was searching for her . . . about the huge black dress and the pasty makeup she wore . . . how Shelley had tossed her makeup into the pond.

"Tell me why Shelley left San Francisco," she said, turning to look at Bart again.

His smile faded. "What if I tell you about the time he tried to climb the Mintons' trellis to get into Melody Minton's room? He was fifteen . . ."

"No," she said sternly. "I want to know why he left San Francisco."

Bart stared at her for a moment. "He'll kill me if he

281

finds out I told you," he said with resignation, moving the chair to her bedside. "Did you know Travis fought in the war?" he asked in a low tone.

She shook her head.

"I'm not surprised he didn't tell you. He doesn't like to talk about it. Of course, he fought for the Union. He was only eighteen when he left. Got himself engaged. He wanted to go ahead and get married, but his fiancée Dorothea, was just seventeen, and her parents urged them to wait. They didn't think he would be gone more than a few months. None of us did. But it was four years.

"Dorothea wrote faithfully, or so she said. Travis never mentioned if her devotion was as undying as she claimed it was. But it was Sarah who missed him the most."

"Who's Sarah?"

Bart smiled, but it wasn't his easy grin. It was a sad smile of remembrance. "Our little sister.

"Poor Travis. He and Sarah were so close, and he . . ." Bart combed his perfectly styled hair with his fingers, mussing it slightly. "God. Travis will kill me."

"Finish what you've started."

"Travis didn't have much of a homecoming. Sarah had been shot the day before he arrived . . . the day before! It was so senseless . . . she was shopping, and these men came storming out of the bank, firing at everything that moved, and Sarah took a bullet in the chest."

There were tears in Annabelle's eyes. "How terrible."

"She was still alive when Travis got home, but she died a few hours later. I think she was just waiting to see him again. Travis was . . ." He searched her eyes as she held her breath expectantly. "He was devastated, and furious. He blamed himself for not arriving sooner. Said if he'd been home it never would have happened."

"That's not fair."

"Well, Travis has always been harder on himself than anyone else." He frowned. "He went after the bank robbers, and caught them. I'll never forget the afternoon he walked back into this house. He tossed a wad of money on the table in the foyer. There was blood . . . blood on his shirt and his hands . . . dried and forgotten.

"Dorothea was here, waiting for him to return. He'd been gone four days, and she waited from sunup to sundown each and every day. But when he did finally arrive . . . he terrified her. He tossed the money on the table and growled, 'That's what four lives are worth, Bart. Sarah and those three outlaws. Eight hundred dollars.' "

"His first bounty," she whispered sadly.

Bart nodded. "Yes. Dorothea ran from the house, broke the engagement, and married someone else. She said Travis had changed too much, that he wasn't the man she'd agreed to marry. Travis went to Mexico for a year, came back for a few weeks, disappeared again. He reappeared for a couple of weeks five years ago . . . I haven't seen or heard from him since then, until he showed up with you."

She wiped away a tear that rolled down her cheek. "Poor Shelley."

"Don't ever let him hear you say that," Bart said quickly. "It was a long time ago," he added.

"But . . . but Dorothea. Didn't she realize what Shelley was going through? Did she think that he could fight in a bloody war for four years and not come back a changed man? What a heartless . . . cold . . ."

"Bitch," Bart finished for her. "I don't know what Travis saw in her in the first place."

Annabelle searched Bart's face solemnly. It was a good face, much like Shelley's, and the memories obviously pained him. After all, Sarah had been his sister, too. He had lost her and his only brother. One dead, the other running away.

"Miss St. Clair . . ." Bart began.

"Annie . . . or Annabelle, please."

"Annabelle. I might be sticking my nose in where it doesn't belong, but it won't be the first time." He leaned forward conspiratorily. "Travis told me that he's leaving as soon as you're well."

"Leaving?"

He nodded. "Maybe you should lean back and . . . take it easy for a few more days. I don't suppose you could manage to look a bit paler?"

Chapter Thirty

"Where is he, Bartholomew?" The haughty blonde in an impeccable blue day dress swept into the library with the air of supreme confidence she'd carried well since she was fourteen.

Bart looked up from his desk, always happy for any diversion that freed him from his endless paperwork. A wicked smile crossed his face. There hadn't been this much excitement in the house for years. "Dorothea." He rose and crossed the room to take her hand and kiss it gallantly. "Whatever do you mean?"

She pushed his hand away and scowled. "I know Travis is back. Why didn't you tell me?"

Bart led the tall blonde to an overstuffed chair and lowered himself in the matching chair beside her. He gave her a pitiful look, an insincere frown. "I've felt so guilty. He made me promise not to tell anyone. How did you find out?"

"Servants talk, Bartholomew. You know that," she snapped.

"Then you know"—He leaned forward and whispered—"that he didn't come home alone."

Dorothea's face reddened. "The opera singer. Yes, I heard."

"Have you . . ."

"Not a soul. I've not even told Herbert."

His smile faded at the very mention of Dorothea's sour brother's name. Herbert was all business, to a fault. He was no fun at all, had no sense of adventure. If he knew, San Francisco would know. Herbert would see to it.

"Then you understand, Dorothea . . ."

The blonde had regained her composure, and smiled at him. It was a small smile, one that would not add wrinkles to her perfect face. "I saw her the last time she sang in San Francisco. She's talented, I suppose, but I don't know what Travis could possibly see in that chubby little girl. Does he know I'm . . . a widow?"

Bart leaned back in his chair. She might as well have asked, "Does he know I'm available?" "I told him." He wanted to tell her that Travis didn't care, and in truth, he didn't seem to. But no one knew better than Bart that his brother had a weakness for Dorothea. A weakness Bart didn't understand. She was beautiful. Possibly the most beautiful woman he'd ever met. But she was also cold and calculating.

"Well?" she asked impatiently. "Is he here?"

"Not at the moment."

Bart relaxed. Perhaps he could turn Dorothea's visit to their advantage. Time was running out. Annabelle had attempted to pretend that she was weaker than she really was, but she wasn't very good at lying to Travis. All he had to do was look at her and frown, and she tried to convince him that she was all right. And she couldn't disguise the fact that her color was returning, and her eyes sparkled. Any day now Travis might decide to disappear, and it could be years before he returned. If he ever did.

"I must see him," Dorothea pleaded. "Marrying Lewis was a terrible mistake . . . I knew it less than a month after we were married. I lived with that mistake for ten years. There weren't any children to fill the lonely hours. When I saw Travis five years ago, I knew there would never be another man for me. I can convince him that we belong together. He still loves me. I know he does."

Dorothea didn't wear her desperation well. Her face flushed and her blue eyes darted from side to side as she avoided his stare. Perhaps she knew he recognized her for what she really was—a rich, bored, spoiled princess, longing for what she had thrown aside years earlier.

"I don't know, Dorothea," he said, indecisively grimacing. "It's been a long time. Travis has . . . changed."

He and Dorothea heard Annabelle's voice at the same time, as she tiptoed down the staircase calling for Shelley. If Bart had been less composed he would have laughed out loud. How perfect! He couldn't have planned it any better himself, and he was a master schemer.

He went to the doorway and called Annabelle in, taking her arm as she entered the room. She'd left her hair down, and it looked as if it had been brushed until it was like silk, straight and thick. She was wearing, and oh how perfect this was, one of Travis's shirts over her tight britches, the loose shirt tied at her waist with a red sash she had obviously found in one of his drawers. A pair of his socks, sagging and much too large, covered her feet. She looked absolutely charming.

"Annabelle St. Clair." Bart led her to the chair he had occupied earlier. "I'd like you to meet an old family friend. Dorothea Cole. She heard Travis was in town and stopped by to see him."

Annabelle graciously greeted the blonde who was visibly shocked. Bart knew Annabelle's appearance had completely thrown Dorothea. There was no sign of the chubby little girl she had mentioned seeing just three years ago.

"Where is he?" Annabelle looked up at him, her smile fading. "When I woke up and he wasn't there . . ."

"He said he was going to town and would be back this afternoon." It was all Bart could do to contain his laughter. Dorothea's face was red, and her lips were pursed tightly. She was unaccustomed to competition.

The stately blonde perched on the edge of her chair, her calculating eyes riveted on Annabelle. "I understand you've had quite an adventure, Miss St. Clair."

Annabelle turned cool eyes to her. "More adventure than I expected to see in a lifetime," she said conversationally. "If it hadn't been for Shelley, I probably wouldn't be here today." She smiled sweetly.

"Who's Shelley?"

Annabelle laughed, a light, musical sound. "I can't get accustomed to calling him Travis. He'll always be Shelley to me." Her words, though innocent, implied an intimacy in their relationship.

Dorothea smiled, and the two women sat there,

grinning cattily at one another, and the chill in the room almost caused Bart to shiver.

"Travis is so kind to those who are less fortunate." Dorothea broke the strained silence. "He always was. I remember how he would bring home birds with broken wings, and kittens who'd been abandoned. He'd fix them up and let them go, or fatten them up and find them a good home. That's just his nature."

My God, Bart thought, the woman could lie, and with such a straight face.

With an unconcerned flick of her hand, Annabelle tossed a strand of her thick hair over her shoulder. If not for the flash of her eyes, he would have thought her unaffected by Dorothea's comment. But instead of reacting angrily, she laid her hand in her lap and cocked her head to one side. "Well, Shelley certainly took excellent care of me when I was . . . well, when I was having difficulties."

Dorothea relaxed visibly. "You must be anxious to return to a normal life . . . back to your career. Paris? Isn't that where you make your home? Such a beautiful city."

"I'm not at all anxious to leave San Francisco," Annabelle said distinctly. "It has a beauty all its own . . . don't you agree?"

A heavy silence fell, and Bart grinned. He couldn't have helped it even if he'd wanted to.

"I have an idea!" he exclaimed. "Since you're feeling so much better, let's have a small dinner party." This was simply too entertaining to allow it to end. "Tomorrow night. You'll come, won't you, Dorothea? All hush hush, of course. Annabelle doesn't want the press to know just yet where she is, you know."

Annabelle lifted an exasperated face to him. "I don't think—"

"What a wonderful suggestion," Dorothea said, standing as though ready to leave. "And you have my assurance I won't breathe a word to anyone, Miss St. Clair."

Annabelle glared at him. "Shelley won't like—"

"Nonsense," he declared, and before he could continue his protestations, Travis entered the room, his countenance dark and frowning, his boots striking against the polished floor with a vengeance.

"Where is she?" he demanded.

Dorothea smiled victoriously. "Travis, darling. you saw my carriage. . . . "

Bart stepped aside, and Travis's eyes landed on Annabelle, her unsmiling eyes lifted to him. His face relaxed when he saw her. "Jesus, Annie. You scared the hell out of me. You're supposed to be in bed."

Annabelle smiled faintly. "I was looking for you."

Travis didn't spare a glance for Dorothea, or for Bart. He crossed the room to Annabelle and took her hand. "Let's go. Back to bed with you."

"I feel much better, really Shelley," she insisted even as he bent to pick her up. "You don't have to carry me." But she smiled as he lifted her, and she wrapped her arms around his neck.

Travis finally turned to Bart and Dorothea with Annabelle in his arms, her head on his shoulder. "Hello, Thea," he said, giving her a halfhearted glance. "Bart." He glared at him. "Later."

With that Travis turned his back on them and strode away with Annabelle in his grasp as if it were an ordinary, everyday occurrence. Near the doorway he bent his head to whisper something in Annabelle's ear, and in response she laughed, low and intimate, and swung one foot lazily in the air.

Bart maintained his composure, but it was difficult. He couldn't have choreographed it better himself. Dorothea was fuming. Travis had all but ignored her. Annabelle had been gorgeous and enchanting, and it was clear Travis didn't have eyes for anyone else.

Bart followed as Dorothea stormed from the room after Travis and Annabelle disappeared. From the foyer they heard Travis's heavy footsteps in the upstairs hallway, and the sound of a door being kicked shut.

With her hand on the doorknob, Dorothea turned to face him. "Tomorrow, Bartholomew." It was clear she'd taken Annabelle's presence as a challenge.

"Eightish?" he asked blandly. Inside, his emotions were in turmoil. Annabelle might be winning, but Dorothea was not one to be dismissed lightly. She was a shrewd woman. A calculating woman.

She had regained her composure. Bart knew that Annabelle had taken her by surprise that afternoon, but tomorrow would be different. Tomorrow, Dorothea would be prepared.

"I've waited too long for Travis to come home to allow some little twit to steal him away," she said coldly. Then she smiled at him confidently. "See you tomorrow, Bartholomew."

Her smile chilled him to the bone.

Chapter Thirty-one

Annabelle opened her eyes, suddenly wide awake. The big house was completely quiet. She turned her head to the side and there he was, sleeping in his chair by the window, the moonlight behind him casting soft light over his tawny hair. Her dreamcatcher was propped in that window, its weblike form eerie in the moonlight.

Shelley still insisted on staying with her, though whenever she commanded it he left the room. But when she woke he was there, having slipped in quietly during the night. As she watched he turned his head so that the moonlight hit his face, and a muscle twitched in his cheek. The smile that had stolen over her face as she watched him disappeared, and she swung her bare legs over the side of the bed. She still slept in one of Shelley's old shirts. It was long on her, falling to her knees, and it was more comfortable than any nightdress she had ever worn, cool, open at the neck, loose and soft.

She stood over him for a moment, watching his face. He was having a bad dream, or at least sleeping badly, and his mouth was twisted into a frown and his eyes moved frantically beneath their lids.

"Shelley," she whispered, crawling into his lap, her legs dangling from the arm of the padded chair, her arms snaking around his neck. She pressed her lips to his cheek, then rubbed her cheek gently against the bristles there. "Wake up, Shelley," she whispered again.

He came awake slowly, not startled or jumpy. His arms found their way around her, and it seemed the most natural thing in the world to wake and find her in his lap, kissing his cheek, whispering his name.

"You were having a bad dream." She snuggled against his chest.

"I was?" Shelley leaned back his head and closed his eyes. He was going to miss her. Too damn much. "I don't remember." It was true that he could recall nothing of the nightmare that had plagued him. He only knew that he hadn't slept well in the house of his birth since Sarah had died there. If he'd believed in ghosts, even a little, he would have thought himself haunted by his little sister.

Annabelle slithered up, kissing the base of his throat and the side of his neck with faint brushes of her lips. She slid her arms down from his neck and started unbuttoning his shirt. Her lips traveled up his neck to his strong jaw and finally to his mouth.

Her lips on his were like an electric shock, the skin on his chest burning where her fingers played. "What are you doing?" he whispered when she pulled her lips away from his to kiss his bare torso.

"If you don't know, I must be doing something wrong," she breathed huskily. "Make love to me, Shelley."

"Goddamn it, Annie." He jumped out of the chair with her in his arms. "Don't do this to me." He tried to drop her onto the bed, but she refused to unlock her arms which held him firmly around the neck.

"I'm not trying to do anything *to* you. I'm trying to do something *with* you." Annie held her face close to his. "I can't believe you don't want it, too."

He tried again and failed to deposit her on the bed. "You've been sick."

"I'm all better."

"Everything's different . . ."

"Nothing's changed," she whispered, and lifted her lips to his. "You're still my passion."

He dropped his knee to the bed, his resolve eroding. One more night . . . Annie was free to do as she pleased. She was fully recovered. She could go back to doing what she loved—singing—and he could leave San Francisco behind again. What would it hurt if he spent one more night in her arms?

He tumbled her onto the bed, landing beside her and bouncing lightly as he started to undress her, the buttons flying through his hands as he expertly freed her from the restraints of his old shirt. She was grinning, a self-assured grin that said "I won" as surely as if she'd shouted it from the rooftop.

Once free of the nightshirt, Annabelle sat beside him and finished undressing him. It had been a long time—much too long—since she'd felt his body against hers. She was hungry for him. Hungry for the touch of his skin against hers, his hands on her body, his lips . . .

She wrapped her arms around his neck and kissed him passionately, every fiber of her being, her heart, her soul, her body, his for the taking. They lay side by side on the big bed, her breasts against his chest, her leg over his hip. They kissed, and kissed, and she didn't ever want to tear her lips away from his. Shelley sucked on her bottom lip, teased her with his tongue, moaned when she did the same to him.

He pulled away from her and lowered his head, kissing her throat, trailing his lips across her skin until his mouth found her taut nipple and then another. When he drew her into his mouth she whispered his name, and her hips moved toward him, rocking gently, until he rolled her onto her back and she spread her legs for him as he held himself above her.

She opened her eyes, and they met the hazel eyes above her that delved into her very soul. She was his. He was hers. He held her there, prisoner of his gaze, as he entered her, torturously slow in his deliberation.

She raised her hips to him enticingly and wrapped her legs around his hips, pulling him ever father inside her as she clung to him. She started to cry out his name when her climax began, and he smothered her scream with a deep kiss. Searching, complete, perfect. Her release tore through her body on endless waves, and she felt Shelley join her in that sweet torture, their lips still locked together, their bodies wondrously joined.

It was so perfect she wanted to cry. She loved him. Of course, she'd known that for a long time, just as she knew that her love was the last thing he wanted. She wanted to take his face in her hands and tell him how much she loved him . . . that she never wanted to be apart from him . . . that she wanted to sleep with him each night, wake every morning to that grin of his, have his babies. But she couldn't tell him any of that, or he would run . . . run so far and so fast that she'd never see him again.

Shelley rolled onto his side and brought her with him, her head resting on his shoulder. He should have realized what was happening. He'd fallen in love with her, and that was the worst thing in the world that could have happened. For her and for him. She was Annabelle St. Clair, and she belonged in San Francisco, and New York, and Paris. She was at home in silk dresses and satin slippers, at dinner parties and the opera. That was who she was. He was just Shelley. A bounty hunter with too much blood on his hands. He was at home in Cheyenne and Kansas City and Brayton. Sometimes he lived with nothing more than dust over his head, one change of clothes if he was lucky, and a bottle of tequila in his saddlebag.

They had no future together. It was good that she didn't love him, that she called him her passion instead of her love. How many times during her illness had she grabbed his hand and said, "I don't love you, Shelley." Enough for him to know it was true. That was good. She wouldn't be hurt when he left.

But he would be. It was going to hurt one hell of a lot. Annie lowered her head and rested her ear against his chest. He brushed the wealth of dark hair that covered his chest away from her face so he could see her clearly, a slice of moonlight across her face.

"Can I sleep here, Shelley?" she whispered, already closing her eyes.

He ran his fingers though her silken hair. "Anything you want, darlin'. Anything you want."

Annabelle turned around, and around again. She was so confused. There were gowns everywhere— tossed over Shelley's chair, laid across the bed. Matching slippers lined the dresser in a neat row, shimmering footwear in every color she could imagine. And now she had to choose.

Lisette had been selecting Annabelle's clothing for her since she had turned thirteen. And tonight . . . tonight was so very important. Somehow she had to convince Shelley to stay. After the night they'd shared, that shouldn't be a problem, but she was unsure. She hadn't seen him all day. He'd been gone when she awakened, absent from her bed, missing from his chair by the window. As soon as the breakfast tray Andrew had brought her had been cleared away, Bart had arrived with a tiny older woman, a discreet dressmaker who took Annabelle's measurements, mumbled under her breath about the lack of time, and smiled slightly when Bart pressed a wad of bills into her hands.

The result surrounded her . . . readymade dresses, surely, but taken in here and there so they fit her perfectly. She was so overwhelmed with choices that she developed a nagging headache that refused to go away. When Rose knocked softly on the door late in the afternoon, Annabelle practically dragged her into the room.

"I'll be helping you prepare for the evening," Rose said primly, frowning at the disarray around her. "Have you decided what to wear?"

Annabelle shook her head.

Rose looked over the array of colors spread across the room. "They're all beautiful. You'll look lovely in any one of them, Miss St. Clair."

"But it has to be perfect," she said desperately, chewing on her lower lip.

A slight rise of her left eyebrow was Rose's only response.

"Not the red," Annabelle said, grabbing the red silk dress from the bed and tossing it aside. It reminded her too much of Cherry Red . . . that little tramp. "I don't look good in pink." That gown landed on top of the red one. A lavender gown followed that one, and Rose discarded a green silk for being much too dark. Within minutes they had narrowed their choices to two gowns, a sapphire blue and a champagne silver.

Annabelle held up the gowns, one after the other, unable to decide. She looked at Rose beseechingly, and the older woman came to her rescue.

Rose laid the two gowns side by side on the bed and they studied them intently. The sapphire blue was low cut and had a full skirt, a flounce at the hem. The champagne was a sleeker, off-the-shoulder style, the material shot with gold threads that caught the light.

"This one," Rose said, lifting the blue gown, "if you want to impress Master Bartholomew." She laid it down and lifted the champagne gown. "This one for Master Travis."

Annabelle smiled for the first time that afternoon, and her headache vanished. "Thank you, Rose." She impulsively threw her arms around the stunned woman's shoulders. "This one it is." She tossed the blue gown over Shelley's chair with the other discarded gowns, and laid the gown she would wear for Shelley across the bed. "Do you really think he'll like it?"

Rose smiled, and wrinkles formed on her face. "I have a feeling it wouldn't matter if you went down dressed in another of Master Travis's shirts and a baggy pair of trousers. But in that gown, you will be irresistible."

Annabelle's smile faded. "What do you think Dorothea Cole will wear?"

"Something garish and in poor taste, no doubt." Rose's suddenly stern face and clipped speech gave away her unkind thoughts about the woman. "You will put Mrs. Cole to shame no matter what you wear." Rose pursed her lips into a tight grimace. "I'm afraid I owe you an apology, Miss St. Clair. It's my fault that Mrs. Cole found out that Master Travis was home, and that you were with him. It was not my intention to spread rumors. You see, I've been . . . well, I spend an occasional day off walking or picnicking with Mrs. Cole's butler, William."

"And you mentioned it to him?" she offered when Rose paused.

Rose nodded, blushing. "I'm terribly sorry."

"I suppose our meeting was inevitable—if not now, in this house, then at a later date. I certainly don't blame you, Rose," she added when she saw the older woman's stricken face. "She's not a particularly warm person, is she?"

Rose shook her head. "No, miss. I meant what I said earlier. You needn't worry about Mrs. Cole."

Annabelle couldn't share Rose's conviction. The cool blonde who had sat across from her in the library just the day before was regal in her carriage, confident, and Shelley had once loved her enough to marry her. And now she wanted him back. Annabelle had butterflies in her stomach, worse than any stage

fright, worse than any pre-audition nerves. There
were many parts for a talented singer . . . but only one
Shelley.

"I should shoot you for this," Shelley said with a bite
in his voice that would have made another man
cringe, but Bart smiled and straightened his older
brother's starched collar. "What were you thinking?"

"Wasn't thinking," he confessed. "I looked at the two
of them sitting there . . . and I couldn't allow it to end.
It was fascinating. Before I knew what was happening, my mouth opened and I asked Dorothea to dinner. Annabelle tried to stop me, I'll give her that, but
I refused to listen. Oh, I asked John—Dr. Smith—to
join us as well. Make it more of a party. No one else
knows about Annabelle being here, so—"

"All right," Shelley snapped. "Jesus, don't you ever
shut up?"

He backed away, feigned hurt on his face. "But my
life is so boring when you're away. Don't deny me—"

"Bullshit," Shelley said slowly. "Boring my ass.
You're the same old Bart you always were . . . out
every night . . . don't need to work, just spend all your
time spending money. Aren't you afraid one day it will
run out and you'll actually have to earn a dollar?"

Bart crossed his arms over his chest and gave his
brother an exaggerated look of disbelief. "I'm crushed.
I've made some fabulous investments, and I manage
my money quite well, thank you."

Shelley smiled, the same lopsided grin Bart himself
used on occasion. "You're a rake, Bart. A rich one, but
a rake just the same. Why don't you marry some sweet
little thing who will keep you in line and help you
spend your money?"

"I've been thinking about that." His smile faded. "Seriously. I'm not getting any younger, and it doesn't look like you have any intention of carrying on the Shelton family name . . . unless you've changed your mind? Do you plan to stay this time? Settle down?"

"Hell, no," Shelley spat. "Annie's feeling better. I'll be leaving any day now." He looked into a gilt-framed mirror and pulled on the restricting sleeves of the black evening jacket he had borrowed from Bart. "Tomorrow, maybe the next day."

Bart refused to look at his brother as he poured a glass of bourbon and studied it intently. "What about Annabelle?"

He faced the long bar, a stiff back to Shelley. The study was quiet for a few long moments, the air heavy with Shelley's indecision and his own anticipation.

"She'll be all right," Shelley said, his words clipped and gruff.

Bart downed his bourbon in one swallow. It wasn't working. His brother, his only family, would disappear again, and this time who knew if he'd ever come back?

"So you wouldn't mind if I . . . courted her, after you leave?" he asked as casually as he could.

"I wouldn't mind at all," Shelley said coolly.

Bart smiled as he turned around. "Fabulous." He raised a newly filled glass. "You say you'll be leaving tomorrow?"

"Or the next day," Shelley said tiredly, his eyes hooded.

Annabelle spent the remaining hours of the afternoon getting ready for the dinner party. She soaked in a hot bath scented with oils Rose provided for her.

Rose washed her hair, and when it was dry she styled it expertly, arranging it atop Annabelle's head, a few tendrils curling over her shoulder.

Thankfully Rose, having employed several girls to prepare the dinner, spent most of the afternoon with her. In between treks to the kitchen to supervise, Rose tried to build up her confidence, assuring her that Master Travis would certainly not have eyes for Dorothea Cole with Annabelle in the room, and it was she who finally slipped the champagne gown on Annabelle's form as Annabelle stared at herself in the mirror.

She'd never had a figure like this. Lisette had been trying to fatten her up since she was sixteen, and had done a good job of it. She insisted Annabelle needed more energy than other young ladies if she was to become an opera star. The pounds Lisette had worked so hard to pack on her had melted away in the months since that fateful night in New York, and Annabelle had a trim shape that almost shocked her.

"Magnificent," Rose declared when their work was complete. "Master Travis doesn't have a chance."

Annabelle took a deep breath and squared her shoulders. Her stomach fluttered. Nerves. A performer of her experience shouldn't be suffering from nerves . . . not for a small dinner party.

Shelley was waiting for Annabelle at the bottom of the wide staircase, dressed in his evening clothes, his face freshly shaven. When she was halfway down the stairs he grinned at her and held his breath, even as he smiled at her. At his first sight of her his chest had tightened, a slender hand clutching at his heart. He was like a weak-kneed sixteen-year-old getting his first good look at a truly beautiful woman, and he knew if he tried to speak nothing but drivel would come out of his mouth.

She stopped on the last step and faced him, her face barely upturned to his. He took her hands and kissed each one, and when he dropped his hands he held onto her slender fingers and leaned forward tentatively for a gentle kiss. It was a tender lover's kiss.

Annie moved back one step, continuing to hold his hands and spreading her arms wide. A bright smile lit her face.

"Look at us, Shelley."

Chapter Thirty-two

Bart sat at the head of the table grinning like a naughty little boy, which he readily admitted that at heart he really was. Travis sat to his left, Annabelle to his right. Dorothea was seated next to Travis, and an obviously adoring Dr. John Smith was at Annabelle's right. The doctor's eyes hardly left Annabelle all evening, and every time she opened her mouth he was enrapt.

If looks could kill, poor Annabelle would have been done in the moment Dorothea had entered the room and sent her a frosty glare. The statuesque blonde was faultlessly dressed, as always, Bart noted, having chosen a dark blue gown that accentuated her eyes. She was elegant and sparkled almost as much as her sapphire and diamond necklace and matching earrings did. Travis barely gave her a second look.

"Miss St. Clair." John leaned closer to her, transparently grateful for the excuse to move nearer the object of his affections. "Do you plan to, perhaps, write about your adventures of the past several months?" His eyes were wide, his attention on the beautiful singer complete as he awaited her answer.

Annabelle's eyes met Travis's across the table, and they both began to laugh. Bart laughed too, not really knowing why, and Dorothea looked on furiously, her eyes narrowed. The doctor looked simply confused.

"Many journals have been published, tales of pioneers making their way west. Women, primarily," John continued. "Surely someone as well known as yourself, falsely accused of murder, fleeing alone across the country . . ." He stopped. Travis was glaring at him, his laughter dying.

Bart wondered, for a moment, if he should interfere. But he remained silent, awaiting the outcome of his little dinner party.

"What do you say?" Travis looked away from the doctor and back to Annabelle. "A book?"

Annabelle shook her head, and her own laughter died away. "I don't think so, Shelley."

The look that passed between them said it all. They didn't need words, and Bart was suddenly jealous— not playfully, but genuinely. Travis had something special, and he was willing to toss it aside for his blasted independence. They had eyes only for one another, unaware and uncaring that he, John, and a fuming Dorothea watched them intently.

"Hell, darlin', Red Wolf alone would make a book."

"Yes," Annabelle said coyly. "But if I told about Red Wolf, I'd have to tell about Swift Eagle . . . and He-Who-Follows."

"Forget that," Shelley said sharply, but Annabelle simply smiled.

"Red Wolf? Indians?" John leaned forward anxiously. "You had a run-in with Indians? How fascinating. What happened?"

"Leave the child alone, John," Dorothea said with mock sympathy. "Can't you see that she doesn't wish to talk about it? It was certainly a very trying time for the poor girl."

Annabelle's eyes were on her plate. "I'm just lucky that Albert decided to tell the truth about what really happened. If not—"

"Oh!" John nearly jumped out of his chair. "I can't believe I almost forgot to tell you. Luck had nothing to do with it."

Annabelle turned to him, and Bart saw the doctor practically preen at having her complete attention for the first time that evening. "I have a patient"—he lowered his voice—"who works for the *Chronicle*, and his sister is married to a policeman who was there when Albert Gibson turned himself in. But that's not exactly what happened." He paused, now the center of attention.

"Annie's not interested in rumors . . ." Shelley began, but John ignored him.

"Anyway, apparently some ruffian had Gibson by the collar, smashed his head on the sergeant's desk, and said, and I quote, 'I don't suppose you'd like to see your lying tongue cut out and tossed in the sergeant's drawer as evidence?' After that Albert Gibson spilled his guts, so to speak."

Dorothea pursed her lips. "How barbaric."

Annabelle looked at Shelley, but he was staring at his plate, toying intently with a potato slice.

"I would certainly be interested to know who forced Albert to tell the truth," Annabelle said, her voice as calm and serene as her face. "I should like to thank him."

Bart watched as Travis raised his eyes to hers. Annabelle gave him a subtle smile. There was a sheepish look on Travis's face, and he couldn't look away from her.

"Whatever would you want to thank him for?" Dorothea snapped. "Threatening to . . . to . . . I can't even repeat it. It's positively savage."

Annabelle fixed a cold stare on the icy blonde. "You don't find it barbaric that Albert stabbed and killed an innocent man, then turned the knife on himself and tried to lay the blame on me? He is the true savage, not . . . not the man who forced him to confess, whoever he was."

Dorothea laid her napkin aside. "I find this conversation is ruining a fine meal. Can't we find another subject to discuss? Something more civilized?"

The room was silent for a few awkward moments, and it was Dorothea herself who broached a new subject. "I hear the Centennial Exposition in Philadelphia is quite amazing. Do you plan to return to the East in time to see it?" She looked pointedly at Annabelle.

Annabelle shrugged. "I haven't planned that far ahead, I'm afraid. The past several months have taught me to take one day at a time." She smiled warmly at the blonde's rigid countenance. "I'm sorry. It appears I'm ruining your appetite again."

Chuckling to himself, Bart began a rousing conversation with John and Dorothea about Custer's defeat at Little Big Horn, a subject hardly more civilized or appetizing than Annabelle's journey across the country. He glanced every so often at Travis and Annabelle who were conspiratorily quiet, exchanging private glances.

At the end of the meal, Bart rose from the table and ushered his dinner companions into the parlor. Andrew poured bourbon for the gentlemen and wine for the ladies. Bart thought he was the only one enjoying himself without reservation, as he watched the evening progress. Annabelle was winning the contest he had most cleverly arranged, and Dorothea was livid. She wasn't accustomed to coming in second to anyone . . . especially where Travis was concerned.

As for his brother, he certainly didn't look like a man who had, hours earlier, relinquished his claim on Annabelle. He stayed near her as she sat on the serpentine couch, and the two of them even seemed to move with a synchronization that was hypnotic. What would it take to convince Travis to stay? Bart wondered. To admit that Annabelle was the best thing that would ever happen to him?

Bart turned his attention to the doctor who was obviously smitten, trailing along after Annabelle like a faithful puppy. John either didn't see or chose to ignore her closeness to Travis, and Bart could only shake his head at his friend's denseness.

He watched as John joined Annabelle on the couch and mentioned the last time she'd performed in San Francisco. Soon they were discussing their favorite operas, the American thirst for culture, and Travis moved away to fill his glass.

Dorothea was there in a flash, leading Travis slowly and purposefully toward the open double doors.

"I must speak to you, Travis," Dorothea whispered urgently. "But not in here. Privately."

Bart pretended not to listen, but inside he was seething. *Tell her to go away Travis. . . . to disappear . . . tell her that you don't want to talk to her privately.* He tried to communicate his thoughts to his brother, even though he didn't believe in such nonsense. He couldn't very well interfere. Some decisions Travis would have to make on his own.

Shelley sighed and set his glass down. There had been a time when Thea's offer would have been attractive. She was still a beautiful woman, graceful and fair, her low-cut gown revealing her ample cleavage, her blue eyes inviting. Just like five years ago. But she'd been married then, and he'd carried a lot of anger. He wasn't angry anymore, thanks to Annie, so he saw no harm in following Thea as she led him to the small stone patio.

"Why are you torturing me like this?" Thea threw herself at him as soon as they were away from the double doors. Her breasts pressed against him, and she held her lips invitingly close. "I never should have married Lewis. I know that, now. I was young and stupid, but I love you, Travis. I've always loved you. We were meant to be together."

He frowned at her. Thea had always been free with her declarations of love. "It's too late, Thea. I'm not the same man who asked you to marry me. That was a lifetime ago . . ."

She kissed him then, pressing her lips ardently to his. She held his head in her hands and clasped him to her, her ardor turning to desperation when he didn't respond.

He didn't move. It was Thea who pulled away from him, stunned and rejected. "Are you trying to make me pay? Is this some sort of revenge?"

He stepped back. He didn't say a word. He didn't need to. There was no feeling left. He didn't hate her, he didn't love her. He didn't even particularly like or dislike her. She was a vaguely unpleasant memory from a life long past, and he watched her storm into the parlor with her head high and her shoulders squared.

The night air was pleasantly cool, and Shelley took a deep breath. Annie would be discussing opera with that stuffy doctor, and Bart and Thea would be watching him like a pair of hawks, so he decided to steal a few quiet moments there on the patio.

By the time Shelley entered the parlor through the open double doors, Thea was gone, and that was fine with him. His last look at her, as she'd realized his rejection, had convinced him that she was truly an ugly woman—inside, where it counts. He leaned against the door frame and watched Annie's back, the line of her neck, the curve of her hip. She was speaking to Bart, and as he watched, she laid her hand on his brother's arm, her long fingers startlingly pale against his black sleeve. Shelley's smile faded quickly. Bart and Annie? Well, why not? Bart lived in her world, appreciated what she loved in a way he himself never could. His brother could offer her everything he couldn't.

He moved forward, unable to stop himself. He hadn't left San Francisco yet, dammit. She stiffened at the touch of his hand on her bare shoulder, but she didn't turn to face him.

"I'm very tired," she said coldly. "I think I should excuse myself."

The doctor moved forward. "Perhaps it's too soon for you to be up and around. I could check in on you in the morning, if you wish."

"That won't be necessary." Annie kept her back to Shelley even as he tried to circle around her. "A good night's sleep is all I need."

Bart was frowning, an expression that rarely crossed his face. Annie's hand remained on his arm, and he circled with her, facing Shelley over her head, the three of them caught in an awkward dance.

Her head down, Annie broke away and practically fled from the room. Shelley attempted to follow, but Bart's suddenly strong hand grabbed him and spun him around.

"Don't you think you've done enough for one evening?" Bart's usually languid tone was clipped and sharp. "Leave Annabelle alone."

He shook off his brother's grip and followed Annie. When he caught up with her she was halfway up the staircase.

"What the hell . . ." he began, laying a hand on her shoulder and forcing her to turn and face him. Her face was ashen, her eyes filled with tears, and his anger disappeared. "What's the matter, darlin'?"

Annie lifted her chin and tried to stare him down. "I am not a wounded bird."

"What?"

"Or a starving kitten, thank you," she snapped, trying to turn away from him.

He caught her arm and spun her around, tossing her easily over his shoulder. She beat her fists against his back, but he ignored her mild assault.

"I don't know what the hell is going on here, but I intend to find out."

He marched back into the parlor, Annie hanging from his shoulder, his arms around her knees, her der-

Linda Winstead

riere in the air. He stopped in front of a blushing Dr. Smith.

"Good night, Doc," he growled. The doctor gathered his composure and bid Bart a hasty good evening.

Shelley deposited Annie unceremoniously on the serpentine couch and stood spread-legged in front of her, blocking her only avenue of escape.

"What's this nonsense about birds and cats?" he snapped.

"Jesus, Trav." Bart attempted to grab him from behind. "Leave her alone."

He glanced over his shoulder. "Stay out of this."

"I don't think I—" his brother began.

"Or I'll wipe the floor with your pretty face, Bart. I swear I will."

"Stop it!" Annie ordered harshly. "Bart, I'll be all right. I . . . I overreacted."

"To what?" Shelley looked down at her and practically yelled. "One minute everything's fine, and the next minute you're telling me that you're not a bird, and you've got tears in your eyes. You know I hate that."

"Bart, can you leave us alone?" Annabelle asked, her eyes never leaving Shelley.

Bart left the room, leaving the door open.

Annabelle stared into Shelley's eyes, wishing that she could read his mind. When she had realized, as she lay in his bed in his childhood home, that he hadn't known her true identity until that night at the Filmores . . . that night she had seen him turn from a warm lover to a distant stranger . . . she'd believed that Shelley was incapable of deceit.

"You were the one person in the world I never ex-

312

pected to lie to me," she said sadly. "That's what hurts the most."

"I didn't—"

"Do you love her?" she asked, resignation in her voice. "Is that why . . . I mean."

"Thea?" Shelley sat next to her. "Is that what this is about, darlin'? I don't—?

"Did you . . . did you sleep with her?" she looked at the folded hands in her lap.

"What?"

"It's a simple question." She looked at him then. "Did you sleep with her?"

"What the hell kinda question is—"

"Did you?"

Shelley squirmed on the couch. "I don't see—"

"I'll take that as a yes." She stood and turned to face him. "I hope the two of you will be very happy."

Shelley grabbed her arm and pulled her back down beside him. "All right. Once. Five years ago. She was married, and I'm not proud of that, but . . ."

"She said . . ." Annabelle began.

Shelley sighed heavily. "You can't believe a word Thea says. She's a manipulator. Always was. I just didn't see it until . . . until I met you. Truth is . . ." Shelley hesitated. Annabelle could read the indecision in his eyes, the uncertainty. "Since I met you I can't even think about another woman."

She stared at him, and there was still a question in her heart. "I saw you kiss her. I went outside to look for you, and I saw the two of you kissing."

Shelley smiled, and she glared at him. He was amused! "Well what would you think if I . . . damn you, Shelley, wipe that grin off your face."

He leaned toward her and tried to kiss her, but she

moved her head to one side. So he took her face in his hands and kissed her pursed lips. "Actually, she kissed me." He tried again, pressing his lips to hers gently. "All I could think about was you, Annie."

"I'm scared," she whispered.

"What are you scared of this time, darlin'?" Her lips softened as he pressed his mouth against hers.

"That you're going to leave." Her voice was little more than a whisper.

She waited for a quick denial, but he said nothing. Instead he pulled her head to his shoulder and took a deep breath.

"Well?" she prompted.

"I never lied to you, Annie. I don't belong here. You don't belong in the world I live in." His voice was resigned.

"I belong wherever you are." She tilted her head back and forced him to look at her. "No matter where that is. I can sleep under the stars, eat beans for the rest of my life, sing just for you . . . all I need are my red boots, my dreamcatcher, and you."

"It's too dangerous. You almost died," he said gruffly.

"People die in the city, too," she argued. She couldn't believe that she was practically begging.

"Annie . . ."

"I love you, Shelley," she blurted out before she could change her mind. "I love you. There. I said it."

Shelley moved her back and away from him, and he frowned slightly as he studied her from arm's length. "I'm the worst man in the world for you," he whispered.

"Hello, Brat." The deep, sonorous voice from the doorway stunned her. She turned away from the shocked Shelley, and toward the well-dressed, dark-haired man who stood leaning casually against the doorjamb with a wry smile on his face.

"Icky!" She jumped up and ran to him and threw her arms around his neck. She planted a quick kiss on his cheek. "I can't believe it. How did you find me?"

He moved her away from him and studied her from head to toe. "You look . . . fabulous, actually. I should whip you good for not letting me know where you were. I've had men looking for you from the moment I found out you'd disappeared. Why on earth did you run like that? What were you thinking?"

"Icky, I have so much to tell you, I don't know where to start." She took both his hands in hers and smiled. "There's someone I want you to meet."

She turned around, one of Icky's hands still in hers. Her smile quickly faded when she saw the empty parlor and the rippling curtains at the open double doors. He'd done it again. That coward. How could he?

Her eyes were narrowed when she turned back around. "Take me home, Icky," she said crisply, and practically ran into Andrew as she fled from the room.

"Give Mr. Shelton a message from me," she shouted at the old man.

"Ummmmm. Master Bartholomew . . . or Master Travis?" He asked slowly, his voice dragging laboriously.

"Master Travis," she snapped. "You tell him that he is a snake. A no-good, low-down, reptile of the worst kind. A degenerate uncouth barbarian. A poor excuse for a man who . . . who . . ." She launched into a tirade in French that had the butler wringing his hands.

"Perhaps Miss Annabelle would like to leave a note for Master Travis?" he asked hopefully.

Linda Winstead

She calmed down suddenly, her composure returning. "Just tell him that I hate him and his canned peaches."

Annabelle ran upstairs and returned moments later with her dreamcatcher, her medicine bag, her cowboy hat, and her red boots.

Nicky was waiting for her by the front door, and suddenly Bart appeared at the opposite end of the hallway.

"Annabelle. Where are you going?" Bart asked, stunned. "Where's Travis?"

She couldn't stand to look at his face, a face so much like Shelley's, and she certainly didn't have any answers to his questions. Without a word she turned and burst through the door into the cool night air.

Chapter Thirty-three

Annabelle woke, after a few hours of fitful sleep, in her yellow room in Nicky's house. She remembered the first time he had brought her to San Francisco from Paris for an extended visit. The room he had presented her, the room he'd had decorated with her in mind, was bright and sunny and frilly, with lace curtains and satin pillows. It was a place she had long considered home.

Nicky was more like a brother to her than an uncle. After her paternal grandfather's death, Nicky had come to live with her and her parents when Annabelle was a newborn and he was barely ten. Her grandfather had been a harsh man, and it often showed in Nicky's stern demeanor. But when Annabelle began to talk and called him Icky, unable to pronounce his name properly, he had retaliated with a rare smile and had called her Brat.

317

They'd been Brat and Icky ever since.

As her uncle reached manhood and left her behind, Annabelle had felt deserted, for a while. But when her parents died it had been her protective uncle who placed her in a musical conservatory in Paris, convinced that she had a gift. He'd hand-picked Lisette and Pierre to look after her when she was away from him, which was most of the time. Still, he visited her often, and at least once every two years sailed her to San Francisco and her yellow room.

Once she had become an adult, those visits grew farther and farther apart, but she cherished Nicky's letters, and poured her heart into her own long messages to him.

But last night she'd barely been able to speak to him, she'd been so distraught. So Nicky had done all the talking, mostly about his wife of less than a year, a woman who couldn't possibly be as beautiful and sweet as he claimed. Annabelle had never met Isabel St. Clair, and was grateful that her uncle's bride was sleeping when they arrived.

Annabelle threw back the white and yellow quilt and forced herself from the bed. The first order of business would be to seek out her uncle and explain everything to him . . . well, almost everything. He deserved an apology from her for not letting him know her whereabouts and that she was safe. She'd been so concerned with seeing that Shelley didn't leave or send her away that she'd been thoughtless where her only living relative was concerned.

There was a plain pale blue dress laid neatly over the back of a yellow padded chair near the end of the bed. Nicky always thought of everything. No detail would be overlooked when he placed himself in charge of a situation.

She crept down the stairs, slowly and noiselessly, hoping not to meet any of the servants, or Nicky's wife. At least, not yet.

She paused at the foot of the stairs and turned toward Nicky's study. If he hadn't changed his rigid schedule, that was where he would be. She heard his voice and slipped quietly down the hall. Who was he talking to? If he was busy, she would creep back up the stairs and wait.

Viewing his broad back through the open doorway, she smiled. More than once, in her mind, she had compared her stoic and determined uncle to a knight of old. Unbendable, undefeatable, inflexible. He was speaking to someone out of her range of vision, and she was just about to turn away when she heard another voice. A familiar voice.

"I wish I'd found her sooner, too, sir. She must have had lots of help hiding from us. Pinkerton's is a most efficient agency."

Annabelle felt light-headed. It was the man who had tried to kill her and Shelley!

"If only I'd known sooner that Shelley's real name was Travis Shelton . . ." He stopped in mid sentence when Annabelle appeared in the doorway. His face paled, and he refused to meet her eyes, the coward. Nicky must be paying him a fortune, she thought, to make this man bold enough to risk running into her.

"Nicky," she breathed the soft words, "What is this man doing here?"

"This is the Pinkerton agent who located you for me. Wendell Yates." Nicky turned to her with a half smile. "I offered a handsome reward to the man who found

319

you, and he's here to collect."

"You're going to give this man money?" She turned to her uncle and presented her coldest face. "He tried to kill me. Shelley, too. He was going to shoot us—"

"You have it all wrong, Miss St. Clair," Yates attempted to defend himself. "If you will remember . . ." He made the mistake of dropping his hand to his side.

Annabelle was certain that he intended to draw his gun and shoot her, and Nicky, too. She ran toward him, grabbing a book from the corner of Nicky's desk. As she descended upon the stunned Yates, she swung the heavy book forward with all her might, slamming the tome into his face.

Blood flowed from his nose, and he howled in pain. He brought both hands to his face to stop the river of blood, and to shield himself from further attack.

Nicky grabbed her from behind and stripped the book from her hands. She was breathing heavily, and her eyes were on the writhing man in front of her.

"I'm terribly sorry, Mr. Yates," Nicky offered, pinning her in his strong arms. "Obviously my niece has been through a frightening experience. I hadn't expected delusions, but I shouldn't be surprised—"

"Delusions?" She tried to free herself but could not. "This man tried to murder me!" She calmed herself with great effort. Nicky was not going to be swayed by emotional outbursts. "I can prove it," she said calmly.

"How?" Her uncle didn't release her, even as she quieted.

"Let go of me and I'll explain," She said almost serenely.

She felt Nicky's arms loosen, and finally he released

her. Yates's bleeding had slowed, but blood continued to drip from his face onto his immaculate suit. He was a mess, and he pressed his hands against his face, trying to stop the blood.

Her eyes delved into the agent's, and he looked away quickly. "Do you deny that you attacked me and my escort while we camped, and attempted to kill us?"

Yates nodded.

"Then why did Shelley stab you—" She made a fist the way Shelley had taught her and punched Yates right where Swift Eagle's knife had pierced his flesh— "right here?"

Yates forgot the pain in his face and grabbed his shoulder, wincing as he dropped to his knees. Nicky jerked her back from the agent and turned accusing eyes on the man who knelt before him.

"You threatened my niece?"

Annabelle knew there was nothing more frightening than Nicky's calm anger.

"I . . . I was tired. My partner deserted me, and I hadn't slept for more than two days. I wasn't thinking straight . . . and I didn't know that she was innocent! No harm was done—"

"You goddamn liar," she spat.

"Annabelle St. Clair!" her uncle shouted.

But she wasn't finished. "You knew exactly what you were doing, you sonofabitch. If Shelley hadn't stabbed you in the shoulder you would have shot us both and left us for dead. Or did you plan on turning my body in for that thousand-dollar reward?"

Yates slowly pulled himself to his feet. "I'm terribly sorry for the misunderstanding. I'm . . . I'm not a bad person," he said defensively.

"I think you'd better leave, Mr. Yates," Nicky

growled. "Mr. Pinkerton will be receiving a letter informing him of my great dissatisfaction with your service."

Yates stumbled to the door of the study, almost colliding with a lovely young woman.

Annabelle turned away from the woman and looked up at her uncle's puzzled face. What had she done? Why hadn't she tried to convince Nicky calmly of her certainty that Yates had intended to kill her?

"Isabel."

Nicky offered his hand, and the woman in the doorway stepped into the room. Her uncle's wife was petite, and her pale pink dress floated around her like a pastel cloud. Her hair was the palest blonde and gathered gently at her nape, her face framed by a few errant tendrils at her cheeks. Annabelle thought that if she wore a circlet of gold on her head she would make the perfect medieval maiden to Nicky's Black Knight. Even the hand she offered to her husband was decidedly feminine, her fingers long and slender, her skin milky white.

Annabelle knew she should stay . . . explain her actions to Nicky, meet his bride . . . but instead she ran past the puzzled pair and up the stairs to her yellow room.

Chapter Thirty-four

Shelley tossed his saddle to the ground and started a small fire. This was true freedom, he thought as he settled by the fire with a handful of wanted posters in one hand and a cup of coffee in the other. A man and his horse . . . no responsibilities, no plans beyond next week, the freedom to travel where and when he desired.

He had almost convinced himself of all this until he reached into his saddlebag and came out with, not a can of beans, but a can of peaches . . . the last of the dozen cans he'd bought in Salt Lake City. He studied it for a moment, the frown on his scruffily bearded face deepening as the seconds ticked by. Without a sound he turned and threw the unopened can as far as he could, listening as it fell through a canopy of leaves far from his campsite and thudded to the ground.

The truth was, he hadn't been able to get more than fifty miles from San Francisco in the two weeks since he'd walked out of the house, leaving Brat and Icky embracing in the doorway. He'd zigzagged from east to west, from north to south and back again, unable to cross the mountains. Somehow he knew if he crossed the Sierra Nevada he would never return. It was so final, so . . . absolute.

He withdrew the *San Francisco Bulletin* he'd stashed in his saddlebag three days earlier. There was an article about Annie on page seven. He hadn't read it yet, couldn't bring himself to. Every time he thought about her he remembered how she had run to the dark-haired man she called Icky, how she'd wrapped her arms around his neck. He hadn't stayed to see what else went on. Were all women so fickle, or only the ones he was attracted to? How could a woman look you in the eyes and tell you she loves you, and then run to another man in a heartbeat?

Maybe what he needed was to read about her, no matter how difficult it was. Maybe if he read all about how wonderfully she was surviving back in the civilized city of his birth, he could forget her and move on. Perhaps he could forget her if he read about her return to her career, social events, the life of a diva. Perhaps.

A great deal of the article dealt with her background, a thorough coverage of her career and personal life, as well as the story of her disappearance. He read every word, reading more slowly when he came to the next paragraph.

Miss St. Clair has refused to grant interviews about her harrowing experience, but stories

*abound. As it is impossible to tell which, if any,
of these stories hold even a grain of truth, this
newspaper will refrain from publishing any of
the accounts until they can be confirmed by Miss
St. Clair. However, we can report that Miss St.
Clair is considering making San Francisco her
home. The opera loving citizens of the city can
only hope her decision will be favorable. Perhaps
her constant companion, Bartholomew Shelton,
can persuade her to remain in our fair city.*

After that he skimmed over the rest of the article.
Constant companion! He noted the dates given for her
scheduled performances, his eyes darting rapidly over
the paper until he came to the final sentence.

*As always when Miss St. Clair is in San
Francisco, she is residing with her uncle,
Nicholas St. Clair, and his bride Isabel.*

Uncle Icky? Shelley tossed the paper into the fire
and watched until it had been consumed by the
flames. It made no difference. She still belonged there,
and he didn't. She would have a better life with Bart
or that ass Dr. Smith or . . .

Shelley laid his head back against the saddle and
crossed his ankles. Sleep should come easily. It always
did. But it eluded him, as it had on so many other
nights of late, as night fell and the stars twinkled
overhead.

What if she'd really meant the words she'd spoken
to him before his hasty departure? Would she leave
behind everything she knew for a man who had nothing? She used the word *love*, but he knew what she

meant. Her passion. She'd get over that, and so would he, eventually. She obviously wasn't pining over him if Bart was her "constant companion."

He closed his eyes and willed sleep to come.

Like a bug in a bedroll.

Like an itch in the middle of his back, one he couldn't quite reach.

"Goddamn!" He rolled up and kicked dirt over the fire. "Hell, I haven't been to Mexico in years," he mumbled to himself, saddling his roan. "Tequila. Senoritas. Long siestas." He jumped into the saddle, wide awake though he'd hardly slept for the past two weeks, and turned his horse to the south.

Annabelle ran her fingers over the many leather-bound volumes on the shelves. Nicky's library was her favorite room in the house, except of course her own yellow bedroom.

She stopped and drew from the shelf the only book that had interested her in the two weeks she'd been here. Percy Bysshe Shelley.

There had been no more violent outbursts, no more profanity since that morning Wendell Yates had dared to show his face in this house. Still, she often found Nicky looking at her with a strange and distant look in his eyes, as if he didn't know her anymore.

Poor Nicky. He wanted so badly to press for details about the months she'd been missing. Annabelle had asked for time, and her uncle was using tremendous restraint in giving it to her.

She started slightly when she turned around and found him standing in the doorway, watching her intently. "Nicky." She gave him a small smile, all that she could manage. "I didn't know you were still up."

"What's the matter, Brat?" Her uncle moved into the room with deceptive lethargy. "Can't sleep?"

She shook her head. "Is Isabel sleeping?"

Nicky smiled gently. "Like a baby."

She tried to imagine Nicky as a father, and couldn't. How would a man who led such a controlled life deal with the chaos of a baby? In his own way, she imagined. He'd probably order the baby not to cry, and not to wake at night while he and Isabel were asleep. And he would expect the child to obey.

"She's worried about you, Brat," Nicky said gently, laying his hand on her arm. "She thinks you're too pale and too thin and far from ready to resume your career."

"What do you think?"

He shrugged his wide shoulders. "I heard you rehearsing yesterday, and you were fabulous, as always."

She clasped the volume to the bodice of her new yellow dress. She hadn't told Nicky any of the details of her trip West, and it was obviously trying for him. He wanted to know everything, but he hadn't hounded her. She had Isabel to thank for that, she was certain.

But Nicky had taken her under his protective wing, as she had known he would, and made his home her haven. He'd threatened every newspaper in town with endless lawsuits if they dared to print a word she did not approve, and had hired a personal maid for her until Pierre and Lisette could arrive. His home was hers for as long as she wanted to stay. He'd been trying to persuade her to return to San Francisco for good.

What was waiting for her in Paris? More notoriety. A return to the way of life she had once loved. Henri was gone, and the idea of returning to Paris left her empty.

"I've been thinking." She approached the subject with more than a little hesitation. "About your offer. I don't want to intrude. You and Isabel haven't even been married a year. You don't need me . . ."

Nicky smiled broadly. "It's a big house, Brat."

"I'll get my own place eventually, Icky." She gave him a genuine smile. "Icky. I did find that personal ad you placed, by the way. It . . . gave me hope, when I needed it most."

Nicky placed his arm around her shoulder. "You only found one? I placed that ad in every newspaper west of the Mississippi for two and a half months."

She laughed lightly. "I found it in a discarded newspaper in the filthiest, most out-of-the-way general store . . ." She stopped suddenly, the memories flooding over her.

"So, when am I going to get the entire story?" He encouraged her with a gentle squeeze.

"Maybe never." She lost her smile. "I was . . . frightened most of the time, until Shelley . . ."

Nicky obviously wanted to urge her on as her sentence trailed away. But he took a deep breath and patted her arm consolingly.

"That Bartholomew Shelton. Should I expect him bright and early again tomorrow?"

"Yes. He's going to show me the bay."

"You've seen the bay."

"Well, he insisted."

"Is this . . . serious, Annabelle?" Nicky walked her from the library and up the stairs.

"Bart?" Annabelle looked up, wrinkling her nose at

her overprotective uncle. "Good heavens, no. He's just a friend."

"Does he know that?"

"I expect he does."

Nicky escorted her to her bedroom door. "I saw another friend of yours today. She raved about you. I didn't even know you were acquainted with Dorothea Cole."

Annabelle made a decidedly unfeminine noise of disgust.

"You don't like her?" Nicky seemed somewhat amused by her strong response.

"She's a goddamn tramp," she said without thinking, and her uncle flinched.

"Annabelle St. Clair," he snapped. "What kind of language is that?"

She turned away from him, the precious volume of poetry clutched in her hands. "It's the truth, Nicky. Just the truth."

Chapter Thirty-five

The gardens of the St. Clair house were much more well ordered and lovely than Annabelle remembered. That was Isabel's influence, no doubt. A gardener tended it lovingly, and not a single yellow or withered leaf was allowed to remain. Roses bloomed there in every color, blood red and snow white, palest yellow and just slightly pink. Only perfect blooms were allowed to remain in the St. Clair garden, and to grace the tables of the house.

Annabelle had convinced Bart to spend the afternoon wandering in the garden, rather than strolling through the park or sharing a picnic by the bay. Every single San Franciscan seemed to know who she was, and stared unabashedly as she attempted to carry on a conversation with Bart. Their conversations were always on the same subject—Shelley. Bit by bit she revealed to Bart some of what had happened as Shelley led her to San Francisco.

No matter how hard she tried to push Shelley from her mind, he was always there! She had tried to hate him, but she couldn't. She knew that she should refuse to see Bart at all. He was so much like Shelley she couldn't help but be reminded. But they had one thing in common that made it impossible for her to turn Bart away. They both loved Shelley.

"Did I ever tell you about Red Wolf and Swift Eagle?" Annabelle sat on a wrought iron bench that had recently been placed at the juncture of four neatly ordered rows.

Bart sat beside her. "Yes. But you can tell me again, if you like."

"No. Surely you get tired of hearing the same old stories about Shelley saving me." She sighed and picked at a nearby red rose, its velvet petals crushed between her fingers. "I swear, Bart, I've tried to make myself believe that he's not coming back . . . but I don't. Not really."

Bart sighed, a bit overdramatically, as he sometimes did. Annabelle didn't understand why he felt compelled to spend so much time with her, watching over her, in a way.

"Maybe you're right, Annabelle. He does love you. I'm certain of it."

She smiled slowly, sadly. "There was a brief time I thought that was true. In a way, I still do. But if he loved me he never would have left. He would be here with me now, or I would be . . ." She hesitated, unable to finish the thought. "Still, sometimes I expect to see him riding up the hill. We were only together a short time, but it seems like it was forever. Does that make sense?" She looked at Bart expectantly.

"I've never been in love." He made himself more comfortable, stretching out his long legs. "I must confess I don't understand it at all. Travis practically deserted you, and yet I have watched your anger die. It's a mystery to me."

"Well." She slapped him on the knee. "I'll have to see what I can do about that. Isabel has a lovely friend . . ."

"No," he answered sharply. "Please promise me you won't play matchmaker."

She smiled wickedly. "Promise?"

"Swear on your very soul."

"I can't do that."

Bart grimaced. "Seems awfully messy to me. I don't think either you or Travis has made a rational decision since the moment he carried you through the front door."

Annabelle returned her attention to the red rose that was shedding its petals into her hand as she plucked mercilessly. "Whenever I was in trouble, Shelley was there. From the first moment I saw him, when that horrid Pinkerton agent had me cornered, it was as if he were watching over me. Then there was the fight with Swift Eagle . . . I thought he'd abandoned me, but when I needed him, there he was." She narrowed her eyes and dropped the petals to the ground.

"When I was drowning, he pulled me to the surface." A thoughtful frown was forming on her face. "I guess that doesn't count, because if it hadn't been for him I wouldn't have been drowning in the first place."

"You never told me about . . . Annabelle, I don't like that look on your face."

She ignored him. "When I was sick, he took care of me. When I was in trouble, he saved me." She looked

332

at Bart, troubled. "Tell me. Was Shelley always"—She licked her lips and searched for the proper words, her mind spinning—"at his best in a crisis situation?"

"I suppose. He always knew what to do while everyone else was panicking." He leaned forward so he could get a better look at her face. "I do not like the direction this conversation is taking."

She leaned back and selected another innocent rose for destruction, slowly plucking the soft petals and rubbing them between her fingers.

There was a cool breeze that made the summer afternoon bearable, and a sudden burst of air forced her hair away from her face, and she smiled . . .

"Oh my God," Bart whispered. "You look just like Travis did when he was about to do something incredibly stupid."

"Annabelle." Isabel's voice floated to them as she appeared, a frown marring her beauty as she studied the petals on the ground. "There's another reporter here, and he's as insistent as all the rest. Nicholas isn't back yet . . ."

Bart stood quickly. "I'll get rid of him." He directed his promise to Isabel. "Why won't they leave Annabelle alone? She's turned them all away at least twice."

Annabelle's hand shot out and grabbed Bart's, and she squeezed tightly. "Wait." She chewed her bottom lip and narrowed her eyes. "Can you keep that reporter occupied for a few minutes?"

Bart leaned over, his face close to hers. "Don't you want me to get rid of him?"

"No. His timing is perfect, but I need time to change."

"Annabelle St. Clair," he whispered. "I don't like this. What are you up to?"

"Trust me, Bart. Stall him. Tell him to be patient and he'll get the interview of his life."

Bart laid a stilling hand on her shoulder. "The last time someone said 'Trust me, Bart,' I got the whipping of my life. I don't know what you're up to, Annabelle, but I don't think Travis would approve."

She freed herself from him easily, standing and spinning around until his hand fell from her arm. "Well, he's not here, is he?" She ran from him, muttering, "At least, not yet."

Chapter Thirty-six

Shelley would have continued straight to Mexico, he told himself, if he hadn't stumbled across information on the bank robber whose poster he carried in his pocket. Two hundred and fifty dollars, and easy pickin's. Bill Withers was just an eighteen-year-old red-headed kid, runnin' scared.

It was almost too easy to track the kid from the settlement where he'd been spotted along the trail to the Sierra Nevada. It was almost too easy, but 250 dollars would buy a hell of a lot of tequila.

The sun beat down on Shelley and warmed him superficially. Inside, he felt cold. He tried to convince himself that that was good. If he could push his feelings deep enough, and bury them in that ice, he would once again be content with nothing more than his roan, the rifle that was slung from his saddle, and the six-shooter resting against his thigh.

When he ran across the camp, he shook his head in disgust. Withers had camped in the open, as though he had nothing to fear.

"Howdy," Withers called as Shelley rode down gentle slope to the camp, kicking up dust as the roan's hooves pounded against the dirt.

One quick look assured him that there were no weapons handy, no pistol at Withers' side, no rifle at hand. There was a woman in the camp, her light brown hair plaited and hanging down to her waist. She had her back to Shelley as he rode toward them, and she was tending a small pot as she squatted by the campfire.

"Dinner will be ready soon," the redheaded kid said, turning his back on Shelley. "You're welcome to join us. Where you headed?"

He didn't answer, and eventually the boy turned back around. One look at Shelley's stern face, and Bill Withers' smile faded.

"You Bill Withers?" He dismounted. What kind of criminal was this? He'd welcomed Shelley into his camp as if he had nothing to hide.

"Yep," Bill answered, his eyes narrowing suspiciously. "Do I know you?"

He pulled Withers' folded wanted poster from his vest pocket and snapped it open. The boy's already pale face whitened, and he lowered his voice.

"You the law?" He seemed resigned to his fate.

Shelley shrugged. "I'm just interested in the two hundred and fifty dollars."

Their voices were low, and the woman bent over the fire seemed intent on her cooking.

Withers ran his fingers distractedly through thin red hair that hung to his shoulders. "I didn't know . . .

about the reward. We was just . . . just . . ." His pale
blue eyes darted back and forth, avoiding Shelley.

"Can I have a minute to tell my wife?" He met Shelley's eyes then, and there was a sadness there much
too deep for his eighteen years.

Shelley watched the back of the woman by the fire.
His hand was on the grip of his Colt. If she came up
with a weapon in her hand . . .

"Sarah Jane?"

Withers turned away from him, and Shelley
watched through hooded eyes, ready to draw his Colt,
as the woman stood and turned around.

Woman was a questionable word, and he dropped
his hand to his side. Sarah Jane Withers couldn't have
been much more than sixteen years old, and as she
turned she placed her hand over her swollen belly and
smiled sweetly.

"Is this gentleman staying for supper, Billy?" she
asked with a gentle Southern drawl. "We got plenty."

The bank robber took her hand and squeezed it
tightly. "No, honey. He's . . . he's takin' me in."

Sarah Jane's smile evaporated and her eyes widened
as she looked at Shelley in horror. "What for? He
didn't do anything. Those men . . . they made it sound
so simple, but Billy didn't draw his gun, he didn't take
a penny of that money."

"He was there," he said coldly. "Tell it to the judge.
I'm just interested in the reward."

"He's a bounty hunter, Sarah Jane," Bill explained
in a surprisingly comforting voice. "He caught me fair
and square, and I reckon he's right. I'll tell the judge
what happened and . . . and . . ."

"We're going back to the farm, sir." Sarah Jane
broke away from her husband and grabbed Shelley's

arm. "There ain't no gold on the ground here, like they said there was. We was just . . . desperate, what with the baby coming and all. That's the only reason Billy agreed to ride with those men. But he didn't hurt anybody. We just want to go home. Billy ain't no criminal. Please, mister."

Shelley turned his back on her. He couldn't stand to have her staring up into his face with those wide brown eyes, paler than Annabelle's, more scared than Annabelle's had ever been. A couple of goddamn kids. In all his years of hunting wanted men, he had never been swayed by a story, and he'd heard them all. He'd had offers of money, double and triple the offered reward. He'd listened as stories of ailing mothers and pregnant wives and hard times went in one ear and out the other. He'd never been swayed. He'd never even considered letting a wanted criminal . . . a bank robber . . . go on his way.

"Where is this farm?" he asked, his words clipped and coarse.

"Kansas," Sarah Jane answered. "It's Billy's pa's farm, and he always said we could stay there and . . ."

"Ever been to Ellsworth?" Shelley asked, his back to the couple as he rummaged through his saddlebags.

"No, sir," Sarah Jane answered seriously. "That's a right wild cow town. My mama wouldn't allow me to . . ."

She snapped her mouth shut when he spun back around to face her. "I've done some stupid things in my life . . . and I suppose I'm about to add to the list."

Sarah Jane paled, and her honey brown eyes widened. She took her husband's arm and backed away two tentative steps.

"No." Shelley would have reached for her arm, but he knew that would only terrify her more. "I'm not goin' to hurt you, darlin'. And I'm not goin' to take your husband in, neither. Goddammit. Gettin' soft in my old age."

Sarah Jane grinned and held Bill's arm even tighter. "Do you mean it? Are you really goin' to let us go?"

He rolled his eyes. "Don't make me change my mind, darlin'. But if you expect to make it all the way back to Kansas you're goin' to have to make some changes."

"What kinda changes?" Bill asked.

Shelley made a disgusted face and held the wanted poster in front of the young man's face. "This is a damn fine likeness, wouldn't you say?"

Withers took the poster and studied it closely. There was no hiding the fact that he was the man in the sketch. The shoulder-length red hair, the sparse moustache, even the shape of his narrow chin was nearly perfect.

"I'm not the only bounty hunter between here and Kansas, and you're gonna have to stop now and again for supplies . . . shave that goddamn moustache for starters," he snapped. "Poor excuse for a moustache, anyway. And cut your hair. Short!" he commanded. "Goddamn red hair," he muttered under his breath, circling around the confused couple. "Boil yourself up some strong coffee and rinse it through your hair. Let it cool first," he said, leaning into Bill's face. The boy was obviously not too bright, and he couldn't have this kid cooking his scalp. "And for God's sake, if someone walks up to you and asks if your name is Bill Withers . . . tell them no!"

Sarah Jane threw her arms around her husband's

neck and began to sob, long wracking sobs that tore from her fragile body.

Shelley looked beyond her head to Withers' face as he stroked his wife's hair and held her close. "What is she doin' that for?"

"She cries a lot lately," Bill said, clearly not quite understanding his wife's outburst, but accepting it just the same. "When she's sad, when she's happy . . . sometimes for no reason at all."

Shelley let them convince him to stay for supper, after Sarah Jane dried her tears. He was still disgusted with himself for deciding not to turn the boy in, but he wouldn't change his mind. The kid was no criminal. What if someone had turned Annie in before the truth had come out?

He told them that once they crossed the Sierra Nevada they would probably be safe. Withers' name and the posted reward were known within the state, but he wasn't big enough to warrant a country-wide search.

"Don't even know your name, mister," Sarah Jane said as she handed him a cup of strong coffee.

"Most folks just call me Shelley," he said, raising the tin cup to his mouth. Bill sat a few feet away, shaving as directed, and he turned surprised eyes to Shelley.

"You're Shelley? I heard of you." It was clear by the look on his face that he was even more surprised about his reprieve, given Shelley's reputation as a bounty hunter.

He gave the young man a formidable look. "And if you ever tell anyone that I had you and let you go, or if I ever hear of you doing anything but farming, I'll be after you in a heartbeat . . . no matter where you are. No matter where I am. Believe it."

Bill nodded his head. Clearly he believed Shelley's threat.

Sarah Jane smiled shyly. "Is Shelley your Christian name? I only ask because we haven't decided on a name for the baby yet, and it would be fittin' to name the baby after you. If not for you, it might not even have a pa around."

"You don't wanna name that kid after me." He grinned, and Sarah Jane blushed at his smile. "Life is hard enough . . ."

"Please, Mister Shelley."

He remembered a time when a tiny, white-faced woman had ridden in front of him, ignoring the fact that they sat thigh to thigh, calling him Mister Shelley.

"Travis," he said with resignation.

Sarah Jane smiled as she sat down beside him. "Travis. I like that. Don't you like that, Billy?"

The young man nodded.

"Travis if it's a boy." Sarah Jane looked as if she should still be playing with dolls instead of choosing a name for her own baby. She had a young face, full of hope and plans for the future, plump-cheeked and wide-eyed. "If it's a girl . . ." She cocked her head to one side. "Are you married, Mister Shelley?"

He stared into the cup of inky coffee instead of looking at the young girl beside him. "Nope."

"Oh. I thought maybe . . ."

"Annabelle," he said softly. "I've always been partial to the name Annabelle."

"Like the opera singer?" Sarah Jane asked lightly.

He raised his eyes to her. "You know her?"

"Well, of her."

Sarah Jane rose and crossed the camp, and began to rummage through their meager belongings. She returned with a newspaper in her hand. "I read all the articles about her fiancé's murder while she was on the run," Sarah Jane whispered with a touch of intrigue in her voice. "And then the real murderer confessed, and she appeared in San Francisco. It's like . . . a dime novel. There's a different picture in this paper than the one they ran while she was missing."

He tried not to appear too interested. "Really?"

"It's much better. I didn't realize how pretty she is." Sarah Jane opened the paper to the page devoted to the story on Annabelle St. Clair, and there it was. A perfect drawing of his Annie. It was a sketch of her face, and she wore a slight smile that was restrained and a bit sad. The artist had captured her almost perfectly, and Shelley felt a tightening in his chest.

"Listen to this." Sarah Jane began to read in a melodious voice. " 'Although Miss St. Clair still refuses to discuss the details of the months she was missing, she admitted to this reporter in a rare interview that she never would have survived her ordeal alone. When asked to elaborate, the stunning diva, dressed in shocking Western wear which included trousers, crimson boots, a hat with a feather in the band, a decidedly Indian weapon at her hip, and a medicine bag around her neck, flashed a wicked smile and asked if I read much poetry. After I admitted that I did not, Miss St. Clair launched into a recitation of the bawdiest limericks this reporter has ever heard, to the shock and dismay of her well-bred aunt, and San Francisco native Bartholomew Shelton, who were present during the interview.

" 'Though unorthodox, to say the least, Miss St. Clair remains one of the finest artists this reporter has ever had the pleasure to hear. She is, somehow, improved for her ordeal, her voice richer, more mature than before her disappearance. It's as though she sings from the very heart. Three weeks of performances at the Opera House begin on the fourteenth. She is not to be missed.' "

Sarah Jane laid the newspaper aside and sighed. "She is so beautiful and talented. I wonder what she meant . . ."

Shelley picked up the discarded paper and stared closely at the drawing at the top of the page. "What's today?" he asked gruffly.

"The date?" Sarah Jane stared at him. "It's the seventeenth, I think. Oh!" Her eyes lit up. "Are you going to San Francisco to hear Miss St. Clair sing?"

"No," he snapped. "I'm going to Mexico. I just wanted to know what day it was, that's all."

The newspaper was open on his lap, and he couldn't take his eyes from the drawing. Would he ever get away from this woman? Hell, he hadn't even tried very hard. He would be in Mexico right now if he'd really wanted to be there.

"Do you know her?" Sarah Jane asked, her eyes narrowed.

"Know who?" he asked stupidly.

"Annabelle St. Clair." Sarah Jane leaned over so she could see his face more clearly. Daylight was almost gone, the sky was gray and shot with pink that would be gone in a moment. "Oh my heavens," she said softly. "It was you, wasn't it?"

"What was me?" He refused to look away from the picture in the newspaper.

"It was, I know it. She asked that reporter if he read poetry . . . and there was a poet named Shelley. My mama used to read poems to me." Sarah Jane licked her lips. "And you're the kinda man who would do that."

He turned his coldest stare on the young woman, but she remained undaunted. "The kinda man who would do what?"

Sarah Jane chewed her bottom lip. "Help a lady in distress. I'll swan, this is the most romantic—"

"Goddammit, Withers." Shelley tossed the dregs that remained in his cup onto the fire and dropped the paper at his side as nonchalantly as he could. "Your wife's got one hell of an imagination, don't she?"

Bill looked up. He had begun to chop off his hair and drop it to the ground, fine red clumps falling at his feet. "That she does. She was the one who had such grand notions about California. We was gonna get rich and live in a big house with a rose bush out by the front porch."

Sarah Jane burst into tears. "It's not my fault," she sobbed. "I didn't mean for this to happen. I just want to go home and have my baby."

Bill dropped the knife and ran to the fire to take his young wife in his arms. "I'm sorry, honey. I wasn't accusin' you, I promise I wasn't." He rocked her back and forth in his arms until her sobbing ceased. She stood on her tiptoes and kissed Bill's smooth cheeks, then kissed him on the mouth.

"I never did like that moustache much." She smiled and turned to Shelley. "I apologize, Mister Shelley. Sometimes I do let my imagination run away with me."

He shrugged. "Wild imaginings, girl. A bounty hunter and an opera singer. That's the most ridiculous idea I ever heard."

Withers laughed, but his wife smiled smugly. "Would you like to keep the paper, Mister Shelley? I've already read it from front to back. Twice."

He shrugged again, as if it made no difference. "I suppose if you're done with it I might pass a little time looking at the articles." He turned away and began to saddle his horse.

"You're not leavin', are you?" she asked, breaking away from her husband, carrying the newspaper in her hands.

"I better get a few more miles down the road. Got a long way to go." He took the newspaper from her and stashed it in his saddlebag.

"Where did you say you were headed?" she asked.

"Mexico, I suppose." He looked down at her swollen belly and frowned. "When are you duc?"

"I got three more months," she said. "I know, I look further along than that. Gonna be a big baby, I reckon."

Shelley hunched in the dirt by the fire and drew a map for Withers, pointing out the Truckee River Pass through the Sierra Nevada and directing him to the Filmore farm.

"They can fix you up with some water to cross the desert with," Shelley said sternly. "Don't you be lettin' that little girl drink any of the water from the Humboldt River, you hear me?"

The young man nodded.

"You tell the Filmores that I sent you, and they'll take good care . . ." It came to him in a flash. They would tell the Filmores that Shelley had sent them, and the first thing Mary Beth would ask about was Annie. Then Sarah Jane would know for certain that her suspicions were correct.

He turned tired eyes to her. "I had a sister named Sarah."

"What happened to her?"

"She died a long time ago. She was a dreamer, like you. Her head was filled with visions of castles and princes, wild imaginings and romantic fancy." His voice was low and sadder than he'd intended it to be. "I do . . . what I do . . . because some savage outlaw shot her. It was senseless and unnecessary. She didn't have to die."

He looked up at the young girl who had managed to pry from him, without even trying, the simple revelation that he had never told anyone. Sarah Jane's eyes were filled with tears.

"Not again, darlin'."

She wiped her eyes and smiled sadly. "I'm sorry. It's just so sad."

"It was a very long time ago."

She frowned at him. "Not your sister. I . . . well, that is very sad, too, but . . ." She pursed her lips and narrowed her eyes, uncertainty in her soft face. "Mexico is very far away," she said simply, and left it at that.

Shelley left them standing there. Even without the coffee to dye his hair, Bill Withers was a changed man. They assured Shelley that before light he would have brown hair.

When he looked over his shoulder, Sarah Jane was waving wildly. Withers had his arm around her shoulders. They had a hard trip ahead of them, but he had the feeling that they would be all right. Little Sarah Jane would see to that.

He pointed his roan to the south. Mexico. Senoritas. Tequila. He rode all night, not pushing the roan but letting the animal set its own slow pace. He was in no hurry, after all. But the night was so damn quiet.

He tried reciting limericks to his horse, but his heart wasn't in it. They were old and stale and not very funny at the moment. Once, in another lifetime, he had known every line Percy Bysshe Shelley had ever written. Bits and pieces came back to him, now and again. Sarah had loved "To a Skylark," and at one time Shelley had been able to recite the entire poem to her. She claimed to love the sound of his voice as she went to sleep, so at night, before he left to fight in the war, he would read to her at bedtime.

He started to recite it again, in the still of the black night, and it came back to him . . . every word, buried deep in his mind. He remembered lying with his head against a wobbly round table, drunk senseless, repeating the long poem over and over again. Some oldtimer had called him Shelley after that . . . and it had stuck. That had been ten years ago.

South, he reminded himself as he watched the sunrise. Still, he was far from tired. Annie deserved a chance to get on with her life, and she couldn't do that with him around. Because if he was close by he wouldn't be able to stay away from her. Mexico. Maybe that would be far enough.

He stopped to water his horse and let the poor roan rest. He opened the saddlebag intending to withdraw a bit of dried meat, but his fingers closed around the newspaper, and out it came.

Alone he could trace the drawing with his finger, study her face as long as he wished. He read over the entire article ... twice ... frowning often. Bawdy limericks? Unorthodox? What the hell kinda trouble was she getting herself into?

Chapter Thirty-seven

Annabelle was onstage performing the final scene of *La Favorita* with that obnoxious tenor from New Orleans. Her hair was unbound, falling past her waist and swinging as she turned. Her white gown was form-fitting in the bodice, with a low-scooped, neckline, and the skirt was full and long, the hem brushing against the floor as she moved to stand in front of the beady-eyed tenor.

She'd read the reviews, which had all been fabulous. The critics declared that, miraculously, she had survived her ordeal and returned to the stage with her voice stronger, more passionate, more emotive. Every night the audience died with her as she sang her final aria.

The first few nights the audience had been full of curiosity seekers—bored, nosy people with nothing better to do than try to get a good look at her, the woman who was San Francisco's celebrity of the moment. Throughout those earlier performances, her eyes had searched the audience, looking for Shelley's tawny head. But eventually she'd stopped looking.

What would she have to do to get him to come back for her? It was a shameless thought, and she had set her pride aside to ask it many times. Didn't he read the newspaper? Had he really turned so completely away from her that he wasn't even reading about her? She did everything she could to get her name in the papers, even going so far as to stand on the mayor's table at his favorite restaurant and sing "Buffalo Gals." Nicky had decided that she was quite insane, and poor Isabel was mortified. What was she going to have to do, get herself framed for murder again? If the tenor laid his chubby little hand on her backside again, she should favor him with the same move that had brought Swift Eagle down. Maybe if she was lucky, that would get her arrested and Shelley would come riding back into town to break her out of jail.

Although she had her doubts, most of the time she was certain Shelley would return for her someday. But when? Thinking about him hurt, and the pain was as sharp as the pain she'd felt deep in her heart the moment she'd turned around to introduce him to her Uncle, and had been faced with an empty room.

Backstage, outside her dressing room, she knew her suitors were waiting. Better than half a dozen of them. In the two weeks she'd been performing they'd been there every night with flowers and candy and jewelry she felt obligated to return. A few of them were actually fairly good-looking, but none of them compared to Shelley. Not one of them warmed her heart, or made her want to laugh or scream or throw herself into waiting arms. Only Shelley awakened her passion.

Her back was to him, and he watched from the wings with his heart in his throat. She moved, and her satiny hair danced, the white skirt of her filmy gown followed her like a vaporous cloud. How could he have ever thought to leave her? She was his, he thought possessively. Damned if he would let her touch another man . . . even his brother.

"Excuse me." A sharp whisper drew Shelley's eyes away from the vision on stage. The little man was a full head shorter than Shelley, but glared up at him with irritation. "What do you think you're doing here?"

He grinned. "I'm waiting for Annie . . . Miss St. Clair."

The little man closed his eyes and shook his head, as if he were dealing with a simpleton. "You'll have to join the others."

"The others?" His grin quickly disappeared.

The man raised a long, bony finger and pointed to his right, and Shelley saw them. He practically growled, and the man who had ordered him to move stepped back warily.

"What the hell are you doing here?"

Bart twisted around, a grin blooming on his face. "Travis. I could ask you the same question." His eyes traveled curiously over Shelley's cleanly shaven face, black frock coat and vest, shiny black boots, and new black hat pushed back on his head.

"What are all these . . . these people doing here?" He spoke in a low voice as he studied each of the men who waited outside Annie's dressing room. Tall, short.

Dark, fair. Pale, soft faces. Impeccably dressed, to a man. In their hands they carried roses in every shade, a tin of candy, a velvet box.

"Our Annabelle has become quite popular since you left so abruptly. Most of these gentlemen are here every night," Bart whispered.

He raised his eyebrow and studied his brother with a piercing glare. "Including you, constant companion?" He looked pointedly at the yellow roses in Bart's hand.

Bart nodded. "Somebody had to keep an eye on her until you came to your senses."

"Hell, I left the last bit of sense I had somewhere in Utah Territory," he scoffed and turned to the group of men . . . Annie's admirers. "What is this, some sort of suitor buffet?"

Dr. John Smith recognized Shelley and gave him an inane smile.

"Doc," Shelley said as though he didn't want to club the man senseless. He even wore a half smile as he moved to stand directly in front of the cowardly man. "Did you bring those for Annie?" He brushed a finger over a budding pink rose. "She'll like that." His grin never wavered as he crushed a single rose between his fingers. Dr. Smith didn't protest, didn't move even as Shelley hooked his thumbs in the waistband of his trousers, pushing aside the frock coat so that his Colt was visible, as well as the silver star pinned to his vest.

"Nice to see you again, Mr. Shelton," Dr. Smith said insincerely, his eyes riveted on the six-shooter.

"That's Marshal Shelton." He leaned in uncomfortably close to the pale man's face.

Bart stepped around Shelley. "Well, I'll be damned." He grinned. "My brother the lawman."

He glared at Bart. "This is as respectable as I get. The job came with a white house with an orchard in the back. A little town about fifty miles south of here." As far south as he'd been able to go.

He was suddenly nervous. What if she said no? He'd practically fallen into the job of marshal in the quiet little town . . . the retiring marshal anxious to move on and searching for a proper replacement. It had been the small white house, the orchard, the wildflowers growing at the edge of the fence, that had sold him. He had even driven a nail into the frame of the window in the bedroom. A place for Annie to hang her dreamcatcher.

He turned away from his brother and faced the line of hopeful suitors. He kept his thumbs hooked in his waistband, the Colt and the star visible . . . and frightening to the group of dandified men. Their eyes were no longer on the exit Annie would take from the stage. They were on Shelley who paced in front of them restlessly. Finally he stopped and plucked a bouquet of red roses from one anxious young man.

"Pretty." He studied them intently. "Not bad . . . ouch!" He pulled away a bleeding finger, frowning. "Thorns." Exactly what he'd been looking for as he'd plundered the bouquet. He glared at the young man, who was now sweating profusely. "You wouldn't give Miss St. Clair flowers with thorns in them, would you?" He scowled at the offending roses, dropped them to the floor, and stomped on them.

Every bouquet was similarly examined, and if no thorns were found, the delicate flowers were invariably destroyed by his search. No one protested.

Shelley took off the lid of a tin of candy one nervous man held possessively. He popped one into his mouth, a small chocolate, and then proceeded to make a face and dump the perfectly good sweets on the floor.

Another man held a velvet box tightly in his hands. He was backed into a corner, and his eyes darted back and forth, searching for escape, and Shelley turned to him.

"What's this?" He snatched the box out of the man's fingers and opened it quickly, before the man could protest. "A bracelet." He lifted the diamond and emerald jewelry and studied it in the light. "Very nice, but do you really think you know Miss St. Clair well enough to give her a gift like this?"

The thin young man stuttered incoherently.

Shelley grinned. "Think carefully about your answer."

The man stuttered and searched for an answer. "I . . . I . . . I don't. No. I guess I don't," he said quickly.

"You don't know?" His smile faded as he returned the bracelet to its box and handed it to the pale man. "I don't know Miss St. Clair very well at all," he said quickly and clearly.

Shelley turned his back on the pitiful men who clamored together. Was that what Annie wanted? Some slick city boy who could give her diamonds?

For a moment, he thought about leaving. It had been a bad idea . . . all of it. The job, the house, returning to San Francisco. He turned away from the entourage to leave. He headed for the door that led to the dark, deserted alley. The door he had come in through. He could hear Bart's voice but ignored his brother's pleas.

Then he did an about face and planted himself facing the stage. It was over. Applause, as enthusiastic as Ann Brown had received after her performance at the

Silver Palace, rang through the hall. It seemed to last forever, and when the performers began to leave the stage, Annie wasn't one of them. She stood on stage, facing the audience, and that caterwauling man took her hand and kissed it.

At last Annie left the stage, and Shelley managed to catch her eye over the crowd. A dozen people rushed to her, until he couldn't see her face any longer, and he put his doubts aside and pushed forward.

The crowd parted for him, until at last he stood in front of Annie. He tried to decipher the emotions in her eyes. Surprise, relief, anger . . . and more.

"I need to talk to you, Annie," he said, ignoring the push around him.

"You can't just walk in and out of my life as you please, Travis Shelton," Annie said softly. "I can't take it."

He took her hand, ignoring her anger. He held her fingers, and felt her resistance melt away. "Come with me, Annie."

He looked to the right. There was Bart, along with the rest of Annie's anxious suitors. He looked to the left, and there was Uncle Icky. God only knew what Annie had told him. The man looked as if he wanted to pounce on him, so Shelley calmly opened one side of his frock coat so the silver star was visible. Nicholas St. Clair's eyes narrowed, but he stayed where he was.

Shelley turned back to Annie. "This won't take long."

"Shelley! Where did you get that? They think you're a sheriff."

"A marshal," he said absently.

He looked closely at Annie's face. Her eyes were narrowed suspiciously, and her red lips were pursed. She was wearing a flimsy-looking white dress that was cut far too low, and she was glaring at him intently. In addition to the red lips, she had rouge on her cheeks, and without a second thought he removed a handkerchief from his pocket and began wiping the color from her face.

"What do you think you're doing?" Annie demanded.

He chanced a quick glance to his left. Uncle Icky was still there, his arms crossed over his chest, his eyes narrowed much like Annie's. Shelley would have to ignore the fact that he had an audience of his own, at the moment.

"The first time I saw you, you had glop all over your face," he said, keeping his voice low. "I didn't like it then, and I don't like it now. Just listen to me before I lose what little nerve I've got left."

He placed the mussed handkerchief back into his pocket, giving her another glimpse of the star above his heart, and he took her hands in his. In case she tried to walk away from him.

"I missed you," he whispered gruffly, and watched as her face softened.

He freed his hand, reached into the pocket of his coat, and withdrew a single, perfect peach, fuzzy and unbruised. He offered it to her on his open palm.

"Shelley," she whispered.

He squirmed, growing warm, the collar of his shirt suddenly tighter. "Well, aren't you going to take the damn thing? If this is a big mistake . . . there are fellas here with flowers, candy, and diamonds. If that's what you want . . . I never shoulda . . ." He was uncharacteristically at a loss for words. The peach remained in his hand, untouched by Annie.

She took a deep breath. "Do you love me, Shelley?" Her soft question held it all . . . hopes and dreams for their future.

"I'm here, aren't I? I came here to ask you to marry me. I brought you this damn piece of fruit because you said . . . and I want it all, Annie. Your heart, your soul. I'll never let you out of my sight again."

"Well," Annie tightened her grip on his hand. "I haven't heard you ask me to marry you, and you still haven't answered my question."

"What question was that?"

"Do you love me?"

"Yes, Annie. I love you, goddammit."

She shook her head, but there was a smile on her face. "We'll need a new pact, you know. You can never say 'I love you' and 'goddammit' in the same breath. It's terrible unromantic."

"You and your pacts. All right. If you're going to sing in front of other people, you're going to have to wear more clothes than that," he snapped. "And I certainly hope that you won't stand on the mayor's table and sing minstrel songs once we get to Santa Clara." The offered peach was still in his hand.

"Teach me how to track a man." Annie laid her hand on his cheek and looked into his eyes.

"What for?"

"Every time I tell you that I love you, you run away. Twice you've done that to me, Shelley. Twice!"

"I don't suppose you'd like to try me one more time?"

She smiled, a real smile with no hesitation, and he knew then that everything was going to be all right. "I love you," she said clearly. "I've loved you from the moment you winked at me as I hid under the stairs. I love the sound of your heartbeat, the feel of your hand on mine. I love riding the sleeping car of the Shelley Railway, beans, tequila, and limericks." She took the peach from his hand and then wrapped her arms around his neck and placed her face close to his. "I love you, Shelley."

He couldn't stop the grin that spread across his face as he lifted Annie off the ground and spun her around. He'd missed her so much, he'd forgotten how wonderful it felt to hold her in his arms, and he couldn't hold her tight enough. When he set her on her feet, he looked over her head and into Bart's amused face.

Shelley grinned and spoke the words that warmed his heart. "She loves me."